Peter sought a few minutes peace with his coffee, but it was not to be. A large mailing envelope had appeared on his desk, his name written on the front in all-too-familiar handwriting. He dropped into his chair and ran his fingers lightly over the script. Peter closed his eyes and wished it had all been a terrible mistake, and Maisie was standing in the door, laughing at the joke. "Caroline, what is this?" he asked, carrying it out to her desk like it was filled with nitroglycerin.

"It's a package," she answered without looking up.

"I can see that." He clenched his jaws so his voice wouldn't shake. "It's from Maisie."

"Really?" Her voice stayed emotionless, and she kept her eyes glued to her computer screen.

"Maisie is dead."

"I know."

This package was a crack in the wall he had erected to protect himself from his grief. "Where'd it come from? Did you put it there?"

Caroline slowly swiveled her chair to face him. "I did," she said softly. "She gave it to me with instructions to give it to you when I thought you were ready."

"Ready for what?"

"She said I'd know. I think she meant when it was time to get on with your life."

He let the package drop to his side. "Who the hell are you to decide that?" he growled. He'd choose when he wanted to get on with his life without input from anyone else.

Maisie's List

by

Beth Warstadt

Best Wishes,
Beth Warstadt

This is a work of fiction. Names, characters, places, and incidents are either the product of the author's imagination or are used fictitiously, and any resemblance to actual persons living or dead, business establishments, events, or locales, is entirely coincidental.

Maisie's List

Cover Art by *Debbie Taylor*

The Wild Rose Press, Inc.
PO Box 708
Adams Basin, NY 14410-0708
Visit us at www.thewildrosepress.com

Publishing History
First Sweetheart Rose Edition, 2020
Trade Paperback ISBN 978-1-5092-3126-3
Digital ISBN 978-1-5092-3127-0

Published in the United States of America

Dedication

To love that transcends place and time
and, as always, to Steve, Kevin, and Brian,
who give everything meaning

Chapter 1

Peter Hunter blew into his veterinary clinic, shoving twelve-year-old Logan ahead of him and dragging six-year-old Lacie behind with their beagle, Buddy, close on their heels. Before his wife died, the clinic had been a refuge from the stresses of his young family, but in the last fifteen months, those stresses had been coming to work with him every day. It had taken plenty of deep breaths and tongue-biting to herd them out the door by seven am, and the sweltering heat of an Atlanta summer morning did nothing to improve his mood. Why did the kids have to go back to school so early?

His office manager, Caroline Spencer, stood up and looked over the checkout desk. "Good morning, Hunters," she said cheerfully.

"Lacie had to change her clothes three times. Three times, and she still isn't done," Peter growled, pulling a bright red hair bow out of his pocket and thrusting it at Caroline. "She made us so late she didn't have time to eat. "

Caroline came out from behind the desk and squatted to pet Buddy. "Lacie, honey, why didn't you lay out your clothes last night?" she asked, her face shining with enthusiastic dog kisses.

"I *did*." Lacie's big brown eyes showed no awareness of the trouble she had caused. "But last night

I liked pink. Today, I like red."

Caroline bit her lower lip, stifling a laugh. "I completely understand."

"I'm glad somebody does," Peter snapped. He'd had another restless night and overslept the alarm, so he had been late starting his morning run. Even though he cut it short, he was still late getting back, and any little thing that disturbed their routine threw off the whole day. He had burst through the door into their kitchen to find Logan, dark brown hair still slick from the shower, eating chocolate cereal out of a stainless-steel mixing bowl and watching the kitchen TV. He was well on his way to being as tall and athletic as his father, and he had a voracious appetite to go with his continual growth spurts.

"Where's your sister?" Peter asked, grabbing a bottle of water from the fridge.

Logan shrugged. "Haven't seen her."

Logan's indifference compounded Peter's irritation. "You could've done something. She makes you late, too. "

"Never does any good."

With no time to argue, Peter took the stairs two at a time and found Lacie standing in her underclothes with her hands on her hips, surveying the catastrophe of clothing covering her bed.

"What are you doing?" he demanded, with what felt like admirable self-control.

"I'm picking out my clothes."

She answered without looking up, her attention completely consumed by fashion decisions.

"Hurry up," he blew out. "We're leaving in fifteen minutes." He had no time to hover and make her move faster. He was already running behind, but he knew he could shave, shower, and dress in fifteen minutes. He wasn't so optimistic about his daughter.

After fifteen minutes to the second, he came out to find Lacie had only made it as far as committing to an outfit. He raised himself to his full height and uttered ridiculous, idle threats, until finally she had clothes on her body. He grabbed her backpack and chased her out the door. Logan already sat in the passenger seat of the SUV, face lit in the waning darkness by his cell phone screen.

Now in the office, Caroline winked at him and accepted the bow. "C'mon sweetie," she said, taking Lacie's hand. "Let's get you a bite to eat and put this bow in your hair. It's almost time for the bus."

"Dad can just take her," Logan offered, following Caroline to the break room. "That's what Mom did when I missed the bus."

Peter spun on his heel and escaped into his office before saying something he would regret. Do what Mom had done? His wife hadn't worked *specifically* so she could be the one handling situations like this. That was not a luxury he had.

He found his computer booted up and his calendar on the screen. He had a full day, not including walk-ins and emergencies, a guarantee that this was his last chance to breathe until five o'clock. He took a careful sip of the steaming coffee sitting on his desk and returned to the waiting room to find Lacie magically transformed. There stood his little girl in her pretty red dress with her auburn hair, so like her mother's, pulled back in a matching bow. She batted her warm brown eyes, the picture of innocence. He took her small hand.

"C'mon, Little Bit. Tell Caroline and Logan goodbye."

"Bye!" She skipped out the door, backpack filled with supplies for the new school year and a brand-new princess lunch box bouncing against her leg.

The bus approached as Peter and Lacie crossed the street. The door opened, and the bus driver greeted Lacie with a kind "Good morning" and friendly smile. Lacie climbed on board with no fear, treating the driver to a brief description of an annoying older brother and a father who didn't know how to tie a hair bow. The bus was only half full, and he realized most parents were taking their kids on the first day of school. He couldn't compound the problem by sending her off with his regrets and apologies to start her day. "Have a good day, Little Bit," he called and waved as the bus pulled away.

Peter returned to find Logan sitting in the extra chair behind the reception desk, typing on his phone with astonishing speed, waiting for the tone of answer, and then punching in his response. *He'd better be texting to check on his ride, or else the phone can stay with me.* "Where's Mrs. Lechleiter?" he asked, his patience stretched to the limit.

Logan shook his phone in frustration. "Justin's on his way. We're going to be late for practice again." He turned accusing eyes on his father. "You know, Dad, you could drive us before you come to the office, and then we'd always be on time. When Mom took me, I was never late."

"Maybe," Peter answered. That wasn't happening. Maisie hadn't needed to be at work by seven o'clock. Instead, he was a thirty-seven-year-old single dad trying to keep all the balls in the air. He wasn't giving up his morning run, and unless Logan took on the task of getting his sister dressed, there was no way to add anything else into their morning.

A horn honked.

"Gotta go." Logan slammed out the door without looking back.

The storm had blown itself out. Having the children leave from the office instead of home was the only practical solution for getting them to school every day, since Lacie's bus passed the clinic, and Logan's ride could pick him up on the way. It had worked last year, but it also made for a very rough start in the morning.

Peter sought a few quiet moments to finish his coffee, but it was not to be. A large mailing envelope had appeared on his desk, his name written on the front in all-too-familiar handwriting. He dropped into his chair and ran his fingers lightly over the script. Peter closed his eyes and wished it had all been a terrible mistake, and Maisie was standing in the door, laughing at the joke. "Caroline, what is this?" he asked, carrying it out to her desk like it was filled with nitroglycerin.

"It's a package," she answered without looking up.

"I can see that." He clenched his jaws so his voice wouldn't shake. "It's from Maisie."

"Really?" Her voice stayed emotionless, and she kept her eyes glued to her computer screen.

"Maisie is dead."

"I know."

This package was a crack in the wall he had erected to protect himself from his grief. "Where'd it come from? Did you put it there?"

Caroline slowly swiveled her chair to face him. "I

5

did," she said softly. "She gave it to me with instructions to give it to you when I thought you were ready."

"Ready for what?"

"She said I'd know. I think she meant when it was time to get on with your life."

He let the package drop to his side. "Who the hell are you to decide that?" he growled. He'd choose when he wanted to get on with his life without input from anyone else.

Caroline didn't move away or lower her eyes. "I miss her, too, but she never wanted you to stop living because she had. It's been over a year, and it seems like the right time for you to read what she had to say."

He stormed into his office and slammed the door. He fell into his desk chair, pressing the heels of his hands into his eyes. He could see Maisie sitting at the kitchen table writing out the grocery list, wearing her favorite gray sweatshirt and blue jeans, stray strands of auburn hair falling loose around her face. Had she been sitting there when she did this?

He took a deep breath. On the one hand, he thought he couldn't stand to pull the scab off the wound of his wife's absence. On the other hand, she had physically handled this envelope. He could touch the page she had touched and the writing she had written.

Buddy laid his head on Peter's feet, compassionate dog eyes fixed on his master's face. Peter looked down at him and said, "I guess there's only one thing to do."

He tore open the package. The clean, rosy smell that had always clung to her hair and clothes wafted out like the captive air of a long-sealed treasure chest. He sat a moment and breathed deeply, allowing the fragrance to create a bridge between them. He dumped out the contents on his desk: a letter and four sealed envelopes written on the expensive monogrammed stationery her mother had insisted match their wedding invitations. Maisie had moved it in and out of the desk drawer for years, always saying what a waste of money it had been. She had finally found a use for it.

My dearest love,

How I miss you! I know you miss me, too.

Miss her? Yes, he missed her. So much that he could hardly bear to hear her voice in his head as he read.

I am so sorry to abandon you with all the responsibilities of the children and the house when work keeps you busy enough. It's not what we wanted, but here it is.

Yes, here it was. He knew it wasn't her fault. She didn't ask for cancer, and she fought hard to beat it. But part of him was still angry with her for leaving.

I'm sure you are not ready to date again. If I had to live without you, I would never want anyone else, but you have the clinic to run and two children to raise. I'm sure you've given it your best effort, but let's be honest. Taking care of the children was supposed to be my end of the bargain. Logan is easy. All you have to do is feed him and get him to practice. Lacie is going to give you a run for your money. You need a woman's help, someone who will love her but be unintimidated by her precious, precocious personality.

I fell in love with you on sight, so there was no wooing involved. This time, it has to be different. You've got baggage, and any woman our age will have baggage, too, so I have selected a few whom I think you

*will like. I know them from your practice, from the kids'
schools, and from the gym. They each have something
different to offer, but they are all good for you in one
way or another. Open them in order, and don't open
number 4 until you have tried the others. If one of them
works out, you may not get that far, and that's okay.*

*Love you in this life and beyond. Kiss our babies
for me.*

Maisie

Peter wished his heart would stop beating.

That morning, he had reached for her only to find
the cool, untouched pillow and neatly tucked sheets
where she used to lay. Before he showered, he squirted
a little of her body spray in the air like a room
freshener. He had given her a lifetime supply of her
favorite scent two Christmases ago because it was on
sale. She had laughed and kissed him and said she
hoped he never got tired of it because she would be
wearing it for the rest of her life. Which she did.

In her lowest moments, she had said he would have
been better off with someone else because she was
socially awkward and a fashion train wreck, but he
meant it when he told her she was being stupid. What
had he done to make her think he cared about any of
that? Fifteen months since they had lost their battle
against her cancer, and he still paused every night
before flipping on the light when he got home. It was a
flicker of hope that, miraculously, she would be
standing at the stove, stirring pots that contained the
evening's dinner. Then Logan and Lacie would push
past him, hit the switch to light up the chaos that was
their kitchen without her, and shove him into the
activities of the night.

Of course, even as they forced him into reality, the kids also gave him the strength he needed to face it. He was so busy with their care and activities added on to his regular work day that he had very little time to wallow in his sorrows. All the other parents knew to call Caroline if they needed anything on his calendar. He had gotten better about checking backpacks and supervising homework, but he was grateful she made sure they finished most of it at the office before they got home.

Another woman in Maisie's place? "No way," he said out loud to Buddy. "I'm not going to do it. Caroline is wrong." He shoved the smaller envelopes back in the larger one and threw it on top of his lunch bag in the bottom drawer. To the ether, he said, "Do you hear that, Maisie? Forget it." If she had actually been standing there, he would have turned his back without a word and marched out. What was he supposed to do when she said such garbage?

He forced it out of his mind and went to the kennel to check on his boarded patients. The carefully sanitized counters and bright white walls were his sanctuary. There was also something soothing in the earthy smell of the animals, the combination of animal foods, surgical antiseptics, and strong, fresh cleaners.

The Cantrells' schnauzer, Louise, revved up her nerve-wracking yammer as soon as he flipped on the lights. "Louise, give it a rest!" he barked back. She ignored him and cranked the volume. As much as he liked dogs—better than most people he knew—Louise stretched his patience to the breaking point. Unfortunately, the Cantrells were retired and travelled a lot, so she was a frequent boarder.

The MacDougalls' old golden retriever, Cinnamon, welcomed him with her ever-present smile and lifted her head to be scratched behind the ears. He sat on the cool tile floor and rubbed her belly so she would turn over, and he could check her incision. He would get the lab results back today and hoped they'd reveal the tumor he removed was benign. She was old for a golden, but she still had some good time left.

Georgette, cat-child to interior decorator Suzanne Martin, cowered in the back of her cage, her usual cat condescension completely undone by Louise's incessant barking. She hissed and stabbed at Peter's hand when he pulled her out to check that her spaying site was clean and infection-free. Animals usually went home from that surgery the same day, but Suzanne was squeamish about anything bloody or oozy, and so she paid for Georgette to spend the night.

Eight o'clock. Next stop, the waiting room. The air vibrated with the stress of people concerned about their pets but anxious to get to work. One of his two vet techs, Lynn, had arrived for the early shift, and they were off to the races. He saw all the waiting patients, one right after the other, in record time.

The routine slowed considerably after nine o'clock, but, oddly enough, that was when staying on schedule became a struggle. Mothers with pre-school children extended what should be quick exams as they tried to control their pets and keep up with active toddlers. Relaxed retirees told fascinating and elaborate stories, and Peter's proper Southern upbringing kept him from rushing them along. His schedule was relieved somewhat by the stay-at-home moms with school-aged children who were all business, trying to get through a lengthy list of chores before their kids got home from school, but they were not the norm. Even with Lisa Park, his part-time vet, and her tech, Samantha, coming in at ten, they still had a hard time staying ahead of the walk-ins, and they never turned anyone away.

Although the office closed for lunch from 1-2, he always had patients overflow into his "break" time. When he came out from his 12:45 at 1:15—a ten-minute exam that took half an hour because of Mrs. Swann's pet hypochondria—Caroline was finishing with the elegant, elderly woman at checkout.

"I'm sorry we ran late, Mrs. Swann," he said, even though it was entirely due to her demand for extra attention.

"That's all right, Dr. Hunter," she said in her classically genteel Southern accent. She gave no indication that she recognized her complicity in the situation. "You nearly always run a little late, so I plan on it when I come." She hastened to add, "You're the best veterinarian in town, though. You're worth the wait."

He forced a smile, torn between irritation and appreciation. He hated when things didn't go according to plan, but it was hard to be angry with someone as kind as Mrs. Swann. He patted her dachshund, Heidi, cradled in her arms, and exchanged a knowing glance with Caroline. "Thanks for your understanding."

He went back to his office, intending to swallow his sandwich whole and update chart notes before round two began. There in the drawer, where he had thrown it over his lunch bag, was the package from Maisie. He carried it out to the reception desk in the empty waiting room. "Are you sure you don't know what this is?" he asked Caroline, squinting as though he could see if she was lying.

"I swear to you, I have no idea what is in that envelope." She held up her palms to show she wasn't hiding anything. "What is it, if you don't mind me asking?"

He debated briefly whether to tell her, but if anybody would understand, it was Caroline. She was good that way. At twenty-six, she had not only survived the implosion of her own family, but she had also filled in all the holes that opened up in his as Maisie's illness took its toll. He decided her counsel on the matter was worth the risk of humiliation. "She made a list of people I should date," he said, slumping into the chair next to her.

Caroline cocked an eyebrow. "And who is on that list?"

"I don't know. She left four envelopes I'm supposed to open one at a time." He handed her the letter to read for herself.

When she looked up, a single tear trailed down her cheek. "She loved you so much."

"I know." He stared out the front window at the passing traffic.

Caroline's voice was choked with emotion. "Sometimes, I feel like she is still here. Do you know what I mean?"

He nodded. He knew. "I can't do it."

She cleared the grief out of her throat. "You can't look at it emotionally. You have to shift into doctor mode and look at it logically. She knew you'd have a hard time, and so she tried to make it easier for you. What she says is true, isn't it? It is very hard to do everything for your family *and* run the practice. Almost impossible."

Peter wouldn't accept her reasoning. "That's no real argument, and you know it. Dating a woman just so she can take on some of my responsibilities? Who'd sign up for that?"

"It's not just about sharing chores. There's also having someone to talk to about things, and someone to distract you when you need to ease your mind for a bit. I believe that was what she was thinking when she planned this." She smiled and handed the letter back to him. "Why don't you see who she suggested? Maybe you'll like the idea better when you know who it is."

He frowned. "All right, I'll look at *one*." He took the letter and returned to his office. He shut the door and stepped over Buddy to get to his chair. He paused to summon more resolve, and then opened the envelope marked with the number "1."

My darling,

You have to get past "What was she thinking?" and move on to "Why not?" I think you'll be surprised at how much fun you'll have. Remember fun?

First up is Suzanne Martin, our interior decorator. I got sick before she implemented her designs, but I like them a lot. Now would be a good time to do it, and you can get to know her while she works.

I know you think art and fashion are frivolous degrees, but she studied interior design at Pennsylvania College of Art and Design, and she has an art history degree from Bryn Mawr, so she's no intellectual lightweight. She moved down here with her husband, who promptly began a series of affairs with his sales reps, clients, and pretty much anything with a skirt he could lift. Her son can be a handful and needs a better role model than his philandering father. You are the best role model I know. She could be helpful in dealing with our fashion-conscious daughter. Let's face it, sweetie, someone who thinks orange is a good color for golf pants is never going to meet Lacie's high standards.

Love you in this life and beyond. Kiss our babies for me.

Maisie

Suzanne Martin. Mother of Georgette the cat. She was coming in right after lunch.

Fine, he huffed to Maisie. *Have it your way. But I'm not making any promises.*

Don't want promises, said Maisie's voice in his head. *I just want you to be happy.*

Then you shouldn't have left, he retorted, plopping his lunch bag on top of her letter.

Chapter 2

Suzanne Martin was sitting in the waiting room when he came out of his office, cat carrier on the floor next to her tapping foot. For the first time, he looked at her as a person instead of a client. She was curvy but petite, with short, raven-colored hair. He didn't usually like short hair on women, but hers was soft and feminine and nicely framed her heart-shaped face. Glancing at Caroline, he nodded subtly toward Suzanne, and she nodded in acknowledgement. Contestant number one.

"Hello, Suzanne," Peter said professionally. "Georgette did great. Come back and see." As he led her to the exam room, he asked his other vet tech, Greg, to retrieve the cat.

Georgette was wild-eyed in Greg's arms. Five hours of Louise's barking had frazzled the cat's nerves, and she was looking to take it out on somebody. Greg held her tight so she couldn't dash away and hide, but blood beaded on a wound on the back of his hand. The tech smiled, unfazed. It was not his first cat scratch.

Peter put Georgette on the exam table and petted her with firm, comforting strokes. "The fever is gone, and the incision has already begun to heal. You can see she's back to her old feisty self."

"Thank you so much." Suzanne put the carrier on the exam table. She took Georgette into her arms and cuddled her like a baby.

"I wouldn't get my face so close to her claws," he warned. "She still looks a little anxious."

"You are absolutely right. Thank you for all you have done." She opened the door to the carrier and Georgette hurdled in.

Peter suspected if the cat had hands, she would have closed the door herself. "It was no problem," Peter answered. This was his chance. "Suzanne, I understand you have a design for redecorating our house."

Her eyes opened wide. "Yes. Your wife and I worked it out before she got sick."

"I'd like to see about getting it done." He forced his voice to sound casual. "It was what Maisie wanted, and I know she was happy with your plan. Can we discuss it outside of work hours? I can't give you my full attention as long as there are patients waiting."

She stood up straight and smiled. "Of course. When do you want to get together?"

When? A question he hadn't anticipated. "Do you eat Chinese food?" He blurted the first thing that came to his mind. "Maybe you could come over tonight, and I'll order out for all of us, your son included."

Her brow furrowed. "You know about my son?"

He had to think fast. Had he known about her son before Maisie's letter? "Of course. He's been in here with you, hasn't he?"

"Not for many years." She lifted the carrier to leave as though their conversation was over.

He wondered why she was so nervous to talk about her son but tucked away the question for another time. "Does six-thirty work?"

"That's perfect for me," she replied. "You picked

the one night we don't have something going on."

He froze. Did *he* have something going on? Dance or football? Math tutor? Parents' night at the school? "Hold on just one second." He excused himself and rushed out to the front desk. "Caroline," he whispered, "do I have anything going on tonight?"

She smirked and looked at him sideways. "Nope. Nothing tonight."

"Great." He dashed back to the exam room. "Tonight's good for us, too," he said, walking her to the checkout desk. "See you around six-thirty?"

"See you then."

When Suzanne bent her head to sign her credit card receipt, Peter glanced at Caroline, and she nodded slightly to acknowledge the mission accomplished. Her gesture of support yanked him into the reality of what he had done, and he regretted his impulsive invitation before Suzanne had even made it to the door. He started to say so to Caroline and ask her to cancel for him, but before he could open his mouth, Caroline said, "No."

"No what?"

"No, I'm not calling her to cancel."

"How did you know what I was going to say?"

"There's panic written all over your face," she teased, grinning.

"Humph," he grunted, and followed the next pet and owner into the exam room.

He didn't have time to obsess over dating like a teenager. He was a grown man with a busy job and too many responsibilities to waste time worrying about such things. He plowed into the afternoon with determined concentration. Every time the impending "romantic" encounter pushed its way into his thoughts, he concentrated hard on what people were saying or what he was saying to them. Some of the pet owners squirmed uncomfortably as he focused too intently on their faces when they talked and leaned in a little too closely to explain what was wrong with their animals.

No matter how doggedly he tried, however, he still had empty time between patients when his thoughts could wander. In between a colicky cat and a puppy that needed its first shots, he remembered that dating required inane small talk and manufactured compliments. At the time, he had not fully realized how lucky he had been to find his life-mate so early, and he recalled berating his fraternity brothers for their ridiculous conversations. Maisie wasn't kidding when she wrote there had been no wooing involved when they were dating. How could she think he would be capable of talking to someone like that now?

Between a turtle who needed a vitamin shot and a Lhasa Apso with a cold, he comforted himself that this wouldn't be a real date. It was dinner at his house with the kids. There wouldn't be any physicality involved. No hand-holding or kissing, or anything else. He could handle that.

Slammed by a wave of memory, he stopped dead in his tracks in the hall. He had never wanted to kiss any woman but Maisie since he was nineteen years old. Every day, she sent him off with a quick peck in the morning and greeted him with another when he got home. Most of the time, they were so busy it was just part of the routine, but every now and then she would stop him, put her arms around him, and make him give her a real kiss. Sometimes, she had to put her arms around his neck to bend him down if he resisted, but he was pretty quick to give in. Afterward, she would hold him tight and lay her head against his chest, even if he dropped his arms because he was ready to move on. After all, he worked hard, and he was tired when he got home, so all he wanted to do was eat and relax. She could be very insistent. She was such a great hugger.

The arrival of Sarah Matthewson with her Jack Russell terrier, Lucy, gave him a much-needed distraction. Sarah had found their family pet lying on the side of the road with a broken leg.

Lucy whimpered as Peter gently probed the leg. "Let's get an x-ray and see what we're dealing with." Using the film as a guide, he set Lucy's leg and sent her home with an antibiotic. "I'll see you back in a week, unless you need me sooner." He gave her his best "don't worry" smile.

"I'm just so happy she's alive," Sarah said, voice trembling. "The kids would have been devastated."

After he escorted Sarah to the door, Caroline pointed at the clock to remind him Lacie got off the bus at two.

"I'll be right back," he said to the people in the waiting room and dashed out the door. He hadn't even thought about how his plans might affect his kids. How would they react to seeing him with a woman who was not their mother? Should he tell Lacie right away? Better to wait until he had them both together. He expected Logan would have a harder time with it, anyway. Lacie missed her, but cried for her less and less. Maisie crept subtly into Logan's conversation often enough that Peter knew she was still on his mind.

The bus pulled up, and his morning guilt resurfaced. He prepared himself for Lacie's complaint that he was the only one who hadn't taken his child to school. Instead, she jumped off the bottom step into his arms squealing, "Daddeee! I had such a good day. I love my teacher, and Curtis Lechleiter is in my class, so he can be my boyfriend again."

Her joy was contagious, and he hugged her tight before he put her down. "I'm so glad." As he had anticipated, the bow was gone, but it didn't seem worth an argument.

When they walked in the clinic and he saw the full waiting room, his stress descended again like rocks on his back. Caroline was on the phone so he scooted Lacie to the break room, where she dropped her backpack in the middle of the floor before being bowled over by an ecstatic Buddy. "Lacie, move your backpack," he commanded and returned to work.

He passed Caroline coming to give Lacie her after-school snack, and as he closed the door to the exam room, he heard her say, "I want to hear every single detail of your first day." He had no doubt his little chatterbox would tell her absolutely everything without a single omission. Her mother wasn't there, but she still had Caroline to listen to her stories. Periodically, he caught snippets of her monologue as she followed Caroline to the waiting room and proceeded to entertain the patients and their owners with her stunning gift for non-stop commentary on everything from being late in the morning to the smelly cheese one of her classmates had for lunch.

Peter heard Logan bound in an hour later and greet Caroline as he walked past the closed door down the hall. A few minutes later, he heard him return and say to Caroline in a voice garbled by a mouthful of food,

"What's on the agenda for today?"

Before she could answer, Peter leaned out the door. "Logan, I need your help here."

Logan made a face at Caroline.

"How about, 'Hello, Logan. How was your day?'" she scolded.

"Hello, Logan. How was your day?" Peter responded without an iota of sincerity. "I need your help holding this mastiff still for his examination."

Logan rolled his eyes for show, but stood a little straighter and dropped his granola bars on Caroline's desk. Peter wasn't a person who showed it, but he was proud Logan wanted to help, and that his twelve-year-old son was strong enough to subdue a muscular, broad-chested animal like a mastiff. With Logan's aid, he had the big dog cared for quickly and easily, and then he released his son to finish the granola bars Caroline had pushed to the side of her desk.

Peter made the mistake of stepping into his office to check his e-mail for lab results and came face-to-face with the picture of Maisie and the kids he kept on his desk. How were they going to react? Should he have asked them first? No, not yet. He was doing what their mother wanted him to do, and they would never guess this was a "date." If he went out without them—and that was a big IF—he would need to explain, but not until then.

By four-thirty, he had only Frodo the Pekingese left in the waiting room, and when he finished with her shots, he found Logan helping Lacie with her math worksheet while tackling his own algebra. "Do you have a lot of homework?" he asked. When he made plans with Suzanne, he had completely forgotten about homework.

"No problem, Dad. Only math. First day of school."

Peter's daily schedule was the same as always, and he kept forgetting that, for the kids, everything was new. "How'd it go?"

"My teachers are pretty cool. This year should be a piece of cake."

They would find out whether or not it was a piece of cake once the homework began in earnest and grades were posted, but for now, the topic was covered. It was time to tell them about Suzanne. "That's good. We have company coming for dinner tonight."

Lacie perked up. "Company?" she echoed gleefully. "Who's coming?"

"Ms. Martin, the decorator. We're going to do the plan she made with Mom."

Logan frowned. "I told Mom I don't want a decorator touching my stuff. She'll make me take down my posters and put up flowers."

"If Mom said so, then we'll leave your room out of it if you want us to."

"I want us to." Logan's voice teetered on disrespect.

"Fine," Peter snapped.

"Fine."

He decided he was going to ignore Logan's attitude. He had been through a lot in the last couple of years without a lot of complaining, and he was generally a good kid.

"I want my room decorated," Lacie chimed in. "Mommy said we could make it all peachy-pink, with a canopy bed and everything."

"Whatever Mom wanted. It was her plan." Hoping to put a more positive spin on dinner, he added, "She's bringing her son, too. I think he's about your age, Logan."

Logan rolled his eyes. "Oh man. Not Dalton."

This wasn't good. Did Maisie know how Logan felt about Dalton? Would she have wanted him to follow through with Suzanne Martin if she had? "Why? What's wrong with Dalton?"

"What isn't wrong with him, Dad?" Logan groaned. "He was cool enough in elementary school, but now he acts like he's better than everybody else because he goes to that stupid private school. He thinks his stuff is the best stuff, and nobody else's counts for anything. His parents have more money than God."

Peter tried to rub away the throb that had begun pulsing behind his eyes. *Did you ever think of that, Maisie? Did you really want me to go out with a woman who has a son Logan can't stand?* Another thought forced its way into his mind. *His parents have more money than God?* Was Suzanne a wealthy woman? Knowing she had a lot of money—which he did not—definitely affected the way he would act toward her.

"How bad can he be?" Peter forged ahead. "He's going to be company. He should be better behaved than if it was just you boys hanging out."

"You don't know him," Logan replied, shaking his head. "He's terrible."

Peter thought they could stand anything for the two hours it would take to eat dinner. "I'm sure it will be okay."

"Ms. Martin is so nice," Lacie said. "I bet she'll let

you decorate your room with video games. Wouldn't you like that?"

"You don't know anything about anything, Lacie," Logan growled. "Dalton's worse than whatever good she would do."

There was no point in continuing the argument with Logan. The Martins were coming whether he liked it or not, and if he wasn't decent to them, he would be grounded without video games and friends for the rest of his life.

Chapter 3

Six-thirty came much faster than Peter had anticipated. Home from the office at five-thirty, backpacks dumped on the kitchen table, papers to be signed fished out and tucked back into agendas which he barely had time to peruse. The agenda checking was pointless because he couldn't keep up with their lists of tasks anyway, but he figured he got some credit for knowing he was supposed to. Before Maisie died, he wasn't aware such a thing as an agenda existed.

Pre-dinner routine accomplished, he scanned the environs, and his stomach did a back-flip. Shoes proliferated like weeds under the coffee table in the family room, easily visible from both the kitchen and the front door. Every horizontal surface was covered with books and papers, DVD boxes, and remotes for every device they had ever owned. The dining room table, where he intended to sit and go over Suzanne's proposals, was invisible under piles of clean laundry, which had been folded but moved no farther. The kitchen was ground zero for the explosion, with unwashed breakfast dishes in the sink and the makings of their lunches left on the counter since they had bolted out the door in the morning. He looked at his watch. 6:05.

"Guys, come NOW," he bellowed. "Look at this place, and they'll be here in twenty-five minutes.

Clean-up mode. Go!"

Logan and Lacie scurried around, pushing papers into piles and pitching books and DVDs into cluttered cabinets. Peter cleared off the dining room table, sending each child upstairs with his or her clothes. "Logan, you can just shut your door, but, Lacie, she is going to look in your room, so try to put everything away." Lacie was desperate for the pink canopy, and he knew she would do her best.

He had just finished throwing the dirty dishes into the dishwasher when Buddy started barking and ran to the front door, his sensitive dog ears announcing the arrival of their guests before they could ring the doorbell. Six-thirty on the dot. "Logan, grab Buddy and take him up to your room." Watching until Logan had the excited dog under control, he took a deep, calming breath and opened the door.

Suzanne Martin looked good. Her denim skirt and white top were fresh and cool, and they flattered her pretty, petite figure. Complemented by a bulging bag of materials over her shoulder and an oversized notebook in her arms, it was just the right look for working but putting him at ease. Did she think he was going to need persuading, in spite of his invitation? He wondered what Maisie had told her about his opinions of her design, and realized he had no memory of them at all.

She was smiling, but when he looked more closely her eyes looked strained. A glance over her shoulder told him why. Her son stood a few steps behind her, still dressed in the navy pants, white shirt, and maroon tie from his expensive private school. His hair was as dark as hers but buzzed on the sides and long in the front, creating a screen over his eyes. His arrogant demeanor and unpleasant expression made Peter dislike him the moment he laid eyes on him.

"This is my son, Dalton," Suzanne introduced him with forced cheerfulness.

"Hello, Dalton." Peter offered his hand to shake.

Dalton took Peter's hand as though he wished he were wearing gloves. He had a cold, limp grasp, and he pulled his hand away quickly. Peter may have thought he disliked him enough at first glance, but this clinched it. He may not be great with schedules and housework, but he made sure Logan had a firm grip and looked people right in the eye when he greeted them. It was an important part of being a man Dalton had obviously never been taught. *He needs a role model,* Maisie's letter had said. No kidding.

"Come in." Peter held the door and ushered them in. Logan had returned and stood with Lacie in a receiving line behind him. "Ms. Martin, I think you know my kids, Logan and Lacie. Logan, this is Dalton" he said. He squinted to give Logan a secret sign. He needed his son to step up to the plate and help out with this obnoxious kid, even if he didn't want to. They were family, and families had to stick together.

"I know him already. Dalton went to Brownsville for elementary school. We were in the same class." He spoke directly to his dad with no acknowledgement of Dalton.

Peter had never seen Logan be so cold to another person. *What had happened between them to make him act that way?*

"Mother, I have *work* to do," Dalton said. The emphasis he put on "work" seemed to imply Logan didn't have work at his public school. "Are we going to be here long?"

"Darling, we just got here," Suzanne pleaded. "Why don't you go and play with Logan for a little while, and if we take too long, you can bring in your work and do it here."

Both Logan and Dalton looked at her as though she had suggested they wear fairy skirts and have a tea party. The contemptuous expressions on their faces obviously unnerved her. "Surely, you can watch television or something," she offered in a much humbler tone.

Take too long? Peter debated whether or not he could call the whole thing off and send the demon child home. Suzanne seemed nice enough, and Maisie liked her, but it was going to be hard to get to know her with Dalton sucking all of the good feelings out of the room. He could talk to Suzanne sometime when Dalton was somewhere else.

But that was not an option. She was here, and there was no way to avoid the evening with them. "That's a good idea. You guys find something you both like. If you don't see anything good on the thousand channels we have," he said to Logan, his voice louder than necessary to discourage any arguments, "pick out a DVD, or play a video game." His hard-and-fast rule of no video games on school nights fell prey to his need for peace. He turned his back on the surly boys and exerted extreme control to change his attitude in speaking to Suzanne. "Let's order food first, and you can show me your plans while we wait for it."

"That's a wonderful idea," Suzanne replied. Relief and gratitude were plain on her face.

Lacie, who had been uncharacteristically quiet,

popped up next to Suzanne and took her hand. "Let's do my room first."

What had Maisie said about Lacie? *She's never met a stranger.* "We've got to order dinner first, Little Bit, then you can take her to see your room."

"I want fried rice without onions."

Peter smiled affectionately. Lacie always ordered the same thing. "Okay, one fried rice, no onions. Suzanne?"

"Where are you ordering from?"

"China Wall." Peter dug the menu out of a pile by the kitchen phone. He was embarrassed to admit how often they ordered out.

"I've never been there," Suzanne said. Addressing Lacie, she asked, "What's good?"

"China Wall sucks," Dalton spat from the family room. Suzanne closed her eyes and grimaced.

"China Wall is awesome," Logan retorted, his tone spoiling for a fight.

"We always go to Lotus Garden," Dalton said condescendingly. "Their chef is actually from China, so their food is more authentic."

"All cooks in Chinese restaurants are from China, idiot," Logan fired back.

Peter swallowed the impulse to teach them both a lesson about the proper way to treat a guest and be a guest. Berating a child in front of his mother wasn't an option, so there wasn't anything he could do about Dalton, but there was plenty he could do about Logan. "Logan. Room. Now."

Given the speed with which Logan complied, Peter realized ruefully that he had done exactly what the boy wanted. "I'm sorry, Dalton." Peter mustered as much sincerity as he could. "Will you be okay by yourself with the remote?" In keeping with his unpleasant behavior so far, Dalton ignored him, cruising through channels like a pro.

Peter turned back to Suzanne. "I'm sorry for Logan's behavior," he offered, expecting Suzanne would reciprocate with an apology for Dalton.

Instead, she put a sympathetic hand on his arm. "Please, don't apologize. Boys will be boys. Now, let's order that dinner."

No wonder Dalton had no filter between his thoughts and his mouth. Having a difficult child was one thing, but accepting his bad behavior was another thing entirely. Maisie had written that Dalton was difficult, but she may not have seen him in all his disagreeable glory, and he had probably gotten worse in the year and a half since she wrote the letter. He couldn't respect a parent who would let her son act like that, and he couldn't date anyone he didn't respect.

Peter expected better from Logan. His son would learn to think before he spoke, or he would stay in his room until he did. He toyed with the idea of ordering Logan something he hated, like broccoli tofu, to pay him back for his attitude, but he had to admit Dalton had it coming. He *was* acting like an idiot.

As soon as Peter dialed, Lacie dragged Suzanne toward the stairs. He heard her voice trailing off as they moved away from him. "Mommy promised I could have a peachy-pink canopy on my bed…"

Once the order was placed, he found them sitting on Lacie's bed, the jumbled pile of clean clothes that never made it to the drawers pushed behind them. They were looking at sketches and pictures in Suzanne's notebook.

"Your mommy had big plans for your room, Lacie," Suzanne was saying. "She wanted you to have everything she wished for when she was a little girl."

Lacie's smile disappeared and her bottom lip quivered. "Mommy and I talked about this when I was a little-bitty girl. She wanted me to have a room where she and I could play dolls and dress-up. We were even going to have tea parties with her grandma's tea set." She indicated a delicate child's tea set made of white china with faded red roses on a decorative shelf on the wall. She pointed at the little round table Suzanne had drawn in the layout for her room. "I won't need it now."

Peter resisted the urge to grab Lacie off the bed and hold her close while she cried out her grief. Caroline was right. They needed to move out of that time of their lives where everything was about missing Maisie, and go forward into a time where they could remember her without everything else grinding to a halt.

Suzanne put her arm around Lacie's shoulders and squeezed. She looked up at Peter, and he saw the hint of tears in her eyes. Maisie may have been wrong about Dalton, but she was right to think a woman could help their family heal. Letting someone else in didn't have to mean shutting Maisie out.

"We can talk about the table, sweetie," Suzanne said, smiling. "Someday, you might want to have a tea party with someone else." She pulled out fabric swatches. "Let's look at these instead. Mom picked out this material for your curtains, this for your bedspread, and these for pillows. Do you like them?"

"I like this one and this one," Lacie replied,

indicating the pink swatches for the curtains and the bedspread, "but I don't like the pillows. They're too yellow."

Peter hid his smile behind his hand. Lacie was more confident of her style preferences than many adults.

Suzanne masterfully suppressed a grin. "We thought they made your room sunny, like a garden. See how they go with the flowers we are going to paint on your walls?"

"Yellow is pretty for the flowers, but I want the pillows to be purple." Unlike Logan and Dalton's argumentative exchanges, Lacie was respectful but firm in her choices.

"We can work with that. I like purple, too." Suzanne's hint of amusement had evaporated.

"And I want climbing roses painted over my door like the real ones at Grandma's. They're red."

"Do you think the red will go with this shade of pink?" Suzanne asked.

"Red roses look beautiful in the sunset, don't they?" Lacie stated as though it was the most obvious thing in the world. "The sunset makes the sky all orange and pink."

Peter chuckled. It was nice to see Lacie get the upper hand with someone besides him. It made him feel less incompetent as a parent.

"Yes, I suppose they do." Suzanne pursed her lips to stifle a grin. "Lacie, you are very smart, and you have a good eye for color. Maybe, when you grow up, you can come and work with me."

Peter did not generally have a lot of patience with his little girl's ramblings, but he had to admit she was a force to be reckoned with once she'd made up her mind. Maybe he should have warned Suzanne that Lacie was not typical for her age. From the moment she was born, she had been very decisive about what she wanted, clamping her jaws tight when she didn't like the food they offered and crawling over toys that didn't interest her.

Suzanne finished her notes and closed her notebook with a slap. "That's settled. I took the measurements when I was here before, so all I have to do is order the curtains, bedspread, and canopy from my seamstress." She turned her attention to Peter. "What about Logan's room, while we're up here?"

Peter shook his head. "Logan doesn't want his room done."

Suzanne tilted her head as though he couldn't possibly mean what he said. "Are you sure? We made a great plan for Logan with sports wallpaper and matching fabric. I have some sketches for you to look at." She opened the notebook to a tab that said *Logan*. "You know, redecorating has the biggest impact on the value of your home if we do all of the rooms at once." She spoke like a teacher leading a student to the correct answer. "That's how your wife planned it."

Peter froze and swallowed his impulsive response. Maisie wasn't here, was she? She never knew twelve-year-old Logan. Who could know how the plans might have changed if she had been here to change them? With dizzying speed, his mood morphed from anger to panic. What was he doing? How could he redecorate the house to look like a place Maisie had never lived? He resolved to satisfy Maisie's request by listening to Suzanne and looking at her ideas, but he didn't have to do anything he didn't want to. "I understand that," he said firmly, "but we have no intention of selling anytime soon. We'll do Logan's room another day."

Suzanne watched him intently while his inner battle raged, but she didn't argue. "What about the master bedroom? Maisie thought you would like it if the colors were more soothing and the furnishings better suited for the space."

When Maisie was alive, new colors and furniture might have been good to share in their private space, but without her physically in the house, it was the one place where he felt most connected with her. He wouldn't stand for anything being moved from where she had put it. "Maybe we should just focus on the downstairs," he said, sweeping his arm toward the door.

Lacie stood up and bounced out, but Suzanne rose slowly and smoothed the bedspread. "You're missing a great plan."

"It's probably lost on me, anyway." He led her down the stairs, Lacie hopping and skipping ahead of them.

Chapter 4

They sat at the dining room table, and Suzanne spread out her sketches for the downstairs rooms, laying fabric swatches and paint cards next to each.

Lacie climbed into a chair to sit at the table with them like an adult. Peter had to admit he could use his daughter's eyes and attitude to make sure they got it right, and he didn't think Suzanne would mind, given the way she had talked to Lacie in her room.

They hadn't made much progress when dinner arrived, and they had to clear off the table. Dalton slouched into a chair without saying a word and opened the food put in front of him. He ate out of the containers instead of on the plate Peter provided, and he made an awkward show of using the restaurant chopsticks instead of a fork.

Logan came down, but Peter handed him his plate and sent him back upstairs. It might not be the punishment Peter had intended, but keeping Logan and Dalton separated eliminated the friction their antagonism added to the evening.

When everyone was seated with their food, Peter realized he had done nothing to see why Maisie thought Suzanne would be a good match. Surely, there was more to it than her talent as a decorator. What was the first step? Get her to talk about herself, right? Wasn't that what people did on dates? "Suzanne, how long have you been an interior decorator?" Was that personal enough?

"Fifteen years. I had just started my career when Mitch and I moved to Atlanta," she replied. "He and I had known each other for years but didn't really connect until a friend's party when we were home from college. He proposed six months later, and in retrospect, we probably got married too fast. I tried having a decorating career while we lived in New York, but the fast-paced demands of the city ate me alive." She looked out the dining room window and spoke quietly. "We had Dalton before I had a chance to establish a career down here, and Mitch said he wanted me to stay home."

Peter remembered what Maisie had written about Suzanne's ex, the hero who ran around with everything in a skirt. Was it acceptable to ask a question that included an ex-husband? He glanced at Lacie and Dalton and felt limited as to what he could say, particularly because they were talking about Dalton's father. Since he couldn't come up with anything else, he decided it was worth a try. "Why Atlanta?"

"His company brought him down to the home office to be a vice president."

"A vice president so young. That's impressive." Immediately, he wished he could take it back. Nothing was impressive about a man who ran around on his wife and abandoned his child.

He stole a glance at Dalton, who had headphones jammed in his ears. He didn't appear to be listening to their conversation, but Peter didn't know if there was actually any sound coming out of the earbuds. It could just be a ploy to cause them to let their guard down and say something he wasn't supposed to hear.

Lacie, on the other hand, looked intently back and forth from Peter to Suzanne. She sat up straight and her eyes were bright, filled as always with curiosity. She wasn't talking, but there was no question as to her complete engagement in the conversation.

Suzanne waved away his unease. "I don't worry about it anymore. It's ancient history." Diverting the conversation into safer waters, she put on a smile and said, "Tell me how you keep everything running so smoothly? It can't be easy to juggle a busy practice and two active children."

Was she kidding? He looked around at the mess he could see and thought about the rest he couldn't. "I wouldn't call it smooth." He smirked. "I'm not sure why, but single mothers seem to handle everything better than single dads."

"I don't think that's true," she replied tactfully. "But it does seem some people are better suited to single parenthood."

"I would call myself not well-suited, particularly to handling a little girl." He cocked his head toward Lacie.

Lacie looked at Suzanne, her big brown eyes serious and sincere. "I can be a handful."

Peter nodded, smiling to hear Lacie repeat what his mother had said. "Logan isn't hard. I know how he thinks. Girls are an entirely different species."

Suzanne and Lacie smiled at each other like the secret greeting for some exclusive club. He had known he was at a disadvantage, but now he felt trapped in a fathomless abyss of manhood. The more he thought about it, the more Maisie's idea made sense. Things with Lacie were only going to get harder. Was Suzanne

Martin the answer to that problem? She seemed to have a connection with Lacie, but her son would definitely make things worse with Logan.

When dinner was finished, Dalton got up without pushing in his chair and slunk back to the TV without a word of thanks. Lacie climbed down and put her dishes in the dishwasher, as she did every night. Suzanne followed Lacie into the kitchen carrying her dishes and the remains of Dalton's dinner. "Twelve-year-old boys," she twittered nervously. "You just can't do anything with them."

Peter disagreed, but he realized that as much as he couldn't understand Lacie, Suzanne was completely clueless about handling Dalton. At this point, however, he still knew very little about her situation, and he wasn't sure how well she would receive his suggestions. He looked for a polite way to usher the perky decorator and her bad-tempered son out the door. This was never going to be the date Maisie had intended. In fact, it wasn't a date at all. Any attraction he might have felt toward her was doomed by the inclusion of the children. "He's probably stressed about all the work he has to do. Maybe you should take him home."

"How much can he have on the first day of school?" Ignoring his not-so-subtle hints, Suzanne shifted her focus to Lacie. "Are you ready to do a little more decorating?" She led them into the dining room and spread out her plan, continuing as though there had been no interruption. "One thing you need to do is get rid of the clutter. Maisie and I talked about that at length. If you look at the plans for the kitchen, you can see I have built-in cubbies with drawers to organize everything and keep it out of sight. Of course, it's better if you throw away papers as you take care of them."

"Yeah, I know," he admitted. "There's just so much stuff. I can't look at it and say what is important and what isn't. Seems like everything the kids bring home has something for me to do, so I'm afraid to throw anything away."

She chuckled. "I know what you mean, but it can be done. You have to take one thing at a time. I see the calendar on your door is out of date." She pointed. "Why don't you get a current one and put things on there as they come up? That way you won't forget. I can get you a great one with lots of space for notes and schedules."

Tucked in his folded arms, Peter discreetly clenched his fists. Maisie's hands had looped the twist-tie around the nail in the door. The calendar stayed.

Suzanne rested her hand on his arm and stroked his wrist with her thumb. "I know it's hard," she said quietly. "I'm so sorry about Maisie."

How had she known what he was thinking? "Thanks," he replied, unfolding his fingers. "I know it's crazy, and we are getting on with our lives, but there are a few things that are hard to let go of." He turned his attention to his daughter, weaving in her seat, eyelids resisting her efforts to keep them open. "Lacie, time to get ready for bed."

The little girl started to protest, but a determined look from her father cut it off. "Can I come back?"

"Sure," he replied. "But take care of everything else first. Brush your teeth and pick your clothes for tomorrow." He turned to Suzanne. "It's a futile idea, but hope springs eternal."

Lacie was moving much more slowly as her day drew to its close. Most of the time, his daughter ran up and down the stairs in the same amount of time it was taking her to drag herself from the dining room table to the hallway.

Peter shook his head. "No matter what she chooses tonight, she'll change her mind in the morning and make us late again."

Suzanne nodded. "Women are known to change their minds from time to time, even little ones."

"Time to time? Try every time. I don't know how to fight it, though. She is always so certain about what she is doing. Maisie knew how to handle her. I'm at a total loss."

"How about if I help?" she offered. "Would you like that, Lacie?"

"Yes, please," Lacie replied, suddenly wide awake. "Ms. Martin is going to help me pick out an outfit for tomorrow, Daddy."

"I want you to promise that if she helps you now, you won't change your mind in the morning," Peter said sternly.

"I promise," Lacie sang. "C'mon, Ms. Martin."

While they were upstairs, Peter cleaned up the rest of the dinner dishes and popped into the TV room to check on Dalton. "What did you find to watch?" he asked, trying to be a good host.

"Nothing," Dalton snarled. "Cable sucks. Our dish is so much better than this."

If Logan ever talked to an adult that way, Peter would be making up chores to take up every spare minute he had for the rest of his life. When Suzanne caught up with him in the TV room, Peter said, "Dalton doesn't like our TV because we don't have a dish like you do."

A shadow crossed Suzanne's face. "We don't have a dish." Her voice was flat. "His father does."

Peter couldn't hold his tongue any longer. "Is he this ungrateful at home?"

"I don't blame him." She sighed. "Mitch took all the good stuff and left Dalton with only me to entertain him. Now that Mitch has re-entered the picture, he has everything Dalton wants, and I have nothing to offer. He has spoiled him for anybody else."

So, Suzanne wasn't wealthy. It was just her philandering ex. Directing her back to the dining room table, Peter thought, *spoiled is right*. Instead, he said, "So he spends time with his dad?" He needed to know if it was possible to have another encounter with Suzanne Martin that wouldn't include Dalton.

"Yes, one weekend a month and two weeks during the summer, either at his condo in the city or on some beautiful beach with wait service that comes right to your lounge chair." She threw up her hands in resignation. "How can I compete with that?"

Her ex-husband must be doing pretty well for himself if he could afford to live in town. He could see that would be hard to beat, but that still didn't excuse Dalton's attitude.

"You and Maisie were lucky, you know," she said with a sad smile.

The sudden shift from her situation to his caught him off-guard. "How do you figure that? I don't feel very lucky."

She put her hand on his and squeezed lightly. "You were a team. You worked together to make things happen. A lot of people never know that kind of love."

He pulled his hand away and leaned back in his chair. She was trying to be nice, and he didn't want to hurt her feelings, but she was pushing into some very sensitive territory. "What makes you say that? No one can see inside another person's marriage."

She shook her head. "No, but some things are so obvious you have to be a man not to see them."

His mother said that kind of thing all the time, and he usually ignored her because her opinions on men had not been reasonable since his father left. Suzanne didn't sound bitter and resentful, so he was more inclined to listen to what she was saying. "What does that mean?"

"You don't need to say it out loud for me to know how you felt about Maisie. It's everywhere in this house." She gestured around indicating the whole house. "You haven't replaced the calendar since she died. You don't want to change your bedroom. You're still driving her car. I'll bet you haven't bought any new clothes since the last ones she picked out for you." She tapped on the notebook in front of her. "Maisie told me you weren't entirely on board with the redecorating idea, and that was before she even knew she was sick. I can only imagine how this upsets you."

Her words were kind, but she was hitting too close to the mark. He had to stop it before it went any farther. He leaned back into the conversation, resting his folded arms on the table. "Upset?" he said as if the idea was ridiculous. "Over draperies and carpet?"

Suzanne turned her face back to the window. "I know about pain, Peter. After Mitch left me, I didn't change anything in the house for the longest time. I even kept his abandoned clothes in the closet, thinking someday he would come back for them. I gave up my family and friends to move down here with him, and he walked out like I was no more to him than the picture hooks on the wall."

A twinge of sympathy nudged his heart. Even when he and Maisie disagreed about money, or the house, or the kids, he never thought about leaving. She had been there with him through school, working to pay their bills while he ignored her for books and lectures and study groups. When he took over the practice from his dad, she cheered him on every step of the way, even when it left her paying for groceries with a jar of loose change. And a man didn't walk out on his children. Her ex-husband was a real scumbag. "That was wrong. He should have kept his pants zipped and taken care of his family."

"Yes," she said softly. "You see? That is why Maisie was lucky. You would never have done this to her."

"She earned it." He matched her quiet tone. "She actually deserved a lot more." Suzanne had accomplished her goal. She had broken through his defenses.

She treated his raw emotion gently. "Children help, don't they?"

He nodded. "I suppose. Between them and work, I don't have much time to feel sorry for myself."

"I know Dalton isn't a pleasure to be around." She sighed. "His father doesn't help. When Mitch has Dalton, he lets him do whatever he wants. He makes sure to be the fun parent, the one who takes him to cool restaurants and arcades. He doesn't expect him to respect me or anyone else." Her voice had an unexpected bitterness, hinting at a deep reservoir of pain she kept carefully hidden.

Peter could see she was fighting an uphill battle. "You have to demand that respect from him. If he isn't fit company, then he shouldn't have any company. No friends, no activities, until he acts right." Even as he spoke the words, he knew it was easy to offer advice when he got to send the child home after dinner.

Maisie had said Dalton needed a good male role model, which was obviously true, but she was wrong to think that man could be him. It was hard enough raising Logan and Lacie. He didn't have the time or energy to take on a bad-tempered, disrespectful, about-to-be-teenager, especially if the boy's father was going to work against him. He needed to get out of the conversation before Suzanne suggested he spend more time with her son to be a good influence in his life. He focused on his breathing to speak with calm control. "Boys can be a handful. I know I was. My mom complained that I was out of control all the time." Now for the switch. "Speaking of sons, I know you have to get yours home. Let's do this quickly, before you have to leave." Executed like a first-class quarterback.

"Of course." She shifted expertly into her professional persona. "Here is the fabric Maisie picked for the valances in the family room and kitchen to match this paint color for the walls. We'll add this table beside your recliner and replace the lamps you have with these."

What the heck was a valance? "Looks good to me," he said quickly. He didn't need to hear about other choices. Not only was he done with the decorating for the night, he was going to accept everything she suggested, anyway. *She has made a plan that includes everything we want,* Maisie had said. "We" want. When she had brought it to him at the time, all he could think about was how much it would cost. If he hadn't been so concerned about the money, Maisie could have seen it done.

Lacie came downstairs in her princess pajamas and crawled into his lap, her interest in decorating waning behind drooping eyelids. "Daddy, I'm sleepy."

"All right, Little Bit. Let me see Ms. Martin and Dalton out, and then I'll tuck you in." He said a silent thank you to the cosmos for his daughter's timing. He stood up and shifted Lacie in his arms so her drowsy head dropped onto his shoulder.

Suzanne did not respond in the way he expected. Looking at her phone, she said, "My goodness, look at the time. We're not done, so why don't you come to my house this weekend? Dalton will be with his father, so we'll have a nice, quiet place to work. I'll even make you dinner. I come from a big Italian family, and I've been cooking since I could reach the stove."

He wasn't fast enough on his feet to come up with a smooth way to turn down the invitation. He was willing to give this thing with Suzanne another chance, but not so soon and not in her territory. He would rather go out someplace emotionally neutral. "I'll have to find a babysitter," he said, throwing a weak obstacle in her way.

"I'm sure you'll have no problem," Suzanne tossed back to him. "If you can't find someone on your own, I have an excellent woman I've used for many years."

Peter admitted she had him beat with the dinner invitation, but there was no way he was allowing

45

anyone who had such poor control over her own child to pick the person to watch his. "Great. I'll keep that in mind."

Her voice became louder as she shifted her attention to the family room. "Dalton, sweetheart, time to go."

Dalton blew past her like a charging rhino. "Finally!"

She pressed on as though she hadn't noticed her son's behavior. "Saturday night, then. Let's say 6-ish. We can have drinks and hors d'oeuvres while we talk more about your plans."

Drinks and hors d'oeuvres? That took the evening to a whole new level. He'd have to show up with flowers, or wine, or something. "Will do. Thanks."

When they were out of earshot, he kicked the door closed and made his way upstairs with his sleeping child. He liked these times when she fell asleep in his arms. It was the little bit left of her babyhood. He laid her gently in her bed, tucked her teddy bear next to her, and turned on her nightlight. He looked at the dancing bears Maisie had put on the walls when the room was still a nursery. Could he stand to paint over them?

Yes, he could. Even if he was having trouble letting go, the kids needed to get on with their lives, and Lacie wasn't a baby anymore.

He stuck his head in Logan's room. "Hey, man, that was way out of line."

Logan looked up from the desk where he was sketching characters from his video games. Buddy lay on the floor next to the desk and got up when Peter opened the door, coming over to greet him. "I know, Dad, but he deserved it."

Bending down to scratch the dog behind the ears, Peter shook his head. "Maybe so, but you can't talk like that, especially in front of his mother."

"Sorry."

He didn't sound sorry. "What happened to make you hate him so much?"

"He was totally cool all the way through the third grade, but then he changed. He said anyone who wasted their time with sports was stupid, and he wouldn't be friends with stupid people. We were happy when he left."

Peter understood, but he didn't want to imply that excused Logan's behavior. "Don't do it again, okay?"

"Okay." All the disrespect was gone from his voice.

"Take your plate and put it in the dishwasher." Peter went down the hall to his own bedroom and closed the door, narrowly missing Buddy's tail as he slid in behind him.

Seriously, Maisie? How did you think Suzanne would be a good choice?

Maisie's voice spoke clearly in his head. *I figured she could make the house the way you always wanted it.*

I never complained about the decorations. I just wanted it to be clean. The kids had their stuff all over the place.

Some of the redesign was supposed to help with that.

She showed me. The little compartment things in the kitchen are good.

I didn't realize the son was so bad. Maybe with a little male intervention he'll be a great kid.

No way. I'm having enough trouble raising my own

children. I don't have the energy left to parent another kid.

Come on. You know I wouldn't have picked her if I didn't think she had a lot to offer you.

I need to bring flowers or wine, right?

Very good.

There was a smile in her voice. Was it really her voice, or was he imagining the conversation? Did it matter? Maisie's side sounded just like her.

As long as they were talking, he decided to vent his irritation. *Lacie changed her clothes three times this morning and made us late. Why did you let her do that?*

I didn't. You did.

How am I supposed to know what's normal for a little girl?

You don't have to know. You're the parent, and you set the boundaries. She's playing you.

I know. Logan is getting an attitude. How do I rein him in and still let him stand up for himself?

I don't have an answer for that one. I never had to deal with him as a pre-teen.

I need you here. You left me with the hardest part.

Not my choice.

I know. If you were right here, right now, I'd take you to bed and...

Fall asleep.

He smirked. *Fall asleep.*

Sleep well, my love. Loved you in that life and beyond. Kiss our babies for me.

Peter stripped off his clothes, left them in the pile where they fell, and dropped into the bed. He expected to be asleep before his head hit the pillow, but sleep wouldn't come. He could talk to Maisie all he wanted, even hear her wisdom in his head, but that didn't change the fact that he had to make his decisions and plans without her. Her suggestion had created the Suzanne situation, but he had to decide how it would unfold in reality.

Did he like Suzanne? There had been moments tonight where he admired her, and other times when he sympathized with her, but he hadn't really discovered anything about her except that she wasn't strong-willed enough to control her son. What would she be like without Dalton?

He ran his hand over the empty space on the bed next to him. Even if she had a great personality and was the life of every party, he didn't see her filling that place. He couldn't imagine anyone being there ever again.

When she was still standing in front of him, he thought he could try again without the lousy son, but Maisie had wanted him to find somebody to love. He didn't see that happening with Suzanne, and it didn't seem right to lead her on when there was no real potential for a romantic relationship. The only fair thing to do was to cancel on her dinner invitation and keep their interactions professional. He congratulated himself on his logical reasoning. Of course, he wasn't very good at those kinds of conversations, but he knew someone who was. Maybe he could get a little help.

Chapter 5

"How'd it go?" Caroline inquired the next morning, as soon as the kids left for school.

Peter threw the file he was reading on his desk. "Not great. Her son is a real piece of work. I don't care how spectacular she is, if she lets him act like that, I can't be around them."

"Bad, huh?"

"Bad's being kind," he replied, residual anger coloring his tone. "If Logan acted like that, he wouldn't leave the house for days."

She shrugged. "He's taking after his father, I guess."

"How do you know about his father?" He had caught her. So, she did know about Maisie's list.

"Everybody knows about his father."

Was that a hint of scorn in her voice? "You don't like her. Why didn't you say so?"

"I didn't say I don't like her. Actually, I admire her. She has done a good job of pulling her life together, and maybe all her son needs is a father figure to whip him into shape."

Again, with the role model? "You guys and your "father figure." I've got my own problems, and I don't want to fix somebody else's mistake. She asked me to dinner, but I'm not going."

Caroline folded her arms across her chest.

"Whatever you want. You're the boss."

He did not appreciate her sarcasm. "Yes, I am. You and Maisie colluded to take control of my life, but I know what I want, and Suzanne Martin isn't it."

"What you want is to not do this at all, but Maisie was right to tell you to try," she commented honestly. "So, Suzanne didn't float your boat last night. Go to her house for dinner, and give her another chance without the son. Maybe she's worth the effort once you get to know her."

Peter frowned. So much for asking Caroline to call Suzanne for him. "Fine, I'll give her another chance." He turned away from the conversation and walked back toward the boarding kennel. "Time to get to work."

Long gone were the days when Peter spent hours twiddling his thumbs, waiting for the next patient to arrive. Between the endless stream of pampered pooches and finicky felines his work days flew by, and the kids pushed him relentlessly through the mornings and evenings, so one day flowed into the next with barely a notice of the passing week.

By Thursday, his promise to Caroline lost its power over him, and he had every intention of cancelling on Suzanne Martin. Before he could, however, he found her standing in the waiting room with a huge basket over her arm.

"You were so kind to have us," she said in a humble, apologetic tone. "I wanted to drop off a little thank-you gift."

He wasn't sure how to respond. His intended cancellation of their dinner was predicated on personal incompatibility and an extreme difference in parenting philosophies. But here she was, looking at him with eager, hopeful eyes, making it impossible for him to dismiss her.

He looked to Caroline for moral support.

"Something in that basket smells great," she said instead.

With a last sideways glance of disapproval at Caroline, he turned back to Suzanne. "You didn't have to do that."

Nodding, Suzanne replied, "I know, but Dalton was awful. You were so wonderful to put up with him."

Wonderful? Had there been another choice? No need to say that out loud. "What's in the basket?"

"Lots of goodies." She beamed. "Chocolate, nuts, protein bars, muffins, and cookies."

He peeked under the red napkin covering the contents and, when he saw what was inside, ripped it off. "Holy cow!" he exclaimed. "Eighty percent dark chocolate? Cashews and pistachios? "Love Your Life" chocolate caramel pretzel protein bars? All of my favorites. How did you know?"

Suzanne glanced at Caroline. "A little bird told me."

Peter visited Caroline with a look that would have intimidated someone who didn't know him so well. She responded with a Cheshire cat grin.

He turned back to the overflowing basket, and his mutinous stomach rumbled. "Did you bake these muffins?"

"Better than that," she enthused. "I got them at *Henri's*. He makes the best muffins you ever put in your mouth. You've got blueberry, banana nut, apple cinnamon, and chocolate. The chocolate ones are so rich they taste like cake."

"Boy, this is overwhelming. Thanks a lot. The kids will have a field day when they get home from school."

She replaced the napkin over the basket and handed it to Peter. She smiled a sad smile, and tears welled in her eyes but didn't spill over. "Yes, well, I owe Logan, too. When you asked us to dinner, I had a delusional thought that he and Dalton might be friends."

"How do you figure you owe him anything? Logan spent the night in his room for what he said." *Because that's what a parent does when his child misbehaves.*

"And I'm so impressed with the way you took care of it on the spot. But Dalton was wrong, too. His terrible attitude aggravated the situation."

If she was expecting a polite denial, Peter wasn't giving one. He looked over her shoulder at the full waiting room and saw his out. "I'd better get back to work. Thank you again. This is all great."

"My pleasure," she replied. His acceptance of the basket seemed to bolster her confidence. "I'll see you Saturday night?"

"Sure." Before she could extend the conversation, he called to the woman cradling a very wise-looking Siamese named Cleo. "C'mon back, Mrs. Groover." As he walked away, he heard Suzanne say, "He's so handsome. Don't you just sit and look at him sometimes?"

"He just looks like Doc to me," Caroline answered.

****

Saturday came much faster than he planned, and he had forgotten to get a babysitter for his dinner with Suzanne. Too bad. He'd have to cancel.

He was in the breakroom settling the kids with

their chicken biscuits when Caroline got to work. They were open nine to noon on Saturdays and closed on Sundays so Peter could give the kids time without having his attention focused on work.

"I have to beg off from Suzanne's tonight. I couldn't find a babysitter." He frowned at Lacie pinching off pieces of chicken and dropping them to a very attentive Buddy perched next to her chair. "Lacie, stop feeding the dog."

"You are not cancelling on that woman." Caroline shook her finger at him. "You know she's probably made all kinds of plans for this dinner. I'll babysit. It's only Lacie, anyway. Logan is completely self-sufficient. We'll order pizza, and then he'll disappear."

Lacie clapped her hands. "Yay! I love it when Caroline stays with us. It's like a slumber party!"

Peter scowled at Lacie for undermining his point. "It's a Saturday night. Don't you have plans with Josh?" He spat out the name like it tasted bad.

She averted her eyes. "Josh is working."

Her longtime boyfriend was a sore subject between them. Peter didn't like the way Josh treated her, but he also didn't feel like fighting, so he let it go. "Fine," he retorted. "But order the pizza early so you have time to finish it. I won't be gone long." He turned his back on her and walked out to his office.

Caroline followed, passing him to get to the desk. "I'll see you around 5:30."

Peter stopped mid-step and turned around. "How do you know that?"

She kept her back to him, shuffling files into a neat pile. "Suzanne had me put it on your calendar."

Peter shook his head and shut his door without a

word. He had no control.

As frequently happened, the stated closing time of noon ran over until one o'clock. This week, it was because Shirley Laufer's poodle wouldn't stop vomiting. By the time the dog spat out the rubber band she'd swallowed, Logan was hopping up and down to get to his game. As soon as he saw his dad shut down his computer, he dashed out to the car with Buddy hot on his heels. Peter tucked a giggling Lacie under his arm like a football and ran out the door. Weekends. Didn't most of the world rest on the weekends? What happened to going home after work and watching his beloved UT Volunteers?

Peter pushed the pedal through the floor of the car and skidded out of the parking lot to get Logan to the park in time to warm-up. He should have known not to worry about time. Every game ran late, and Logan's 1:30 start was pushed back to 2:15. Peter did the calculations in his head. Two fifteen to 4:15, barring interruptions, and there were always interruptions. Twenty-minute drive home, so no later than 5:00. Half hour to shower and dress. Caroline would arrive at 5:30. He could do this. If he had to, he could skip the shower and put on extra deodorant.

Fresh air and sports worked their magic on him. He felt the stress go out of his body as he yelled or clapped over every play. From the corner of his eye, he watched Lacie playing in the dirt next to Buddy until she tugged on his sleeve.

"Daddy, can I have a Ring-Pop?"

"That's garbage, Lacie. Get something else," he replied, handing her a dollar.

She returned with peanut M&M's, which at least

had some protein.

The team won on Logan's touchdown, but there was no time to hang around and celebrate. Peter shook the coach's hand, grabbed Lacie with the hand also holding the dog's leash, and pushed Logan ahead of him to the car. He broke land speed records to get home and allowed himself three seconds of satisfaction when he stepped in the door at five o'clock on the nose. Maisie would have patted him on the back and called him "reliable as Greenwich Mean Time."

He dashed up the stairs, spun through a shower, then came to a grinding halt in front of the closet. The last time he had been on a date with a woman he wasn't married to was the night he had proposed to Maisie. They went to see their favorite band, Dreams of Home, and he had worn blue jeans and a T-shirt. He didn't think that was appropriate dress for a date with a stylish woman like Suzanne.

Fortunately, Maisie had known enough to leave him clothes that made him look good.

"This green shirt makes your eyes pop," she had said.

He didn't know what "popping" eyes meant, but it seemed to be a good thing.

"Wear it with khakis," she had directed when he tried to put it on with blue jeans.

Green shirt, khakis, popping eyes. He ran down the stairs right as Caroline came in, bottle of wine in hand.

"Here." She held it out to him. "I figured you'd forget."

"You figured right. Thanks."

"You look perfect, but your hair's too neat. Run your fingers through it to muss it just a little. Don't you think, Lacie?"

Lacie had walked in from the family room where she was watching her favorite movie, *The Ice Queen*. "Yes." Lacie held up her arms so he would bend over. She rubbed her little hands through his hair. "That's better," she said. "You should go now."

He shared a knowing glance with Caroline. Lacie wanted him gone so she could drag her favorite babysitter up to her room to play.

Logan also strolled in from the family room.

Peter wasn't sure what he'd been doing, but he was sure his son hadn't been watching *The Ice Queen*.

"Hey, Caroline. What're we doing about that pizza? Can we order dessert, too?"

Peter pulled two twenties out of his wallet and handed them to Caroline. "You'd better order one pizza for Logan, and another one for you and Lacie. Is forty dollars enough?"

"More than enough," she replied. "They're running a buy one, get one half-off special. That should be plenty to get a dessert pizza, too."

His kids were in good hands. "Okay, then. Wish me luck."

"Good luck," she called over her shoulder as Lacie pulled her up the stairs.

Chapter 6

Suzanne's home looked like one of the magazine "idea" houses Maisie had dragged him to year after year. It was pale yellow, like buttercream frosting, with white trim, blue shutters, and a nice-sized front porch. The bushes were well-trimmed, not overgrown like his, and there were neat little flowerbeds filled with matching white flowers on either side of the steps. All-in-all, great curb appeal.

Peter lifted his foot to the bottom step, stopped in mid-air, and lowered it to the sidewalk. The house was fresh and tidy, as though the resident led a serene, well-organized life, the complete opposite of his own. He had spent so much time disparaging her disagreeable son that he hadn't given any thought to her perspective. What must she have thought of the chaotic environment at his house? He had never actually asked her out on a date, and yet she seemed to know instinctively that was what he had in mind when she invited him to dinner. Did she think she was the person to bring order to their lives? Maisie's letter had said he might not need all four people on her list if one of the first ones fit the bill. Was Suzanne that person? Was he clinging too stubbornly to Maisie's memory to see it?

A vision of Dalton's snarling face rose in his mind's eye. Suzanne might be pretty and well-organized, and she might be the perfect match for

Lacie, but she clearly was not a good mother for a boy like Logan. Except...what if Maisie and Caroline were right, and Dalton's problem was his lousy father? Would she be a good mother if the boy had a good father?

He tapped his fingers on the bottom of the wine bottle cradled in his arm. With a clear head, he found the prospect of an evening with another adult and no kids appealing. As a date? The jury was still out on that one, but the idea wasn't as terrible as it had seemed when he first read Maisie's letter. *You wanted me to try, so I'll try.*

He climbed the steps and rang the bell. It gonged like a big grandfather clock. He heard steps, and the door opened to reveal a different Suzanne than he had known at the clinic or his house. Her shimmery aqua shirt was cut off the shoulder and her jet-black jeans fit her like a second layer of skin. He had noticed her eyes before, but tonight they reminded him of a Caribbean Sea. He guessed that was what Maisie meant by clothes making eyes "pop."

"Peter," she said brightly, "I'm so glad you're here. Please, come in."

"Thanks." He had to brush against her to get through the door. Her seductive appearance threw him off his tenuously achieved balance, and he sucked in his breath to minimize contact. "I brought wine."

"Why, thank you. And it's already chilled." She took the bottle and looked at the label. "How did you know this is my favorite? Shall we have a glass while we talk?"

"Something smells delicious." Peter followed her into the kitchen, where he expected to find all the debris of a home-cooked meal. Not so. Three large windows flooded the room with light. The pristine white counters and cabinets looked as though they were newly installed, or else part of a model home, and the island in the center was clear except for a wire mesh basket of fruit and a pitcher filled with fresh flowers. He recognized the aromas of garlic and oregano, and he saw the saucepan, but there wasn't a drop of tomato sauce on the stove. He used the corkscrew she handed him and filled the glasses she set out.

Suzanne drank from hers and gave an exaggerated sigh. "That is so good, and it complements the meal perfectly. How did you know?"

I didn't. Caroline did. "Just a lucky guess."

Suzanne led him into the living room, wine glasses in hand.

The living room was as immaculate as the kitchen. The sofa pillows showed no signs of wear, and there was no hair to indicate a cat lived in the house. He tried to imagine his built-in shelves like hers, the clutter gone and organized with carefully arranged knick-knacks. There was one black and white picture of Dalton as an angelic small child, squatting and peering with innocent curiosity at a fluffy white bunny. There was no foreshadowing of the surly pre-teen he would become.

Suzanne perched on the sofa, waiting for Peter to sit down.

He remained standing and made a show of admiring the room. He tried to pinpoint why he was so uncomfortable in a place that was free of all the things that drove him crazy about his own house. "Nice place. Is this what Maisie wanted our house to be like?"

She nodded. "Similar, but with more family

pictures and mementoes scattered around. She couldn't bring herself to get rid of it all."

"Huh." He tried to imagine it, but he couldn't get past the sheer amount of stuff they had, even when Maisie was alive. He visualized their family room littered with the papers and the shoes and the DVDs and the dolls and the sports equipment and the carelessly framed photographs…and like a bolt of lightning striking he understood. The problem with Suzanne's house, the reason he felt uneasy, was the silence. Not only that there was no television or radio or yelling kids. The cool colors and perfectly placed furniture made no noise at all. They told no story and showed no signs of life. Everything about Suzanne was neat and polished, which should be very calming, but instead he felt restless and out of place. Her voice brought him back to reality. "Once you get rid of the clutter, it's very close."

He had always been told his facial expressions gave away his thoughts, but Suzanne's comment indicated she wasn't reading him correctly this time. He wasn't about to tell her that her house was impersonal and lifeless. He stalled commenting on her assumption by examining the collection of photos on the baby grand piano. Without pausing to measure his words, he observed, "You look different in every picture. How come?" As soon as the words were out of his mouth, he wished he could take them back.

Her smile faded, and she brushed an invisible crumb off her pants. "I thought if I tried, I could be appealing enough to make Mitch want to stay."

The pain in her voice told him he had hit the raw nerve that he had feared. How could he ease the sting of his impulsive observation? "You're smart and talented, and you look great. He couldn't see that?"

She recovered her composure. "Thank you, Peter." Suzanne tucked one leg under her and leaned back against the ample pillows. "I was a fool. Now I know that was never going to happen. I lost him as soon as I said 'I Do.'"

"Looks like you've done okay for yourself." He took a seat on the opposite side of the sofa. "You know what they say, 'The best revenge is a life well lived.'"

"Yes, I suppose I have, but he stole something I want to get back."

"What's that?"

"My self-esteem."

"I don't know why you'd have a problem that way. You have made a real success without him." They were wading into a pool of emotion that made him uncomfortable, and he needed to get back on solid ground. He shifted his gaze away from her vulnerable expression and looked around the room. "It all seems so new. Have you been here long?"

She raised her head, drew in a breath, and blew it out slowly. "Let's see," she said, smoothly adapting to his change in mood. "We built this house shortly after Dalton was born, so twelve years."

"Twelve years? You keep it great."

Suzanne smiled. "I use it as a showplace. I can't expect people to hire me if my own house isn't well-decorated."

"Good point. But I have a feeling it would be like this even if you didn't have to show it." The more they talked, the more he recognized that the perfect house was Suzanne's way of claiming control of her life.

"It's true, I like to have a place for everything, and everything in its place, but my plan for you is a lot less formal. Your family's lifestyle is very different from mine." She chuckled. "Maisie was always running out the door to this thing or that for you or the kids, and, as you know, she didn't care much for housekeeping. I suggested my cleaners to help with that, but she didn't think you could add on the expense, particularly after paying for all of the new elements I put in the plan. I told her you might change your mind after you saw the finished product."

"She was right about that." He had never understood why a stay-at-home mom couldn't keep up with toilets and sinks, not to mention laundry. He often told Maisie that if she would do a little bit every day, it wouldn't pile up. His suggestion usually resulted in icy silence for the rest of the night. Since she'd been gone, he had discovered exactly how hard it was to keep all those balls in the air. "I could use a good cleaner now," he admitted. "During the week, it's all work, and on the weekends, it's all kids."

"I'll get you the name of my service before you leave," she offered.

"Thanks."

The shared moment had eased the tension between them, but with the subject exhausted, Peter couldn't think of anything else to say. He took several sips from his wine glass and held it up to the light as though he was a connoisseur evaluating its quality.

After a few long minutes, Suzanne asked, "Did you always want to work with animals?"

Peter grabbed the topic and ran with it. "I knew I wanted to be in medicine of some kind, but it wasn't until I got to college that I realized I don't like people very much." *Too much honesty.* "Present company excepted, of course."

"Of course." She smiled.

"Anyway, my dad was a vet, so it made a lot of sense. Turns out that whatever makes a person genetically predisposed to work with animals I got in spades."

"You are wonderful at it. I can't imagine going to anyone else."

Her acknowledgement leveled the playing field between them, and he relaxed into the pillows behind him. He may not be good at her job, but he was very good at his. "Speaking of which, where is Georgette?"

As if on cue, Georgette came slinking around the sofa and rubbed against Peter's leg. Peter reached down and scratched her head. The cat jumped between and past them to the sofa table and perched, still as a statue, to stare out the window.

"It's amazing there's no cat hair or scratched furniture or smell. I would never guess you had an animal in this house. And there's no sign a child lives here. How do you do that?" Another misplaced observation. Peter hoped his comment wouldn't lead them into further discussion of her ex-husband's mishandling of Dalton.

She sighed. "When he's here, Dalton keeps all of his belongings in his room. I can show you, if you'd like."

When he's here? She had said he was only with his dad one weekend per month. What was she NOT saying? "Sure." Being careful not to slosh the wine out of his glass onto the pristine white carpet, he followed her up the stairs, where pictures of Dalton's childhood were displayed like an art gallery. "Cute kid."

Suzanne inflated like a party balloon. "He was a beautiful child. People said he should be a model, but Mitch wouldn't have it. After he left, I was too devastated to do anything about it."

They reached the landing, and Suzanne paused to allow Peter a chance to see her decorating. from a different perspective. The cathedral ceiling gave him a bird's eye view of the living room, which looked even more like a magazine feature from above.

She opened the door to Dalton's room.

Peter had expected it to be neater than Logan's rumpus room, but this was absolutely sterile. The bedspread and curtains were made of blue and white striped fabric, and there was a framed antique poster of an America's Cup race. There were no sports or music posters pinned to the walls, no books or magazines or clothes scattered on the floor, and no pictures of teams or friends. While it was true Dalton might have different interests than Logan, this room looked like he had no interests at all. No interests and no friends. Logan's room was a mess, but it was definitely his space, and anyone who saw it would have a complete catalog of the things that were important to him within seconds, including the picture of his mother by his bed. Had Logan come with Maisie to see Suzanne's decorating skills when she hired her? That would account for his strong reaction to letting her make changes to his room.

"So, what do you think?"

Peter cringed and bit his lip. He may not be the smoothest guy in the world, but he had learned his lesson about saying the first thing that came to his mind. "It's really something."

"I had a similar plan for Logan's room, but Maisie didn't feel like he would accept it. I have a new one you and Logan might find a better fit. I can show you, if you'd like," she ended hopefully.

In the face of this kind of "redecoration," he was on his son's side, but he didn't want to be rude. "Sure." Peter swallowed, trying to sound more enthusiastic than he felt.

"Great. Come down to my office." She led the way back down the stairs and, after a quick stop in the dining room to drop off their wine glasses, he followed her through an inconspicuous door on the other side of the living room.

For the first time since he arrived, Peter felt like he was seeing signs of life. While he could hardly call her office messy or disorganized, there were drawings tacked up all around with swatches of fabric and magazine cut-outs attached. Shelves were loaded with decorative pieces of every kind from miniature Greek statues to silk flower arrangements in a kaleidoscope of colors. Neat stacks of paper and magazines covered her desk. He felt like he was seeing a "behind the scenes" feature of a movie.

Suzanne led him to a table with designs for his house spread out across the top.

She stood so close that her hair tickled his chin, and her flowery perfume made him lightheaded. She was small and soft and feminine, and he was suddenly aware that he had not been this close to a woman in any non-work situation in a very long time. They may not be making the love connection Maisie had intended, but

Suzanne was very attractive. He had to admit he was enjoying being alone with her without Logan and Lacie demanding his attention.

In spite of the attraction, he was no longer the seventeen-year-old boy who couldn't keep his hands off Maisie. He didn't want to act on those feelings. That would open a can of worms he wasn't ready to have loose in his life. He sidestepped away from her to point out a room in the back corner of the plan. "Is this an office?"

She followed, sliding into the space between him and the table. "Yes, it is."

He held his breath to stave off the effect of her fragrance. "What about the stuff that's already in that room?"

"The children can keep their toys upstairs in their bedrooms. Maisie said you'd never been happy with how messy it is."

"It's still a landfill," he admitted. Of all the rooms she had on the plan, he couldn't deny that one truly needed some attention. It had been bad enough when Maisie was alive, but after she died, he had just shut the door and ignored it. It was more of a storeroom for old toys than anything else at this point. He grabbed on to the diversion. "Can you show me more about what you want to do there?"

"Sure." She took his hand to lead him across the room. "I have some drawings over here that will help you visualize my plan."

He pretended interest, hearing her voice but not her words. He had to get out of the situation before her closeness took them to a more intense level of intimacy. He tapped his finger on the drawing. "I like this a lot.

Let's start with that room."

"Of course." She seemed pleased to have won the point. "I have the measurements already, and I can set the carpenter to work on the storage units on Monday. Once you see what we can do in there, you'll be more enthusiastic about some of the other rooms."

Peter was rescued by a rumble from his stomach. "I'm starving. When do we eat?" Not smooth, but effective.

Suzanne sighed and looked at her watch. "Your timing is perfect. The chicken finished baking two minutes ago." She seemed disappointed to leave the cozy office, but she held his hand as she led him to the dining room. "Have a seat," she said. "I'll be right back."

"Are you sure I can't help?" Peter called to her in the kitchen.

"No thanks," she answered through the door. "Won't take but a second."

Relieved to have a moment alone, Peter blew out a breath. He needed some time to transform into an animated and entertaining dinner guest. He shook his head. *Like that would ever happen.*

Chapter 7

Peter refilled their wine glasses with the bottle she had put on the table, took a sip, and rolled it around in his mouth while he tried to plan how the rest of the night would go. Since he couldn't anticipate her responses to any of his "brilliant" conversation starters, like "Where does your family live?" or "Is Georgette your first pet?" he dismissed each idea until he had nothing more stimulating to say than, "Boy, this looks really good" when she finally returned with their plates.

"Thank you." She not so much sat as posed on her chair and delicately lay her napkin in her lap. "I picked an easy meal so we could focus on the plans."

"Right. The plans." The plans had been an excuse for getting to know her, and he felt guilty for not treating her efforts with more consideration. "You did a great job, by the way. I'm afraid I'm not the best person to review them. I guess you've figured out decorating is not really my thing."

Suzanne smiled. "Maisie said as much when we first started, which is why I was surprised you showed an interest in any of this." She took a deep breath and exhaled slowly. All pretense was gone as she looked directly into his eyes. "Why are you here, Peter?"

He squirmed. "What do you mean?"

"With everything else you have going on in your life, why did you pick now to connect with me and start this project? I'm surprised you remembered it existed at all."

In all of the potential conversations he had envisioned, he had never considered the truth a viable option. Now that it was here, what could he say? He looked over her shoulder and fixed his gaze on the light reflecting off the crystal in her china cabinet. His voice was low, as though he wasn't sure he wanted her to hear what he was saying. "Maisie loved things that sparkled, and she was always looking for the next rainbow." He redirected his focus to Suzanne's face and saw sympathy and compassion in her eyes. "She wouldn't be happy for me to live constantly looking for her to come through the door, and if she saw me doing it to the kids, she would kick me from here to the moon."

Suzanne continued to listen without comment. That was both good and bad. He didn't know a lot of women who could stand the dead air long enough to allow the other person to collect his thoughts without jumping in. On the other hand, if she wasn't going to supply any prompts to direct the conversation, he would have to keep it going on his own. There was no way he would tell her about Maisie's list. That wasn't something he would ever share with anyone except Caroline. He had to adapt the truth to a story he was willing to tell.

"I'm still finding Maisie's things all over the house." He pointed his fork at her. "This can't be a surprise to you." He scooped up a bite of pasta.

Her chuckle was surprisingly deep and sincere. "Maisie definitely knew how to fill her living space."

He swallowed. "Your designs are one of the things I came across, and coincidentally you were picking up

Georgette the next day. When I looked at you for yourself instead of just as Georgette's owner, I thought you were someone I'd like to spend time with. Updating the house seemed like a good way to break the ice."

Suzanne nodded. "I guess you didn't see Dalton as part of that picture, did you?"

He took another bite to stall, and then decided to stick with honesty. "No, I didn't. I understand he is his father's son, but I can't excuse his bad behavior even for that. I'm sorry."

"You're not my first date, Peter…this is a date, isn't it?"

"Yes." He nodded. There was no point in denying it.

"Yes. You're not my first date, and you're not the first to tell me you can't deal with Dalton."

With all the cards on the table, Peter felt he didn't have anything to lose. "Why do you let him talk to you like that? For that matter, why did you let him talk to me like that? He's just a kid. You're still the one calling the shots."

Suzanne's misty eyes fixed on something he couldn't see. "It doesn't feel like it. Mitch may not be telling me how to look or what to buy anymore, but as long as our son believes what his father says about me, he won't respect anything I say."

Peter knew this wasn't an argument he could win, and it wasn't really his place to get involved, anyway. "It tells me a lot about your ex-husband that he thinks Dalton's behavior is acceptable. He's not a guy I want to know."

Suzanne relaxed, and gave a little laugh. "No, he's

not. He's got a lot of money, but he doesn't like to share. Greed is another thing that makes him a terrible parent for a twelve-year-old boy."

"Suzanne, you are very talented. I may not have the eye of a professional, but I know when something looks good. It is obvious you have worked hard to build a business for yourself, and you have been pretty successful. On top of that, you are a very nice person, very compassionate and understanding." He wasn't usually funny, but he felt a little vet humor was appropriate for the moment. "Plus, Georgette likes you, and cats are very discriminating judges of character."

She didn't laugh. "But...?"

"You're a mother, and you come as a package with your child. So do I."

She nodded. "Yes, we do. Sometimes I try to remember when it was so much easier to make decisions. I liked something and did it, or I didn't want to, so I didn't. Now, everything is based on how it will affect Dalton."

"Yeah. I can't even get to work in the morning without making sure two extra people are dressed and fed. Once upon a time, I rolled out of bed, went for a run, got dressed, and I was out the door in less than an hour. Now, it actually has to start the night before." He rolled his eyes.

This time, she did laugh. "Lacie is so smart and beautiful. She will always keep you on your toes because you will never know what to expect."

"You aren't kidding about that. Any advice?" She may not have a daughter, but she helped Lacie pick out clothes that she actually wore the next day without argument.

"I'm afraid not. Every day is going to be a new day with her. My advice is to relax and enjoy the ride." She seemed to be considering her next words, then her eyes darkened and she hung her head. "I really can't give anyone advice, can I?"

"Maybe not for a 12-year-old boy, but you definitely nailed it for my daughter. I'll take every little piece of direction you have to offer."

"Thank you for saying that, Peter. Lacie is a precious girl, and I will be happy to spend time with her whenever you think it will help."

"It's great of you to say so, especially since I can't make the same offer."

Suzanne sat back in her chair. "I understand, but do you at least have any advice for me?"

"Only that you remember who's the boss and don't show any weakness. Kids smell fear."

"It's a little late for that, I'm afraid." She looked toward the picture of Dalton with the bunny.

He put his hand on hers. "It's never too late, Suzanne."

She smiled sadly. "I don't suppose I can convince you to show me how it's done."

He removed his hand and sat back. "I'm hardly an expert, but even if I was, I've got my hands full with my own kids."

They both knew what that meant. Suzanne came with Dalton, and he came with Lacie and Logan, and there was nothing else to say.

Suzanne was a very nice woman, but once they took the children out of the conversation, Peter found they didn't have much to talk about. He could talk about football, baseball, basketball, or hockey. The closest she got to sports was tea and scones during Wimbledon. He spent his days sticking thermometers up animal butts, and she was too squeamish to take Georgette home after spaying. She knew the properties of every fabric known to man and whether or not it needed to be dry cleaned. He threw everything in the washing machine on cold, and if it didn't come out wearable, he threw it away and bought another one.

When the evening was over, Suzanne walked him to the door, and he thanked her for the great meal. They planned the next time they'd get together to talk about the house, and she offered to take Lacie to lunch and shopping the next weekend. She waved goodbye as he pulled away.

As he drove home, Peter reflected on his "date" with Suzanne. It certainly wasn't anything like the dates he remembered when he was younger. But, as Maisie had said in her letter, there had been no "wooing" involved with her. She had picked him, and he never had to think about it at all. It was rare enough to have that kind of relationship once in a lifetime. He knew it would never happen again.

In the family room, Caroline was unfolding herself from her position on the sofa, and Buddy, who had obviously just been pushed off her lap, was stretching on the floor. On the television, Princess Kate's snow monster chased her sister, Lizabeth, and her friend, Ian, out of her ice castle in *The Ice Queen*.

What had his life come to that he recognized a princess movie at first glance? "You know, we do have other movies."

She waved away his comment. "I know, but I like it. How'd your evening go? You're home a little earlier than I expected."

"Where are the kids?" He looked up, as though he could see through the ceiling.

"Lacie is asleep, and Logan is in his room. How did it go?"

How did he summarize his evening and first real date? "It was okay. She's nice. Her house is great."

She blew out something that might have been a laugh. "Her house is great? That's all? No magic?"

"What?"

"Magic. Sparks flying. Weak knees."

He pressed his fingers into his forehead, rubbing hard. Magic? Women were always saying crazy stuff like that. "Weak knees? Men my age don't get like that over women. How much do I owe you?"

"When have you ever paid me? You don't owe me anything." She folded the blanket and placed it neatly on the back of the sofa. "It's nice to have a fellow *Ice Queen* appreciator to share the movie with."

"Until she fell asleep." He knew his daughter. She watched the same movie before bed every night, but only made it fifteen minutes in before she was snoring on the sofa.

Caroline smiled. "That's okay. It was fun, anyway. 'Night, Doc." She moved to the door.

"You know, you can call me Peter."

"I know," she replied softly, blushing.

His breath caught in his chest. In her blue jeans and T-shirt, she stirred the same feelings Suzanne had awakened in her more stylish, flirtatious way, but the attraction to Caroline grabbed him deep and squeezed hard. He knew it was inappropriate for an employer to feel that way about an employee, and this particular employee had started working for him while she was still in high school. Now she was twenty-six to his thirty-seven, and the age difference was not so important, but she was still too much of a little sister for him to feel comfortable having romantic thoughts about. Employee, little sister, wrong. He had to get out of it fast. "Goodnight, Caroline. And thanks. See you on Monday."

"See you then."

He turned out the lights and went upstairs with Buddy close on his heels.

He opened Lacie's door. In the dim light of her Ice Queen nightlight, he could see his daughter sound asleep on her stomach with her stuffed bear just peeking out from under her arm. He eased in soundlessly and gazed into her sweet, precious face. Stroking away a stray hair, he leaned down and kissed her lightly on the forehead.

Under the next door on the hall, Peter saw Logan's light was still on. He tapped on the door and pushed it open without waiting for a response. In the midst of strewn clothes, dog-eared sports magazines, and leftover dinner dishes, Logan stretched out in his bean bag chair, talking through his headset as he played some war video game. Peter knew he gave Logan too much gaming time, but the kid would always be outside if that choice was available, so he didn't worry about it. He walked in without a word and put on the extra headset so he could listen in.

"My dad's on," Logan warned.

"Who's there?" Peter asked.

"It's just me, Dr. Hunter."

He recognized the voice of Logan's friend,

Michael. He was a good kid, and he had good parents. "Hi, Michael. Don't you guys think it's getting a little late?"

"No way, Dad," Logan said emphatically through the headset. "It's only ten, and it's not a school night."

"Thirty minutes," Peter instructed. "It's not good for you to stare at the screen so long. You should read instead."

"Like reading is better than video games." Logan rolled his eyes.

"Okay, Dr. Hunter." Michael's voice was a good bit more respectful than Logan's.

He took off the headset and walked out of the room. As he closed the door, he heard Logan say something disagreeable, but he decided to ignore it.

Peter made his way down the hall to his own bedroom, kicked off his shoes, plumped up the pillows, and stretched out on the bed. He patted the space next to him for Buddy to jump up and lie down.

Why did you pick Suzanne? he thought to Maisie. Even if it was his imagination, he craved the sound of his wife's voice.

You wanted a great-looking house, and she has a great-looking house.

Seriously? You thought I could make a relationship based on someone's ability to keep a clean house?

She's not a maid, Peter. She could change the whole character of our house. She could make it uncluttered, organized, and serene. We had our biggest fights because you were unhappy about the house. Remember?

It wasn't like I was going to leave or anything. It just needed to be picked up. You and the kids always had junk all over the place.

Yes, and now you do.

He chuckled. *Yes, I do. Sorry about that.*

It's nice you finally realized it.

But seriously, how could you think I expected a museum?

It seemed like that was what you were asking for.

That's you talking garbage again.

Watch it, buster. Be nice to the dead girl.

Not funny, Maisie.

Sorry. So, you didn't like her house. That doesn't make or break a relationship. What went wrong?

I didn't say I don't like her house. I said it wasn't necessary for ours to look the same.

Is her son the only real problem?

He is part of it, but he is a symptom. She is great for Lacie, like you thought she would be, but she and I don't have anything in common. We both love our children, but our philosophies of child-rearing are so different that the conversation is a very slippery slope. It doesn't matter if Dalton's behavior is the husband's fault, she should never let him get by with acting the way he does.

Were you attracted to her?

I don't know if I feel comfortable commenting on that to you.

Come on. I deserve to know if I got that part right.

She was pretty enough, and she did make me think that maybe I could date again. But it will never be like it was with you. I couldn't keep my hands off you.

I never wanted you to.

Peter rubbed his hand over the empty side of the bed. *That is what I miss most. Not being able to touch you.*

You need to be touched. That is why I want you to find a living woman. I didn't know her son was so bad. I never saw that side of her.

Yeah, well, maybe you don't know everything.

That's just one miss. Give me a little credit. No one ever knew you better than I did.

True. God, I miss you.

Are you still going to use her as a decorator? She is very talented.

Yeah. She's going to help me get rid of the mess in the playroom.

A fresh coat of paint for the family room and kitchen wouldn't hurt, either. What about the next person on the list?

When I get to it.

That is your classic brush-off. You need to keep going on this now that you are underway.

I don't know. Maybe.

Maybe is better than nothing, I guess. Promise me you'll check out number two.

He felt drowsy. *I promise. Sometime.*

Go to sleep now. Loved you in that life and beyond. Kiss our babies for me.

Chapter 8

Peter felt he had given Maisie's first choice a fair chance. Suzanne was nice enough, and certainly attractive, but there was none of Caroline's "magic." He had tried, it didn't work, and he didn't feel obligated to rush into the unknown behind door number two. There were more interesting things to occupy his attention.

Every year, the community had the Labor Day Festival on the Square, and every year, Hunter Animal Clinic sponsored a "Most Beautiful Pet" contest. It had grown into quite an event, with some people dressing up as dogs or cats to enter as contestants. The pictures of the winners—both human and non-human—were framed and displayed on the "Wall of Honor" in the clinic. When Maisie had first suggested it five years before, Peter had forbidden it as animal abuse, but in typical Maisie-fashion, she ignored him when she knew she was right. He commiserated with the indignant-looking animals, but he had to admit it was a great time, and since the pets got lots of treats for their humiliation, it wasn't so bad. Peter hoped they enjoyed the fact that the human contestants looked far more ridiculous than they did.

This Labor Day, Peter woke up at his accustomed 5am, even though it was a holiday and his alarm wasn't set. He lay in the dark a few minutes, staring up at what would have been the ceiling if there had been any light to see it. *It's Labor Day*, he thought. *Such a nothing holiday to the rest of the world, but Maisie loved it as much as the Fourth of July or Thanksgiving.*

At last year's festival, she'd only been gone a few months, and he had been struggling to put one foot in front of the other. He had dismissed the matter entirely from his overwhelmed brain until Caroline offered him a different perspective. Maisie had invested so much time and effort into the event, setting up a modeling runway like a New York fashion show and soliciting prizes like pet portraits from professional photographers, that it was a highlight of the festival all five years she had done it. Local news crews had made it the annual closing story on their Labor Day broadcasts. It had become a tradition for the holiday and a legacy for Maisie. "This is the essence of who Maisie was. It's important we celebrate the way she danced through life. Important for us and important for the kids. Their memories of her should be filled with joy." Caroline won her case with her inarguable closing remark.

This year, they didn't even discuss it. Caroline took care of all the logistics so all he had to do was show up and emcee. Her style was not quite as bouncy, but her enthusiasm was equally as catching. She had designed the *Maisie Awards* for "Best in Show," "Most Glamorous," "Most Unusual," etc, and for the humans, "Most Realistic" and "Most Ridiculous." Peter still felt a twinge of unease at doing it without Maisie, but he remembered what Caroline had said and knew his wife wanted them to go on without her.

After all, that was the point of her list.

As he had for the last year, Peter pushed his

feelings aside and cleared his head with his morning run. He was surprised the house was still quiet when he got back and went directly upstairs to get his children moving. He found Lacie sitting in her bed reading *Green Eggs and Ham* to her stuffed rabbit. "Good morning, Little Bit," he said, leaning against the doorjamb. "Are you hungry?"

"Can I have waffles?" She rolled her legs over the side of the bed and slid down to the floor.

"No time for waffles today. You'll have to have your favorite cereal." He leaned down to kiss her on the head as she brushed past him. "I'll meet you in the kitchen as soon as I get Logan."

"Logan likes staying in bed late now. He's almost a teenager," she commented as she disappeared down the stairs.

Almost a teenager. Who had put that thought in her head? Probably the boy in the next room, lying with bedcovers up to his chin and the pillow over his face. "Logan," he said, knocking on the open door for extra noise as he walked in. "Time to get up."

The pile of sheets and blankets didn't move, but a muffled voice came out from under the pillow. "No school, Dad."

"No, but the festival starts at noon, and we need to set up for the pet show."

Logan yanked the pillow off his face and stuffed it behind his head. "I don't want to do the pet show without Mom."

Peter leaned against the wall to steady himself and search for the right words. "I thought so too, but Caroline pointed out that Mom loved it and would have wanted us to do it. It's a really happy memory, and we need focus on the good times when we remember Mom."

"I don't want to forget her."

Peter sat down on the bed and put his hand on the covers over Logan's legs. "Do you really think you could ever forget her?"

"I don't think so, but sometimes during the day I realize I haven't thought of her for hours. She used to be always on my mind, all the time."

"If she was alive, you wouldn't be thinking of her all the time. An almost-teenage boy isn't supposed to be thinking about his mother every minute of every day. In fact, most boys your age probably don't think about their mother at all, until their stomachs growl."

"Yeah, well, most guys can ask their mom to make them a sandwich. I can't ever do that again."

This was a voice Peter had never heard from Logan. Was bitterness possible in such a young person? "I miss her, too. You know I do. But Caroline is right. Just because we are happy when we think of her doesn't mean we're forgetting she's gone. It's the best way to remember her. Really, the only way to remember her. Going to the pet show we can talk to the folks who knew her, and they'll tell new people how the whole event was your mom's baby."

"But now it's Caroline doing it. They'll give her all the credit."

He was *almost* a teenager, but for now, he was still a child looking to be comforted.

"How long have you known Caroline? Only all your life. Do you think she would let that happen?" He knew he was winning the argument with Logan as she had won it with him.

Logan smiled. "Nope."

Peter stood up. "And after the beauty contest comes football."

Logan threw his legs over the side of the bed and jumped up. "Football, football, football," he said, as though it was the only word he knew.

Peter chuckled. "We have to have breakfast first."

Logan dropped to his knees to look under his bed. "Food. Football. Food. Football," he chanted, pulling out a crumpled T-shirt. He held it up triumphantly. "My lucky shirt. I'll be down in five."

Peter looked at the clock when Logan walked into the kitchen. Ten minutes instead of five, but good enough. Lacie was eating her bowl of cereal like the delicate princess she thought she was, one tiny fruit ball at a time. The box of Logan's favorite chocolate cereal and the gallon of milk sat on the counter in front of his seat alongside his usual stainless-steel mixing bowl and spoon. "I'm going to take my shower. When you're done with breakfast, finish getting dressed and brush your teeth so we can go."

"Ok, Daddy," Lacie replied, swinging her legs on the tall stool.

Logan was already transfixed with the sports report on the local news channel, but held up his spoon to indicate he heard and understood.

There wasn't any real need to rush, but Peter wanted to maintain their forward momentum so he showered quickly. He found them in the family room, everything done but their shoes, disagreeing on which channel to watch. "TV off, guys. Help me load the car."

Lacie carried her little chair and a picnic basket she had packed to share with her friend, Curtis, while Peter and Logan loaded everything else.

They arrived at the park to find it bustling with activity as people set up the vendor booths around the perimeter of the open green space. When the developers revitalized the town center twenty years before, they had anticipated the current emphasis on "Live, Work, Play" designs. They tore down the ugly, empty strip malls on the streets in front of the town hall to create an open park lined on the right and left by rows of shops with condos on the upper floors. The beautiful lawn opened on the fourth side to community athletic fields where the afternoon football games would be played.

Caroline was supervising the rental company putting up the runway for the pet contest. Her flushed cheeks made her face beautiful, but Peter dismissed the thought immediately to help her set up the table with the awards.

Logan pulled out the picture of Maisie that Caroline had brought to sit in the center of the trophies. Peter stopped what he was doing to watch his son wipe the glass clean with the hem of his T-shirt and put it in its place with quiet reverence. Logan turned around and nodded at his dad to acknowledge their shared moment of memory.

The picnic food was also a tradition for the employees of the Hunter Animal Clinic, and each person brought the thing they made best, or bought best, if the talent of cooking eluded them. Caroline had set up a table with a red checked tablecloth to hold the potluck. A consummate baker, Caroline's dessert was the first item on the table. Peter deposited his own bucket of fried chicken at the other end, then picked up her container and cracked the top to peek inside. He closed his eyes and took a deep whiff of the contents. "Brownies," he said reverently, as though he was seeing the face of God.

"Oh, my goodness," Caroline laughed. "It's not like you haven't had them a hundred times before."

"Never enough." Peter smiled.

The first vet tech, Greg, walked up carrying a cooler with his young wife following closely behind with their chairs. "This year, I made brisket and corn."

Peter held up his hand for a high-five. Greg was duly proud of his acknowledged position as grill-master.

Across the lawn, Peter saw the other tech, Lynn, who was a vegan, approaching them with a plate of raw cut vegetables and a dip. She was followed by her teenage son, carrying a bowl of fruit and reminding Peter she was older than she looked.

Peter's part-time vet, Dr. Park, seemed to appear out of nowhere. "This year, I brought homemade veggie dumplings so Lynn can have some, too," explained the tiny Asian woman with an accent that said she hadn't been in the United States for very long.

The table was almost full, with just enough room left for one more dish, which was provided by the arrival of Dr. Park's tech, Samantha.

"Potato salad," she said, placing her covered bowl in the empty spot.

With all the food in place, Caroline took the microphone that sat on the speakers by the runway. "Come one, come all, to the "Most Beautiful Pet" contest," she called.

From all sides of the park, people came carrying or leading pets of all types and sizes. They were mostly dogs, both purebred and mutt, but there were also two brave souls cradling unhappy-looking cats. Eight-year-old Sammy Furrier held a box which Peter knew held a large turtle, and Logan's friend, Michael, was toting a handled cage with his pet ferret, Reggie.

Peter recognized Ron Taylor dressed as a sheep dog, complete with flopping ears and a toy sheep on a leash. George Line looked completely ridiculous as a poodle in a red tutu, and both men sauntered up with smirks on their faces.

"You'll never find a dog as good-looking as this old sheepdog," Ron said, poking himself in the chest.

"No dog has ever beat a poodle for sheer style," George countered. "What do you think, Peter?"

"I think we need to see the whole group before I can make any comments." Peter gave an exaggerated bow and ushered them to the base of the runway. "Gentlemen, let's get this party started." As always, many of the pet owners took the contest very seriously and had their dogs brushed and curled like they were competing in the Westminster Dog Show, while others dressed them comically as business people, super heroes, or fairy princesses. One white bulldog was even a unicorn. Each person and pet was appropriately appreciated, and even those who didn't win a trophy received a certificate of thanks for their participation.

Show over, it was time to eat. Peter made a show of holding Logan back so everyone else could get their share of the food before he went through. He filled his own plate until it threatened to collapse in the middle and relished every bite. When he finished, he grabbed the container of Caroline's brownies and tucked them into the crook of his arm, daring anyone else to try and

get one. They were so dark and rich that Peter didn't
even chew. He closed his eyes and let each bite melt in
his mouth. Brownies were a good reason to fall in love
with a woman, but she was his Caroline, part employee,
part little sister, all tied up with a worthless boyfriend.

Peter noticed that said boyfriend, Josh, was
missing. He wasn't sorry. Josh was a jerk after too
many beers, and Caroline usually made a hasty retreat
before he did something inappropriate in front of her
co-workers. Peter could never figure out why someone
as attractive and talented as Caroline stayed with such a
loser, and he often told her so.

After food, football was the order of the day. Men
of all ages and skill levels joined in and tried valiantly
to keep up with the younger, faster boys. Peter was in
good enough shape not to embarrass himself, but even
he couldn't hope to catch Logan. Once his boy got the
ball in his hands he was a blur, tearing past even the
high school players. His only handicap versus the older
boys was his height, but if he continued to grow to
match his dad, six feet plus wasn't far off. Football
coaches watched him with greedy eyes.

They played football until near dark, then scattered
back to their families to watch the fireworks. Having
the farthest to drive, Dr. Park and Samantha begged off,
and Greg and his wife were off to the side, making-out
like the newlyweds they were. Grateful for Josh's
absence, Peter pulled up a lawn chair close to
Caroline's. Lacie climbed into his lap, and Logan
stretched out on the ground in front of them with his
buddies, Michael and Justin. For one brief, shining
moment, all was right with the world.

Before the fireworks started, Peter took the chance

to have a semi-private conversation with Caroline. "Where's Josh?" he asked casually.

"He couldn't make it this year." She looked down at her folded hands. "He started a new job as a waiter, and holidays are their busiest days."

"Waiter? I thought he was a computer tech for some big company." Peter remembered Josh boasting about the importance of his job at last year's Christmas party.

Caroline still didn't meet his gaze. "That didn't work out."

Even though his efforts had never paid off, Peter felt like he had to try again. "Why do you stay with him? You deserve so much better."

She lifted her face to look at him, her eyes shining with tears. "Thank you so much for saying so. It means a lot. Really, it does." She gazed, unfocused, into the distance. "When we started dating, he wasn't like he is now. We had a lot of fun. He changed when he started drinking so much." She threw up her hands. "I guess I'm hoping he'll change back." She looked at him for reassurance.

Peter nodded. He knew guys like Josh never "changed back," but he didn't want to cut the hope out from under her.

He was spared further need to comment by the first explosion and raining sparks. He poked Lacie in the side, trying to annoy her awake, and put his mouth right up to her ear to whisper, "Wake up, sleepy head. Time for fireworks." He looked up to see Caroline watching him with a sweet smile. She gave a contented sigh, and he poked Lacie again to push her into awareness. As the little girl rubbed the sleep from her eyes, Caroline reached over and gently brushed the hair from her forehead. Within seconds, Lacie was wide awake and sitting forward in her father's lap, oohing and ahhing with everyone else. The booming music and exploding colors drove all other thoughts from Peter's mind. When the final cannon blast of the *1812 Overture* echoed all around them, the crowd erupted into deafening cheers and applause.

The elated throng moved in a congested, but cheerful, mob toward the exit. Peter's group shook hands and gave hugs as each person pared off toward his or her car. With their SUV in sight, Peter threw Logan the keys to race ahead with Lacie hot on his heels. Only he and Caroline were left to walk slowly after the children.

"I like you better without Josh," Peter said, on impulse.

"It *was* fun." Caroline nodded. "A great, stress-free day."

Peter frowned. "Stress-free? Even with the dog show?"

She rubbed his arm. "A labor of love, Doc."

When they reached their cars, Peter pulled her into the customary hug, but held her a little longer than he had the others. He looked down into her face. "Please consider leaving Josh. I don't like the way he treats you. Honestly, I'm scared of what he might do."

"Don't worry, Doc," she said with forced cheerfulness. "He's all bark and no bite. When it's just him and me, we get along great."

"Maybe," Peter responded, unconvinced. "Just think about it, okay?"

"Okay." She squeezed him before letting go and

getting into her car. She cranked her engine and waved as she drove by.

When she was gone, he turned to look at his own car. Logan had started the engine and sat in the driver's seat with Lacie in the back like Miss Daisy.

In spite of his concerns about Josh, it *had* been a good day.

Chapter 9

"You haven't mentioned a date in a while," Caroline commented as she shut down the office for the day. Halloween decorations overflowed a box on her desk, ready to be put out the next day. "What's going on with Maisie's list?"

Peter stopped mid-step. He had hoped she would ignore the topic if he didn't mention it, but he had never really believed she would let it go. He pivoted to face her. "I tried and it didn't work out, so I'm done." Peter squinted at her, daring her to argue.

Caroline was too short to get right up in his face, but she got close enough that he couldn't look away. "You know that's not what Maisie wanted," she scolded. "She gave you four choices to allow for some of them not to work."

"I don't want to." He stepped away and crossed his arms like a petulant child.

She moved back to the desk and shut down her computer. "I understand that, and so would Maisie. But she was right when she said this would be good for you. Don't you feel a little bit better about it now that the first one is out of the way?"

"I guess," Peter replied with a decided lack of enthusiasm. He went into his office and kicked the door closed. Buddy popped out from his usual spot under the desk, tail wagging. "Hey, Bud," he said, scratching the dog's back. He settled in his chair and opened the drawer where the envelope sat, untouched since the August interlude with Suzanne Martin. "Am I ready to try again?" he asked Buddy, who lay down with his head on Peter's feet.

The brown spots over the beagle's eyes twitched back and forth.

"You're right." Peter nodded. "Caroline'll never give me any peace until I do it." He pulled out the big mailer and took out envelope 2.

My dearest darling,

If you're reading this, things didn't work out with Suzanne Martin. I'm not surprised. She was never the best candidate because you don't have much in common, but I thought you would appreciate her sense of style and her fashionista sisterhood with Lacie. Guess not.

You have plenty in common with our next candidate, Donna Lechleiter. Her older son, Justin, has been on Logan's football and baseball teams every year, and her younger son, Curtis, has been in Lacie's class in preschool, so I'm sure she is still close by, organizing activities and parties. She also has an older daughter, who is going into high school as I write this, but I can't remember her name, and she's not around much, anyway.

Donna kicked out her husband. She doesn't make any bones about telling people he didn't measure up to her exacting standards. Don't worry about that happening with you. She has a lot of respect for self-made people and for professionals, and you are both. Wayne is still involved with the children, and you will see him at various events and functions, so maybe you'll do a male bonding thing and get some more information out of him. He always seemed like a good father to me, but I can't say how he was as a husband.

Whether you make a love connection with Donna or not, she is a good person to have in your corner because she knows everyone and everything. She can tell you where the kids need to be, and when, and how they need to be dressed. I'm guessing that has been a challenge for you since I've been gone. As far as the other details go, you're on your own.

Love you in this life and beyond. Kiss our babies for me.

Maisie

Caroline knocked on the door and didn't wait for a response before opening it. "'Night," she said. Seeing the envelope on his desk and the letter in his hand she leaned against the doorjamb, her backpack over her shoulder. "Is that the next one?"

"Yes." He dropped the letter on the desk and leaned back. "It's Logan's team mom. I'm seeing her in an hour at the game." He shook his head and asked as though Caroline had some magical insight into his wife's mind, "How did Maisie arrange that?"

Caroline smiled. "It's just a lucky coincidence. She wrote it over a year ago, and they hadn't posted the football schedule yet."

He glared at her. He was not happy to do this, but he would, because…because…why? Why would he do this? He didn't want to. But Maisie wanted it. "I can't think how I'm going to make this work, but I guess I've got to try."

"That's all she wanted. You're pretty smart. You'll figure it out. Besides, with Donna Lechleiter, all you have to do is start a conversation. She'll seize the opportunity and orchestrate everything else."

"You know Donna, too?"

"Everybody knows you can't be trusted with a schedule," she teased, spinning around to head out the door. "And Donna seems to be in charge of every activity you need to know about."

"Right. See you tomorrow."

"Good luck," she threw over her shoulder.

"Thanks."

Logan and Lacie were finishing their homework at the break room table. Peter paused a moment in the doorway to take in the scene. Logan helped Lacie figure out which pictures on her worksheet ended with the "er" sound. His open laptop displayed a short paragraph.

He hated to disturb them, but they had to get moving. "Hey, guys, time to go. We've got a game at seven."

"Can you read this quick, Dad?" Logan asked. "The topic is Define Your Greatest Strength."

That was kind of an adult thing to ask of a twelve-year-old. "And what do you consider your greatest strength?"

Logan nodded at the screen. "Read it and find out."

Peter leaned down to read.

Some people don't discover their greatest strength until they are adults because they don't have to use it. I've already found mine because my mom died when I was young. Through that experience, I discovered the word "resilience." A person who is resilient is able to experience bad things and go on with life. It is hard to be without my mom. She was so great and did everything for us. My dad is trying hard, though, and he and my little sister and I are still a family, and we still do all the regular stuff. We are resilient.

Peter dropped into the chair Logan had vacated. He bought time by pretending to still be reading while Logan waited. Finally, he responded in the only way he could without betraying his emotion. "That is a great paragraph, Logan. Good job."

"Thanks." He pushed "Submit". "Let's go. Can we hit Arby's for dinner? I want potato cakes instead of fries."

"Okay, but we need to drop Buddy at home first." Potato cakes instead of fries. Another fast food dinner.

****

Peter selected a parking space far from the entrance to the fields to buy a few extra minutes of walking time to steel his resolve. He had met Donna Lechleiter a dozen times over the years at class or team parties, and he had a vague impression of her as an electric ball of efficiency, bouncing like a pinball from food to activities to trophies, but he had never really looked at her as a person separate from her usefulness to his family.

Donna was in her customary spot directly in front of the "Welcome to Five Forks Field" sign, the tailgate of her van open and spread with a red-and-white checked tablecloth. No fast food for her children. Did she do that every time? As soon as her son, Justin, saw Logan, he jumped up, and they ran full out for the field with Lacie and Curtis, her younger son, trailing behind.

When he got close enough for her to hear, he whistled his appreciation of her tailgating skills. She straightened and visited him with an 'I'm-so-pleased-you-see-what-a-good-mother-I-am' smile. She was tall for a woman, coming closer to looking him eye-to-eye than most. She was well put together, body taut and ready to spring into action, even in jeans and a t-shirt with 'Team Mom' across the front.

"Dr. Hunter," she said. "Would you like to join me? There's plenty."

"Call me Peter," he offered. In fact, there was not plenty. It looked like she had packed exactly the right amount of food for herself and two children, but he wondered if she could snap her fingers and make more appear. On their plates were the end stubs of sub sandwiches that must have overflowed with vegetables because only lettuce fragments, a few shredded carrots, diced cucumbers, and tomato seeds remained. Sandwiches with vegetables were clearly a healthy improvement over the fast food burgers and chicken nuggets that were the game night fare for his own kids. Peter stretched his neck from side to side to relieve the tight stress that came with the idea of adding another food-making chore into his day.

She offered Peter a cookie from a large, full-to-overflowing plastic container. "Please have one. Most of them are for the snack after the game, but I have a few more than we need for the boys."

It would be rude to turn her down, so he took one off the top and examined it closely. They were so perfectly sized that he wondered if she counted the number of chips she put in each. Maisie's cookies had always been lumpy and oddly shaped but delicious, and he expected Donna's cutout appearance would equate to a cardboard taste. He took a bite, and they tasted as good as they looked. He felt a tug of disappointment

Maisie couldn't beat this perfect woman in the cookie baking challenge. "Boy, these are really good," he said, taking another when she offered.

"It's simple," she replied as she packed up the remains of their feast. "It takes no time at all, and I think homemade are so much better than store-bought. Don't you agree?"

Peter nodded, his mouth full of cookie.

"The boys have so many activities that we were eating fast food every night." She pressed lids back on the containers. "I knew they weren't getting good nutrition just from the vitamins they took every day, so I started packing our dinners."

I'm supposed to be giving them vitamins every day? "Right," he said quickly.

"They still get fast food on Fridays." She leaned in as though someone might overhear her and care. "I don't want them to feel deprived." She handed him the container of cookies and pulled out a cooler. "Bottles of water to keep the team hydrated."

Peter's inner Southern gentleman reared his head. "I should carry the cooler instead. It's heavier."

She waved him off. "Not to worry. It has wheels. All I have to do is pull."

They walked together up to the field. If she thought it was odd for him to walk with her, she never let on.

"You know, I swing by your office every morning to pick up Logan for football."

He remembered Logan's complaint that she was always late. "Yes. Thanks a lot for doing that."

"I could take Lacie, too, if you'd like. That's what I do with Curtis. The elementary school is on the way to the field, so I just drop him off. He and Lacie are in the same class. Isn't that lucky?"

He didn't like the idea of making both children late, but he also didn't want her to think he was unappreciative. "Yes, it is. Thanks for the offer. I'll keep it in mind."

"Please do." She paused and shifted the cooler handle to her other hand. "Our friends, the Morrisons, have a Great Dane named Beauregard. By any chance, do you see them?"

Peter did know Beauregard, a 150-pound gentle giant who thought he was a lap dog. "Yes, I do. They were in just last week."

"Isn't it a small world?" she said, as though they had just discovered they were cousins.

"It is," he said politely.

"Our friends, the Austins, also have some sort of mixed breed named Lucky."

She was missing the most important part of that story. Lucky was a rescue puppy who'd been found chained in someone's backyard with no food or water. She was one of five dogs the Austins had saved. They also used humane traps to catch feral cats and have them neutered. "Yes, I see Lucky, too."

"We don't have a pet. Curtis is allergic." She lowered her voice. "I wouldn't have one, anyway. The Austins' house smells like a zoo. I'd be afraid for my children to sleep there. They might get some sort of disease."

Peter was so surprised by her comment that he stopped walking. "You think they'll get a disease because the house smells like animals?"

Donna turned to look at him as though her comment could not be contested. "No, of course not.

But you can get diseases from dirty animals, can't you?"

Peter shook his head, and bit back a reply that would imply she was ignorant. She was in more danger from kids who sneezed without covering their mouths. When he answered, he spoke slowly to keep his vocal tone neutral. "Sure, but not house pets. All the Austins' animals have had their shots, and the dirt from the yard isn't usually dangerous."

"That's good to know. Still, germs are everywhere." She patted a bulge in the pocket of her jeans. "That's why I carry hand sanitizer wherever we go. You should, too."

Seriously? Peter thought and then reconsidered. She packed her kids' dinner instead of getting fast food. She gave them vitamins. She knew a lot more about being a mom than he did. On the other hand, he'd been around animals all his life and never caught so much as a cold from them. Should he set her straight? Nope, no harm in hand sanitizer. "That's a good idea."

Donna stopped rolling the cooler next to the aluminum bleachers and climbed up to sit. Peter put the cookies on top and moved to follow her. "Oh, no, bring the cookies," she said firmly. "Ants."

Peter tried to balance the cookies and climb on the bleachers, then thought better of it and put them on one of the benches. She shot down and took it back to her seat before he even had a chance to pull himself up. He sat next to her, the cookies between them. "Are you Lacie's room mom, too?"

"Actually, this year I'm the secretary for the PTA. Dawn Mendez is their room mom. Did you get the last notice about Teacher Appreciation Week?"

He mentally flipped through the stack of papers he had collected from Lacie's backpack. Was one of them about Teacher Appreciation Week? "When did you send it?"

"I put it in the PTA newsletter that came out the end of last month, and Dawn just sent out a flyer on Tuesday."

"I'm sorry, but I don't remember," Peter admitted. "I'll look for it when I get home."

Donna put a comforting hand on his arm. "Please don't worry about it. I know you have a lot on your mind, and not a lot of practice managing a family. What can I do to help?"

"Thanks. Right now, it would be great if you tell me what Teacher Appreciation Week is."

She laughed. "Of course. It's a week where we show our appreciation for the teachers' hard work. We do a different thing for them every day."

"Like what?"

She ticked off the items on her fingers. "On Monday, we bring in her favorite candy. On Tuesday, each family sends in one flower that will be combined with all the others to make a huge bouquet. On Wednesday, the students are supposed to draw pictures of themselves to collect into an album for her. Thursday is her favorite drink, and Friday the PTA brings in lunch for the whole staff. We'll set up a café in the auditorium, and the fourth and fifth graders will wait on them. It's a lot of fun, and they feel very much appreciated when it is all done."

By the time she said the last thing, Peter couldn't remember the first. "Did you organize all that?"

"Not me alone, but I am on the Teacher

Appreciation Week committee." She must have sensed his anxiety, because she jumped right in with, "Don't worry about it, please. It's not meant to add stress to anyone's life. It's supposed to be fun. I can send in double of everything so you don't have to remember it at all. I can even run by and drop it off the night before so Lacie can give it to Ms. Allen herself. Unless you let me pick her up in the mornings."

"I don't want you to have to do that," Peter replied. "It's my responsibility to get it done, and I need to do it."

"Nicely said, but my offer stands. If you realize, even at the last minute, that you can't do one of the things, don't hesitate to call me. I always have extras, just in case." She paused. "Would it help if I called your secretary to leave you reminders?"

Did everybody know he couldn't keep a schedule? "Caroline's not a secretary. She's my office manager. But yes, it would help for her to put it on my calendar."

"No problem. I'll e-mail her the flyer when I get home."

Peter was generally too busy to dwell on the quality of his parenting, but Donna's efficiency cast a spotlight on his inadequacies. He admired her and resented her at the same time. "You seem to have it all under control."

"I have lots of experience." She visited him with a self-confident smile.

"How do you have time for everything?" he asked sincerely. "Do you work, too?"

"I sub at the school and do some tutoring on the side. My ex-husband is still paying for the house and living expenses for the children, plus a little bit of alimony to cover what I need for myself. Wayne and I agree that it's better for me to stay home, since he is never available to do anything for them."

Her face was still smiling, but her voice was sharp.

"I see." Peter did not want to get involved in a conversation about her ex-husband.

"My children are my life. In spite of Wayne's shortcomings, I will always be grateful he gave them to me."

Her statement was so genuine, so deeply felt, that Peter couldn't think of anything to say. He was rescued by Lacie's banging up the bleacher seats to ask her routine, "Daddy, can I have a Ring-Pop?" to which he gave his routine answer, "That's garbage, Lacie. Get something else."

He pulled out his wallet, but before he could hand Lacie her dollar, Donna interjected, "Sweetie, all that candy will rot your teeth. Let me get you a snack out of the cooler."

"That's not necessary." Peter was caught off-guard and worried about the correct response. Should he say yes, which was what he wanted to do? Was he supposed to refuse but be appropriately appreciative? Should he offer to pay for the snack?

"It's no problem at all," she responded, moving swiftly to the cooler. "See? Here comes Curtis for his."

Donna whipped the hand-sanitizer out of her pocket like a quick-draw sharpshooter.

Curtis and Lacie held out their hands without question to receive a squirt each.

"Is Lacie allergic to peanuts?"

Based on the fortune he had spent on peanut M&M's, it didn't seem likely. "No."

"Sit here while you eat," she instructed. Peter was astonished to see the children obey without question.

Donna climbed back to her seat and handed Peter a granola bar. He didn't recognize the wrapper. "I've never seen this kind before."

"I get them in the health food section. Have you read the labels on the popular ones? The amount of sugar and salt is unbelievable."

I'm supposed to read the labels? He always bought the same things Maisie had bought, replacing what she left in the pantry. Had Maisie read the labels?

"And don't worry," she added. "The fruit snacks are sweetened with actual fruit purée."

He was supposed to be worried about the ingredients in fruit snacks? Didn't the word "fruit" mean they were healthier than candy? What else was he supposed to be worrying about? "Thanks," he said, overwhelmed at the amount of information he didn't know about raising his children.

"It's my pleasure," she said brightly.

Unlike the delicious cookies, the granola bar did taste like cardboard, but if it was healthier, it was worth the sacrifice. Wasn't it?

Lacie and Curtis finished their snacks and returned to the hole they were digging next to the bleachers. "I keep old clothes in the car just for the football field," Donna commented. "That way, Curtis doesn't ruin his good ones."

"That's a good idea." *Vitamins, check. Hand sanitizer, check. Healthy granola bars, check. Read labels, check.* Peter glanced at Lacie, who was getting dirt all over a school-quality pair of leggings and top. *Extra clothes in car, check.*

"Are you originally from around here?" Donna asked, maintaining her constant stream of conversation.

"Uh…no." Peter was still mulling over his parental shortcomings. "I was born in Knoxville."

"Tennessee!" she squealed, as though he had said he was from Disneyland. "It is so beautiful up there! My family went to Dollywood one summer and absolutely loved it."

"Yeah, Pigeon Forge is nice, but it gets a little crowded in the summer." Truthfully, he'd rather stab himself in the eye than get stuck in the tourist traffic jamming the single main street through the mountain town.

"Was Maisie from Tennessee, too?"

"Yeah. We grew up there."

"Grew up together?"

"Yes." He didn't want to talk about Maisie. Not after he was suddenly faced with how inadequately he was filling her place. "Look," he pointed at the field. "Justin is in as quarterback."

Donna sprang up suddenly like someone had pushed her start switch. "Go, Justin! Show 'em how it's done!"

Diversion achieved. Their personal conversation came to an end. Peter loved watching Logan skillfully execute the plays the coach had taught them. Justin was second string, but Logan was on the field all the time, receiving the ball and dashing through lines of blocking guards. Peter had played the same way when he was Logan's age, and sometimes as he watched his son, he could feel the phantom ball in his hands and the pounding of his heart as he raced ahead of the defenders toward the goal.

After they were home and Logan and Lacie were asleep, Peter stretched out on the bed again, patting the place next to him for Buddy.

The beagle looked accusingly at Peter from the floor.

"Sorry, guy. We'll take you to the game with us on Saturday, okay?"

Satisfied, Buddy jumped up on the bed and took his accustomed place.

Scratching the dog between the ears, Peter's head dropped back onto the pillow. *I'm doing everything all wrong.*

Maisie's voice answered. *No, you're not. You're doing a great job.*

How do you know? Are you watching from heaven?

Yes, I am.

You didn't tell me I'm supposed to read the labels.

That's why I suggested Donna for you. She's the best mother I know.

Hand sanitizer and granola bars don't make her a better mother than you were.

That was the right thing to say. But there were a lot of things I let fall through the cracks that she's got covered.

Is one of them Teacher Appreciation Week?

No, I did pretty well with that one.

Thanks for the heads up.

It wasn't the top thing on my mind at the time. Sorry.

I'm sorry I didn't pay more attention when you were taking care of all of this. Now that I'm the one, I can see how hard it is to keep all the balls in the air.

Don't worry about it. Nobody knows what they're doing with kids. Mostly, they turn out okay anyway. Who is Lacie's teacher this year?

Ms. Allen. Don't you know that in heaven?

Smart Aleck. Logan had her, too. She loves sunflowers, and her favorite candy is popcorn flavored jelly beans.

It must truly be her talking to him from Heaven if she could tell him things he didn't already know, right? He wanted it to be her with every fiber of his being. *Thanks.*

No problem.

I miss you.

I miss you, too.

Even in "heaven?"

Even in Heaven.

Donna's mothering skills make me feel inadequate. I'm not sure I want to spend time with her.

There is more to Donna than just mothering. Give her a chance. She likes to help people. Once you let her help you, I think you'll find she decreases your stress.

Okay, I guess.

Loved you in that life and beyond. Kiss our babies for me.

Chapter 10

"How was Donna?" Caroline asked after the kids blew out the next morning.

"There wasn't much to it in the way of a date," Peter admitted, dropping into the chair next to her behind the desk. "But I did discover what a lousy parent I am."

She swiveled around to look at him, her brow creased in surprise. "What's wrong with your parenting?"

He sighed. "For one thing, I'm supposed to be reading the food labels."

"C'mon, Doc. You know about nutrition and food additives. I've heard you talking to people about garbage dog food for years."

"Yes, but that's my job. When I took on full-time care of the kids, I needed *something* to be easy, so I kept buying whatever Maisie had in the cabinets. The kids liked it. I liked it. Problem solved. How could I know she wasn't careful about what they ate?"

Caroline straightened like someone had poked a finger in her back. "She *was* careful, and she *did* read labels. But she wasn't prone toward fads, and she didn't think all "health" foods were better. Your kids have always been healthy, haven't they?"

"Yes, they have." Processed sugar or not, they hardly ever missed a day of school.

She leaned back in her chair. "Relax. Read a few labels if you want to feel better. You're doing fine. How many men do you know who bring their children to work with them to catch the bus? Logan and Lacie are great kids. Wherever she is, Maisie is proud of you."

Common sense. Caroline had a way of putting things in perspective. That was why he talked to her. She was one of those guardian angels that would sit on his shoulder and stop him from saying stupid, inappropriate things.

At the game on Saturday, Peter discovered that being friendly with Donna pulled him into the social circle of football parents in a way that had always eluded him. At first, his characteristic reserve held true, but eventually, the camaraderie broke through and he was talking to the others like old friends. Buddy helped as a conversation starter, both because Peter had to sit on the bottom bleacher and because some of them hadn't known he was a veterinarian until Donna made a point of it.

Most of them had known Maisie, and, once they realized he was okay with it, she bobbed in and out of their conversation like a fishing lure.

"Maisie was great in a crisis," said Ron Williams, father to twins Robert and Ryan. "Remember when Adam Moskowitz hit Curtis with the baseball bat? It bled like a son-of-a-gun, but Maisie was right on it while the rest of us were still trying to figure out what happened."

Donna's body went rigid. "I could have handled it, but Maisie was sitting closest so she got to him before I could."

Peter shook his head. "She never said anything about that to me."

Donna waved her hand as though swatting away the subject. "Peter, are you still taking those children out for fast food before the games? You know it is so easy for me to make a little extra. I can make some for you, too. After all, we can't forget Dad." She bumped him with her elbow like they were sharing a secret.

Did he detect a flirtatious tone in her voice? He looked around to see if anyone else had noticed, but the others had suddenly become enthralled with the game. "I can't ask you to do that. I just need to be better about planning."

"Nonsense," she replied, brushing away his refusal. "I'll have it ready when you get here on Tuesday night. Do you like pasta salad?"

"Pasta salad?" At a kid's football game?

"You know, pasta with mozzarella, salami, pepperoni, onions, tomatoes, and olives? I make it all the time. My kids love it."

She *did* mean pasta salad at a football game. "I'm not a big fan of olives," he admitted.

"Is olive oil okay?"

"Sure." Were they really having this conversation?

"Great. Let's call it a plan."

He was embarrassed, but her will was too strong. He surrendered without further argument. "Thank you, Donna. Let me pay you for the food."

She held up her hands to stop him. "I'd have to buy it anyway. It's really no problem."

He looked at the others, but everyone was working hard at pretending they didn't hear them. He wondered if he and Donna would be the subject of the gossip mill when they were out of earshot. The thought didn't seem to bother her, so he guessed it shouldn't bother him, either. "Thanks. Thanks a lot."

****

After Logan and Lacey left for school on Monday, Peter told Caroline about Donna's plan. "She made me an offer I couldn't refuse." He rubbed his chin in a Godfather imitation.

Caroline chuckled. "She's got your number, Doc."

"What do you mean?" He crossed his arms and leaned against the doorframe to his office.

"She's analyzed your weaknesses and moved in for the kill." Caroline went to the wall of files behind her desk to pull records for their returning patients.

"Kill?"

"She has identified you as a potential mate."

Peter smirked. "We're not breeding. She's just making pasta salad."

"Pasta salad, huh?" she teased. "She's pulling out the big guns."

"What are you talking about? It's a salad." He turned his back on her and shut himself in his office.

Caroline's comments put Peter on his guard when he pulled into the football field parking lot on Tuesday. From the look of things, Donna had been there for a while. She had camping tables and chairs set up, a low table for the children and a higher one set for two adults. "Seven Nation Army" blasted from the radio. In spite of his wariness, the music took him back to college. He and Maisie had found a CD player with two headphone jacks so they could listen to the same music, and "Seven Nation Army" had been one of their favorites.

Donna's food reminded Peter of a fancy buffet with chicken salad on croissants, the promised pasta salad, freshly cut watermelon, and lemon squares dusted with powdered sugar for dessert. He had been to a lot of tailgates, and this one was more like the set up for a college or pro game than the parking lot of the local recreation fields. Maybe Caroline had been right. Maybe Donna had an agenda beyond the kindness of feeding a family with no mother. He *had* detected flirting during their last encounter.

Logan filled a plate and joined Justin, who had already started. The boys were like vacuum cleaners, sucking up the food without tasting it. Peter and Donna shared a smile, connected by the common experience of parenting preteen boys.

Lacie and Curtis were paying less attention to their food than the action figures Curtis had brought to share. Lacie finally took a bite of the pasta salad and turned up her nose. "Blegh," she said, spitting it out on her plate.

Peter rushed in to soften the offense. "The food is really delicious, Donna. Lacie is kind of a picky eater."

Donna appeared unaffected. "Don't worry about it. My oldest child is a girl, and she is still finicky about her food."

The boys wolfed down two lemon squares each and wiped sticky hands on their pants before standing up to sprint to the field.

"Thanks, Ms. Lechleiter," Logan called back as he ran after Justin.

Curtis ignored them and the lemon square on his plate, fixated on the action figure in his hand.

Lacie, on the other hand, was savoring every small, delicate bite.

"Do you like it, Lacie, honey?" Donna asked, prompting the appropriate response.

"Yes, I do," replied Lacie. "Thank you very much."

Donna turned her full attention on Peter. "How about you, Peter?" she asked, as if his licked-clean plate wasn't an answer.

"Not at all," he joked. "You can see what I didn't like left on my plate."

She beamed. "I'm so glad. I left out the olives just for you."

"I noticed. Thank you."

"Mom, can we go?" Curtis asked. He'd lost interest in the action figures and had been waiting impatiently for Lacie to finish eating.

"Sure, honey." Donna snapped the lids on the food containers.

As the younger kids ran toward the football fields, Peter kept an uneasy eye on them. "You let him go just like that, without someone to watch him?"

"I can see them all the way to the sidelines," Donna said like she was instructing a new parent.

He looked again and saw that what she said was true. Lacie and Curtis had reached the bleachers where other parents were already sitting to watch them. Donna's confidence was contagious, and for the first time in a long time, Peter didn't feel compelled to dash after them. He leaned back in his chair to finish his sweet tea. "Seven Nation Army?"

Donna's face broke into a genuine, unaffected smile, eyes sparkling. "Once I told the boys it came from Jack White misspeaking "Salvation Army" as a kid, they were hooked."

"I'm impressed," he said. "It never occurred to me to share my music with them. Of course, it never actually occurred to me to listen to "my music" anymore. In the car we're committed to kids' radio, and I forgot all about it. Who else do you like?"

"My tastes are pretty eclectic. Sunspots. Summer at the Beach. Life on Mars, but only the *Friends in Heaven* album. *Stuffed Pigs* and *Simple Moments* were both sub-par. Dreams of Home is my favorite group. In college, my girl posse owned the floor when we danced to "Long Time Coming.""

"Those are all great bands," he said, impressed. "That music takes me back to my college days."

"You like Dreams of Home?" She froze in the motion of folding the tablecloth. Talking music made her an entirely different person.

"I did fifteen years ago," he replied. "Maisie and I saw them in concert. Are they still around?"

Her eyes lit up like a Christmas tree. "They're coming to Atlanta next Friday. Would you like to go?"

She had caught him off-guard, and he choked on his answer, "With you?"

"Absolutely. Seems like nobody else has heard of them."

She was almost pleading. Even if he had wanted to, he didn't see how he could refuse her. He had a glimpse of young Donna, sashaying carefree around the campus with her girlfriends. He would have been friends with that Donna in those long-ago days. "Sure." He hadn't done anything without considering time, babysitters, or money in two years, and he was ready for a little liberation.

"Great! I'll order the other ticket right now, before

you have a chance to change your mind." She was on her phone and done before he threw away his trash. "How about we do dinner before? I know a place that has the best burgers in town."

"Sounds good." He wasn't sorry to have boarded this train, but he did feel like it was barreling along without brakes.

The remains of their picnic disappeared like magic, and they were walking up to the field, cooler in tow, before he could blink.

"Who else did you listen to?" she asked like a cooing teenager. "Pearl Jam?"

"Uh, yeah," he agreed, flexing his memory muscles.

"Red Hot Chili Peppers?"

"Sure."

"Foo Fighters?"

He chuckled. He and Maisie had gone to concerts by these bands and many others, sometimes with friends, sometimes alone. He liked remembering the years when they were dating, and the person he'd been at the time. Instead of being bent with the burden of loss and responsibility, he stepped lighter for knowing how lucky he was to have lived it.

Peter leaned down to lift the cooler over the curb, and when he stood up, Team Mom Donna had returned. The hint of pursed lines shadowed her top lip.

"Hi, everybody." She waved at the parents on the bleachers. A folder of flyers covered with football graphics materialized out of thin air. She handed one to each family representative in the stands. "This is for the end of season party," she said. "What do we want to do about trophies?"

"They're too old for trophies they didn't earn," grumbled Ron Williams.

"Then what do you propose as favors instead?" Donna shot back.

"Why do they need favors?" Jim Morse countered. "This isn't a tea party. Their reward is that we paid for them to play football."

"Is that the way everyone feels?" she asked, her jaw set in disapproval.

"Is there something inexpensive we can give them that isn't a trophy?" asked Joan Williams, the peacemaker.

"A medal?" Donna was not going to be denied.

"How about nothing?" Ron agreed with Jim.

The men dug in, and the women squirmed.

Peter was amused. He had never known there could be so much drama in middle school sports.

"How about monogrammed tags for their gym bags?" Joan offered. "We'll use the team logo on one side and their initials on the other. If they don't want to put it on their gym bags, they can put them on their backpacks." She cringed, waiting for someone to yell at her, but no one did.

Donna sighed. "Fine. Is everyone okay with that?"

The response was less than enthusiastic, but no one disagreed.

Joan's shoulders relaxed. "I'll be happy to take care of this. I know a place that can do it very reasonably."

"That's all right, Joan. I have a place I've worked with all the times I've been team mom. He's cheap and fast." Donna dismissed Joan's offer without discussion.

No one spoke for the rest of the game. Peter wished

the Donna he had seen in the parking lot would make another appearance. He wondered which version of her would show up for their "Dreams of Home" date.

****

Peter didn't have the chance to tell Caroline about Donna and the concert until the next day at lunch. On days when they had time for a real break and everyone else went out, Caroline would bring her lunch bag into his office and sit on the opposite side of his desk. He laughed out loud when Caroline choked on her sandwich at his mention of the musical date with Donna.

"You like Dreams of Home?" she sputtered. "Since when?"

"I wasn't always a drag," he informed her. "Once upon a time, I was young like you and had fun."

"Young like me?" she replied. "You're not that much older than I am."

"Eleven years."

"It may be eleven years on paper," she shook her sandwich at him. "But working for you has aged me considerably."

She didn't look aged. Yes, she was older than the teenage girl who had come to work for them ten years before, but she had simply matured into a lovely young woman. "Are you saying I'm hard to work for? "

"Sometimes." All the teasing was gone from her voice. "You set our standards pretty high. It can be a little daunting to reach them."

He sat back and crossed his arms. "I just want everyone to be professional. I don't ask anything from you all that I don't expect of myself."

"That's true," she agreed. "But you can be pretty

117

hard on yourself."

"I suppose." He sat up and rolled his trash into a ball. "Anyway, she bought the ticket before I could even blink."

"I told you she had your number. She's even wilier than I gave her credit for."

Peter couldn't tell if she admired Donna or considered her manipulative. He was going with manipulative. "You are more cynical than I gave you credit for." He lobbed the ball into the trash can by the door with his best free-throw shot.

"When's the concert?" she asked, putting the top on her salad container and packing it in her lunch bag.

He cocked an eyebrow. "You mean she hasn't called to put it on my calendar?"

Caroline's mouth hinted at a smile. "Not yet."

He felt triumphant that he finally knew something she didn't. "Next Friday." He stood up to go back to work, stepping around the desk to wait for her while she finished cleaning up.

Standing so close, she had to tip her head back to look up at him. "That's soon. I'm surprised there were tickets left. Lucky for you, I'm free to babysit."

Looking down at her accentuated his sense of her as a little sister, and he felt a wave of affection. "Not for free," Peter replied. "I don't want you to feel used."

She laughed. "*Now* you're worrying about my feeling used? I've been babysitting for you for ten years."

"Yes, and I used to pay you for it. What happened to that?"

"I got older, and you gave me a real job so I don't need the money. You're not using me if I offer.

Besides, I didn't finish *Ice Queen* the last time. Maybe if we start in the middle, Lacie will make it farther before she falls asleep."

"Then you've got to let me do something for you. How about I pay for you and Josh to go out to dinner?"

Caroline's face fell. "Josh and I broke up."

She looked so unhappy that Peter carefully kept his expression neutral to hide his pleasure. Was she truly finally rid of the albatross around her neck? "Why didn't I know?"

"Because you were doing what you always do, Doc. Kicking butt and taking names."

Peter smiled. "Then I guess we'll have to think of something else."

Her face relaxed. "I guess so. What time?"

"She wants to go out for dinner first."

Caroline chuckled and shook her head. "Of course, she does. What time?"

He was a little irritated by Caroline's attitude. His voice dripping with sarcasm, he said, "Since she hasn't called you, I guess I'll have to ask her myself."

"You do that." She pitched her trash into the garbage can as she walked out.

He didn't have to wait long to ask. Later that day, he followed Sally Morrison and Beauregard the Great Dane out to the waiting room to find Donna standing by the reception desk. "Donna? What a surprise." He looked to Caroline for explanation, but she shook her head. "Is everything okay?"

"I'm here with Sally," she replied with the confidence he was starting to recognize. "We're going to lunch after she takes Beauregard home." She shifted her attention to Sally. "Did Peter tell you his son plays football with Justin? You know Logan, don't you?"

"Of course, I do. He's been in my Sarah's class at least three different times over the years."

Peter was too busy to get into a long exploration of every time Logan and Sally's child had done something together since they were two years old. "You ladies have a nice lunch."

Donna didn't budge. "Peter and I are going to a concert together," she informed Sally, looking to Caroline for corroboration.

"I put it on his calendar," Caroline confirmed. "But Dr. Hunter didn't remember what time."

"The concert begins at seven, and we need time for dinner." She glanced at the other occupants of the waiting room and spoke in a louder voice. "I thought I'd introduce him to a restaurant called *Fender's*. They have the best burgers you ever put in your mouth."

Sally put her finger to her cheek. "Do you really think so? We like *Burger Bar*. *Fender's* has such a limited menu."

Just like with the trophies, Donna allowed no discussion. *"Burger Bar* is good for what it is, but *Fender's* is an experience."

"That's okay," Caroline offered, looking at Peter with an affectionate smile. "Dr. Hunter is a hamburger purist. Just give him ketchup, lettuce, and tomato, and he is good to go."

Peter nodded, wishing Donna and Sally would leave. This tense, personal conversation should not be taking place in front of his waiting patients.

As opposed to showing gratitude for the support, Donna fixed her attention on Caroline like a hawk on its prey. "You keep his personal calendar and know what he likes to eat? That is over and above for an office manager."

"I've worked for him a long time," Caroline replied, professional persona back in place.

Peter had run out of patience for the tension-charged air. "I'm sorry to cut you off, but I've got patients waiting. What time for dinner?"

"Five o'clock should do it. I'll pick you up, since I know where everything is."

That made Peter step back. He may have been out of the dating game for a while, but he still held on to some of the traditions. A man should drive. "I think I can get us to a restaurant and the concert venue. It's at Olympic Park, right?"

"Yes, it is," Donna soothed. "The restaurant is close but hard to see from the street, and it's so much easier if I get us there."

Peter didn't feel like arguing. "Five o'clock it is. See you then." Enough said. "Goodbye, Sally. I'll see you and Beauregard next year. Mr. Kane, bring Chaser on back. I'm sorry for the wait."

Leading Mr. Kane and Chaser, his border collie, to the exam room, Peter overheard Donna ask, "So exactly how long have you been working for Dr. Hunter?"

Chapter 11

As Caroline was shutting down the office on Friday afternoon, she called to Peter, "Hey, Doc. Dr. Park's son is playing football at the high school tonight. Can I take Logan and Lacie?"

He came out of his office holding his lunch box and briefcase. "Are you sure you want to deal with them out in public like that? Keeping up with them in a crowd can be stressful."

"Have you ever been to a high school football game? Your kids are very well behaved compared to most. Logan's friend, Michael, and his parents will be there because his brother is starting. Lacie will be completely captivated by the cheerleaders, and they will love her. We'll be fine."

He had been to high school football games, but it had been back in his own high school days, and he had always been on the field with Maisie in the bleachers, cheering him on. He sighed at the happy memories and toyed briefly with the idea of cancelling his date to go with Caroline and the children. Maisie's voice whispered in his head, *Remember fun?* If the Donna who showed up was the one who had gushed over the band, it would be a good time. "Sure. Thanks." He handed her enough money for entrance fees, plus food for herself and the children.

"C'mon, guys," she called into the backroom. To

Peter, she said, "Do you think you can dress yourself without Lacie's help?"

"Very funny." He waved her off, but when Lacie walked up, he asked, "What do you think, Little Bit? Khakis and the blue button-down?"

"Wear blue jeans and the purple shirt," Lacie replied confidently. "I like that purple shirt."

"Sneakers?"

"I like the brown boots."

Caroline gave him a thumbs up. "She's right about the purple shirt. It looks great. Highlights your eyes."

He held the door open for them to leave and made a note to look in the mirror after he was dressed to see if his eyes looked any different.

Having successfully dressed himself in the Lacie-approved fashion, and unable to see any difference in his eyes at all, Peter was still wondering whether College Donna or Team Mom Donna would show up when the doorbell rang at 5:45. He opened the door and was greeted by pre-husband, pre-kids, fangirl Donna in all of her sparkly glory. Although her black shirt had faded to charcoal and was very tight, the words "Rockin' the Night Away" were still vibrant in hand-painted glittery gold. Multi-colored sequins had been embedded in the paint, and there were obvious spots where one or more had fallen off.

Her shirt made him happy, though he couldn't exactly say why. Maybe it was because it reminded him of the great concerts he and Maisie had seen. Maybe it was because it made him think of old friends who had existed in the fan frenzy of their college days. Maybe it was because it had been a long time since he had been to an adult occasion where hand-decorated clothing was appropriate. God knows, he hadn't been dressed in neat jeans and a purple polo back then. In those days, he and Maisie thought they were dressed up if they wore clothes first thing out of the wash. "Nice shirt. I bet it's seen some great shows."

She giggled. "This is my concert shirt. I made it myself. The glitter and sequins reflect great off the stage lights. Of course, it didn't use to be so tight."

Now, in addition to young, enthusiastic Donna, she was also suddenly busty, sexy Donna. Peter wasn't sure he was ready to handle it. It was unintentional seduction, at least, he thought so, and her excitement for the music was more enticing than any overt advances would have been. It occurred to him he was about to make his first new concert memory in fifteen years. *This is what you wanted, isn't it, Maisie? Life going on, even if it has to be without you?*

On the ride downtown, Donna asked a lot of snoopy questions, but he had to admit she was a good listener. "I know you said you and Maisie grew up together, but did you date the whole time?"

"Uh, no. We didn't start dating until college." He didn't feel inclined to elaborate, but he was nervous about an uncomfortable silence.

He needn't have worried. Donna was the conductor of this train. "And you guys went to a lot of concerts?"

"I wouldn't say a lot. We didn't have enough money to go to big concerts. Mostly, we saw the smaller, lesser-known groups at venues around town."

"I know what you mean about that. We were so poor we brought lawn chairs to sit outside and listen to the music."

"We did that, too." Peter laughed. "I miss those

days sometimes. Things are a lot simpler when you have no money. The answer to everything you want to do is *no*."

"Yep, but we still managed to have a good time, didn't we?" She paused for a beat, then asked, "What do you do for fun these days, Peter?"

Fun? What was fun? Logan's football? Fireworks on Labor Day? An early morning run? "Probably the same as you," he replied. "There isn't time for much that doesn't include the kids." He didn't want it to sound like he was unhappy about spending time with Logan and Lacie, so he hastened to add, "But they're good enough, aren't they?"

"Yes, they certainly are. They are my life. But I do think it's okay to do something without them sometimes, don't you agree?"

"To be honest, I hadn't thought about it until you suggested this." After Maisie died, even though their demands drove him crazy, he couldn't bear to leave Logan and Lacie for long periods of time because he was haunted by the fear of losing them, too. He focused his inner eye on them having fun with Caroline at the football game and relaxed with the knowledge that he trusted her completely. She was family, and she would watch carefully to keep them safe.

Donna pulled into a city parking lot. "Isn't this convenient? There's *Fender's*." She pointed. "And we can walk to the park from here without it costing an arm and a leg."

"Yeah, this is great," Peter replied, distracted as he scanned the line of storefronts. "I don't see the restaurant. You said it's close?"

Donna smiled an "I-know-something-you-don't-know" smile. "It's right there, in between the bank and the clothes store."

He looked again. There was an inconspicuous door with a frosted window and *Fender's* written across it in stylized script. As they crossed the street, he looked up and saw people sitting at tables in the second story windows. He followed her through the door into a dimly lit stairwell echoing with muffled crowd sounds and with another identical door at the top.

When he stepped inside, he looked around and could think of only one thing to say: "Cool."

"Yes, it is," Donna replied reverently.

The walls were covered with framed, autographed concert posters and t-shirts, and there were glass cases with assorted music memorabilia. Only one sign by the door did not reflect the festive mood. "Sex, ~~drugs~~, and rock and roll!" it proclaimed with the word "drugs" marked out. "Drugs dull the music" admonished a handwritten sentence below.

"I knew you'd like it. I recognize a fellow music appreciator when I see one." Donna looked around as though she had designed it for them personally.

"Welcome, welcome!" said a man with shaggy white hair and a beard, whose sparkling eyes made him look like a mischievous Santa Claus. The black Bonnaroo T-shirt pulled tightly across his generous belly was pure rock and roll. "I'm Nate. Welcome, welcome." He led them through the noisy dining room to the only unoccupied table. "How about a beer?"

Channeling his college days, Peter asked for the cheapest brand he could remember. "I'll have a *Red's*." The point wasn't the quality of the beer, but the taste of the memory. Nate's grin told Peter that he understood.

"That's a good one. I'll have the same," Donna said with a smile.

"An excellent choice," affirmed their host. "It's still one of my favorites after all these years."

The background music came from a loop of old concerts shown on the ubiquitous TVs visible from every vantage point. On the menu there was no long list of sandwiches with clever names, only "Build Your Own Burger" and "Build Your Own Salad." Donna ordered a burger with everything on it, but Peter kept his plain, just as Caroline had predicted.

After Nate left to put in their order, Donna sighed and smiled. "Do you know this is my first date since Wayne left? It never occurred to me I might find someone who shared my taste in music, and music really needs to be shared, don't you think?"

Peter nodded as the young waiter put their drinks on the table. "I agree."

"Is it your first date, too?" She swirled the amber liquid in her glass and held it up to look at the light through it before taking a sip.

His night with Suzanne certainly counted as a date. "No, it's not. But there's only been one other." He took a slow sip and swished it around in his mouth before swallowing. He put his glass down on the table and blew out a sigh. "That is just as terrible as I remember," he laughed.

Donna held up her glass to clink. "Absolutely awful."

Peter touched his to hers. "To the great memories that go with awful beer."

"Amen." Donna put down her glass.

When she looked up, something undefinable in her

expression put him on his guard. "So, Caroline has been with you ten years? She must have been pretty young when she started." She squinted as though it would help her assess the truth of his answer.

"Uh, yeah," he replied, carefully keeping all emotion out of his voice. He was not going to get into a deep discussion of his relationship with Caroline. "She didn't start out as an office manager. She babysat the kids so Maisie could work the front desk."

"I see." She nodded wisely, as though she saw more than he had said. "You must be pretty close with her."

The hairs on Peter's neck stood up. Donna was not invited to make assumptions about or comment on his relationship with Caroline. "Caroline is a member of the family." He leaned forward to take control of the conversation. "Where did you say you went to college? What did you study?"

"I went to Tallulah State up in the mountains. My degree is in accounting, and I worked with Marchon, Hicks and Jones when I first got out of school."

He was relieved Donna respected the subject change. "Marchon, Hicks and Jones? That's pretty impressive." Some of the more affluent members of his family had used the prestigious, old money, accounting firm.

"They took me right out of college. I was an accounting star," she replied, tipping her nose in the air in an exaggerated show of pride. "That's how I met Wayne. I had actually been promoted above him, but I stopped working after Justin was born. Shortly after that, Wayne decided to start his own accounting firm." She shook her head. "His timing was always lousy."

"You didn't work with him?" It was obvious her career was a source of pride, so why didn't she pursue it?

She wiped the table with a napkin, even though it looked perfectly clean to Peter. "I don't need to tell you how demanding two children can be if you're going to raise them right. Just when I got Justin and Audra into school and thought I might do a little work on the side, Curtis came along. Even though he's in school now, without a husband who will help, I really don't have time for anything else."

"Audra is your oldest?" He remembered Maisie's comments about the existence of an older child she never saw.

Donna nodded. "She's a junior in high school, and we're just starting to look at colleges. With her grades and all of her accomplishments, she can get into almost any school she wants." Dark clouds passed across her glowing expression. "As long as her father will pay for it."

"Good for her." Peter dodged discussion of the ex-husband again. "Is she babysitting tonight?"

Donna chuckled. "Unwillingly. Audra doesn't exactly have a high opinion of her little brothers. They'll make themselves scarce after they eat, to avoid her displeasure."

Peter thought of Logan's indifference to Lacie in the morning. "I can't imagine leaving Lacie with Logan, even though it's a couple of years away. Logan wouldn't show his "displeasure." He wouldn't pay any attention to her at all. She could set the house on fire, and he'd never notice until the flames leapt in front of his video game."

Their conversation halted with the arrival of the most beautiful burger he had ever seen. The juices from the meat permeated the bun, making it hard to pick up and requiring the entire stack of napkins the server put on the table. The French fries on the side were skinny and fried to a perfect crisp, like the ones he usually tried to pick out first from the bunch. Peter sat back after every bite to draw out the experience as long as possible. He needed to bring the kids here, particularly Logan. All Americans needed to have a perfect burger at least once in their lives, and they would never get something like this off of his grill. "You were right about this place," he admitted to Donna. "When you said 'best burger in town' I had my doubts, but this lives up to the hype."

"Wayne and I discovered it back in the days when we were first working together." She wiped hamburger juice off her hands. "Then I started coming here with my friends whenever Wayne gave me a reprieve from the kids."

He noticed that Wayne often came up in her conversation, even though her comments were nearly always disparaging. Maybe she was more hurt than angry. "You and Wayne stopped coming together?"

"Did you and Maisie go places together after you had kids?" she countered.

"Not much. And she never asked for a break. Maybe I should have offered…" he trailed off, wondering if there was something Maisie never told him.

"Maybe you should have. But if she didn't ask, how were you supposed to know? Could you read her mind?" Donna took his hand where it rested on the table. "I never saw her unhappy, and never heard her say a word against you. Even when she was sick and she had to be feeling terrible."

"I should have tried." Even though alarms were going off in his head warning him against it, he asked, "What happened between you and Wayne?"

She dropped his hand and went back to eating. "He loved his work more than he loved us. I gave him plenty of chances. I warned him that if he couldn't find a way to spend time with us, he didn't need to be part of our lives."

Peter took a bite of his burger. He was also guilty of not making time for his family until Maisie became too ill to do everything herself, but she never complained. On the other hand, Donna set a standard that would have been hard for him to meet. He shook himself out of his funk and came back to cheerier conversation. He wanted to get back to happy, carefree Donna. "Do you remember the first time you saw Dreams of Home?"

Donna relaxed, and he felt like he could see her becoming younger before his eyes.

"Of course, I do. It was the 1999 Homecoming Tour here in Atlanta. Let me tell you," she leaned in as if she was telling him a secret. "I had a major crush on Marcus Home. I would have had his baby."

Peter laughed. "That's pretty serious," he said. "It's a good thing he didn't take you up on it."

"My girlfriends held me back. I was ready to jump up on the stage, but they didn't think it was a good idea."

"Hard to imagine Team Mom Donna as Fangirl Donna," Peter teased.

"You'll get a look at her tonight. If Marcus is still half the stud he was in 1999, I'm available." Donna winked. "You don't mind, do you?"

"Of course not. It will make a great story at the next football game. 'I was out with Donna, she climbed up on the stage to dance with Marcus Home, and that was the last I saw of her.'"

"Exactly," she replied, sitting up straighter and puffing out her chest.

When they were finished, Nate sent them off with enthusiastic slaps on their backs. "Make sure you do exactly what I would do."

"That was a great burger," Peter said, patting his stomach. "Thanks." He wondered what other non-kid-oriented restaurants were out there to explore. Maybe on more dates with Donna? Her confidence and assertiveness were intimidating, but she was good company and he felt a camaraderie with her as parents who had a rock and roll past.

"My pleasure." Donna grinned. "I had a feeling you would appreciate Nate's place. Not everyone does."

The horde streaming toward the huge, open plaza grew more closely packed with every block until they were shuffling instead of walking. The high-rise office buildings that framed the venue created funnels for the surging mob, but once into the big, clear space there were plenty of open areas for sitting or lounging. For a concert this size, of course, no one would be sitting for long, and Peter was afraid they wouldn't be able to get close enough to see the band. He needn't have worried. Donna was a master at darting and dodging through the dense throng, maneuvering them into position right next to the stage.

The opener, Arthur's Lobotomy, was playing bravely on, in spite of the jostling and noise of the crowd as it settled into place. Peter had never heard of the band, and its members were much too young to have been part of his college experience. Still, he was close enough to hear them over the bustle, and he liked their sound. He pulled out his phone and made a note of the name to search it on his computer when he got home.

Suddenly, it hit him like Nate's slap on the back. He stared down at his phone. He was making note of a band. Where had this Peter been hiding for the last fifteen years? When was the last time he had paid any attention to music or cared about the name of the performer?

Donna was already dancing and waving her arms over her head. She had caught the eyes of the vocalist, and he seemed to be singing directly to her. The team mom, room mom, PTA mom was gone, and an adoring groupie had taken her place. Her enthusiasm was infectious. Peter wasn't going to swoon like a starstruck teenager, but he did surrender to the pleasures of the music and watching Donna dance to the pounding rhythm.

The stage went dark, and the crowd froze like statues. Donna grabbed his arm and squeezed so hard he could feel his pulse throbbing in his bicep. Only because he was standing so close to the stage could Peter see the shadows of the band members taking their places. A single spotlight blinked on, highlighting Marcus Home standing at the microphone, head bowed over his acoustic guitar. He was a little grayer, a little softer around the middle, but Peter thought he looked pretty good for an old guy.

Marcus played the soft introductory strains to the song that put them on the map, "Bully the Bullies," and the crowd held its breath, taut as an overwound clock spring. With one last gentle strum, he put down the acoustic and took up the electric guitar on a stand just out of sight in the shadows. The stage exploded into a blinding deluge of light and sound, and the audience sprang loose, cheering and jumping in a frenzy of musical ecstasy. They never sat down, never cooled down, never calmed down during the entire two hours the band played or the extra encores willingly given to adoring fans. These guys knew how to play an audience.

Peter's characteristic inhibitions were vaporized by the booming music and blinding lights. His heart pounded in time with the throbbing bass. He danced with the girl to his left, he danced with the girl to his right, he danced with the girl behind him, but mostly he danced with Donna. They pulsed and undulated to the rhythm of the strings and the beat of the drums. He twirled her into his body and out again. They sang, they laughed, and they cheered.

Surrounded by the mass of bodies filing out of the park, they held on to their ebullient energy. Their buoyant steps matched the rhythm of the music ringing in their ears. The crowd thinned out, waving to strangers who had become friends, as they made their way back to the parking lot where they were one of two cars remaining.

Nate Fender was locking up. He saw them bouncing down the street, grinned, and gave them a "thumbs up" sign.

Donna had the classic, original Dreams of Home album on CD in her car, and they sang to the music all the way home. She sang with abandon, squeaking a bit on the high notes and dropping without warning into the lower range of the harmonies. Her carefree spirit liberated Peter as well, and he sang along with just as much joy, if not quite the volume.

Donna pulled up to Peter's house and sang to the end of the song before she killed the engine. She beat a rhythm on the steering wheel. "That was one for the record books," she croaked.

Peter couldn't remember the last time he had felt so free. It was well before Maisie died. Before the kids had been born. Before he had taken over the practice. "Thanks for suggesting this, Donna. I had a great time."

"You are so welcome," she said, releasing her seatbelt. She pushed up the armrest and slid closer to him.

Peter tried to put more space between them but backed into the door. "I didn't think cars had bench seats anymore."

Donna patted the leather upholstery. "There aren't many, but Wayne found one that does. When we bought this SUV, he wanted it as much like a muscle car as possible. I have to say, this is one time I appreciate his taste." She closed the gap so their legs were touching and looked up at him from under heavy lids. "It reminds me of making out with boys when we were in high school," she said in a husky voice. "Did you do that, too?"

"Make out with boys?" he teased, hoping to neutralize the electrically charged air.

A low, guttural sound came from her chest, which he thought was a kind of chuckle. "You know what I mean."

He knew what she meant. The last time he had made out in a car, he and Maisie had generated so much heat the windows had fogged completely. His sister had pounded on the glass and interrupted them before anything serious happened, but as he closed his eyes now, even with Donna so close, he got goosebumps at the memory of Maisie's warm breath on his neck and the tickle of her hair on his nose. Donna was great company and a lot of fun, but he could not "fog the windows" with anyone else when Maisie's memory was so vivid in his mind.

Peter reached behind his back and pulled the door handle. "I do know what you mean, but I don't think my back can take the contortions anymore. Can yours?" He eased out of the car. "This was the best time I've had in a long time."

Donna leaned across the space he had vacated. "Enough to do it again?"

"Absolutely," he replied, closing the door gently. "I'd like that."

She sat up behind the steering wheel and rolled down the window on his side. "There's a Pearl Jam tribute band in the City Park next month."

He sensed she was testing him. He leaned in the open window. "There is no one I'd rather go with."

Donna looked happy again. She fired up the engine and turned up the music. "See you soon," she called gaily, waving as she pulled away.

Peter waved back and congratulated himself on his skillful handling of the situation. The music still rang in his ears as he walked into the house, beating the rhythm of the percussion on his legs.

"Looks like you had fun." Caroline stood up from the sofa and folded the blanket she had over her lap.

"It was outstanding. I'd forgotten all about music and how it makes me feel." He pulled Caroline into a dancing embrace, twirling her out and back as he had Donna at the concert. When she rolled back, her face was inches from his, and his mouth was on hers before rational thought had a chance of exerting control.

Caroline didn't pull away. She wrapped her arms around his neck and clung to him as he lifted her off the ground. Crushed against him, she was soft and warm, and she tasted like popcorn and fruit punch. He instinctively backed to the sofa to bring her down with him.

When his calves hit the solid furniture, reality crashed in. He lowered her to the floor but kept his arms around her and dropped his head against hers. "I'm sorry," he muttered hoarsely.

"Don't be," she whispered. "Music does that to me, too."

He had kissed Caroline, and he liked it. He wanted to do it again.

No, that was wrong. She was like his kid sister. She was his employee.

But she fit him perfectly, like she had been turned out of a mold to match his body. He couldn't help it. He leaned down and kissed her again.

She pressed into him and returned everything he gave her.

Stop.

What had he always said about workplace

romances? They gum up the engine of a finely tuned machine. How often had he said that "so and so" should keep his pants zipped and his mind on business? But...

No. No "buts."

Using the full force of his strength of will, he dropped his arms. "I'm sorry. I shouldn't have done that."

"That's okay, Doc." She stepped back and turned her face away. "I should be going."

He could see she was trembling and reached out to squeeze her shoulder, but he pulled back when he remembered he was the one who'd made it happen. "Will you be okay going home?" He didn't know what he could do with the children asleep upstairs, but he felt compelled to say it.

"It's no problem, really. Josh will be looking for me."

Josh.

Peter had always disliked Josh because of how he treated Caroline, but this was different. She was going home to Josh, and he wanted her to stay here with him. It was wrong on so many levels, but it was true, nonetheless. He swallowed and struggled to sound like a concerned brother, not a jealous competitor. "I thought Josh was gone."

"Nope. He's promised to change, and I believe him."

That one statement set off blaring alarms in his brain. Abusers always apologized, always promised it would never happen again. He had no evidence Josh had ever actually done anything to her, but her naïve insistence that he was going to be better—and the thought that he had done something to be better about—made Peter want to put his arms around her and hold her in the safety of their house. "Caroline," he said quietly.

She didn't turn around. "I've got to go. I'll see you Monday."

He was too unsettled to pursue it. "Text me when you get there so I know you're safe."

Without looking back, she nodded and was gone.

He trod heavily up the stairs. How would he face her on Monday? Should he pretend like it hadn't happened? Would she let him?

He checked on his sleeping children and dragged himself into his bedroom, the euphoric feeling from the concert completely evaporated. He needed to talk about it all with Maisie—Donna, the concert, and Caroline—but it didn't seem right. Caroline belonged to them both, and kissing her felt like cheating in a way the other women did not.

In the darkness, his mind replayed the memory of opening the clinic door to find a high-school-aged girl standing in the rain, cradling a forlorn little bundle. Hair dripping and clothes soaked, she'd stepped in and pulled aside the wet blanket to reveal the limp body of a gray tabby.

"My cat is sick," the girl pleaded. "Can you help her?"

Peter had stayed up all night to save the cat for the sad girl who seemed to be all alone in the world.

She would have been better off if she was. Caroline's mother drank herself into oblivion every night. Her father was completely disengaged, shutting himself in his office with his computer instead of seeing to the welfare of his children. Peter and Maisie had stood by her side when her grandparents came to take away her brother and sister before Family Services placed them in foster care. Caroline stayed to take care of her mother, but Peter, Maisie, Logan, and eventually Lacie, became her real family. She spent more and more time with them and less and less at her own house, until one day she went home to find her mother dead. Her father left, and Caroline had never seen him since.

She was so much more than an employee.

Chapter 12

Peter was pulled out of a deep, dreamless sleep by the sliding of a chair, the banging of a cabinet, and the clatter of dishes in the kitchen. Either Logan or Lacie was up and getting breakfast. As he rubbed sleep from his eyes, the memories of the night before hit him like a tidal wave.

Donna.

The concert.

Caroline.

Life was so much easier when he stayed home.

He staggered down the stairs and found Lacie in her pajamas sitting at the kitchen counter, eating a bowl of cereal and watching cartoons. She greeted him with a cheery, "Hi, Daddy! Did you have fun?"

Not feeling particularly cheery himself, he nonetheless couldn't take it out on his little girl. He cleared the sleep out of his throat. "Yes, I did, Little Bit. How are you this morning?" He kissed the top of her head as he crossed the room to the coffeemaker.

"I'm great," she replied. "How come you're still wearing the purple shirt?"

He ran his fingers through his hair. "I was too tired to change when I got home last night."

"Okay." She took a bite of her cereal. "Daddy, can I play on the playground at the football game? You can see it from the seats."

He may have just woken up, but she had clearly been awake long enough to determine the issue that would dominate her day. "Hold on." He grimaced, unable to clear the unaccustomed cacophony of feelings from his head. "Let me get some coffee before we talk about that, okay?"

As the warm, dark fluid brought everything into focus, he turned his attention back to her request. She was right that he could see the playground, and it was far off to the side, away from the dangers of the rampaging players and balls flung like missiles. But that also meant he would be hard-pressed to get there fast enough if she was hurt. "I'll think about it." The parental stock answer.

"Okay." She turned her attention to the television like she was satisfied.

Peter wasn't fooled. He had about half an hour before she asked again. Then fifteen minutes before the next one. Then ten. Then five. Then she would be pleading relentlessly, "Please, Daddy. Please, Daddy. Please, please, please, please. Puh-leeze!" He had to down his caffeine fast and kick his brain into a higher gear.

He leaned against the kitchen counter and sipped his coffee, watching Lacie eat her breakfast. Since Maisie died, he had talked with Caroline when he couldn't confide in anyone else. About the kids. About the clinic. About being overwhelmed. Right now, his gut felt like the inside of a clothes dryer with feelings rolling and bouncing around, but how could he ask for her help when she was the cause of his turmoil?

And if he did talk to her, what would he say? He *should* say it was a mistake, and they *should* forget about it, but he couldn't summon the resolve to do it. Something deep inside didn't want to burn that bridge, no matter how wrong it was.

He took another drink of coffee and noticed Lacie had raised her bowl to drink the fruit-flavored milk out of the bottom. He needed more time to think, and she would demand his attention if hers was not occupied. He grabbed a banana off the counter and handed it to her. "Here, Lacie. Eat this, too."

"Okay, Daddy." She turned her attention back to the TV and pulled absently at the stem of the banana.

It would be easier if he opened it for her, but that would defeat the point of buying time. He had cancelled Saturday hours for the clinic because of the early start of Logan's football game, so before he faced Caroline on Monday, he would meet Donna at the field today. Based on her hopeful expression in the car, she wanted to take their relationship further, but did he want to encourage her? He'd had a good time at the concert, and she did bring music back into his life. She knew a lot about raising children and balancing all the different aspects of their lives, an appealing quality in any woman he considered dating. That was certainly why she was on Maisie's list. Maisie had wanted him to be happy, but she had known that passion at this stage in his life was secondary to responsibility. Was it worth another try to see if they were compatible on a date without a concert? Donna appeared to be exactly what his family needed.

If only he hadn't kissed Caroline. He had held her in his arms for only a few minutes, but it had created a complication his wife could never have foreseen. His feelings for her were something entirely new, a desire that was not a replacement for Maisie but uniquely hers, and entirely inappropriate. *Maisie, why couldn't you have let me be alone, happily wallowing in my self-pity?* A run would help clear his head, but he looked at his watch and saw there was no time.

Lacie had used her spoon to dig into the banana through the peel, and she was digging out her last bite.

Peter drained his cup and poured another. "Come on, Little Bit," he said, lifting her down from the counter stool and turning off the television. "Go get dressed while I get Logan up. We've got to go."

He followed her up the stairs and knocked on Logan's door, opening it without waiting for an answer. "Logan," he called, his voice loud enough to penetrate his son's deep sleep.

Buddy lifted his head, jumped off the bed and stretched, and then came over for Peter to bend down and scratch him between the ears.

"Logan, get up. We've got to be at the field in an hour."

The mound of sheets and blankets rolled over and his son's head appeared at the top. "What?"

"Football."

Logan threw off the covers. "I'm up." He rubbed his hands open-palmed over his face.

Satisfied Logan would stay awake for football, Peter took a quick shower to wash away the concert smell and got dressed. He stuck his head in Lacie's room, ready for the outfit-choosing fight, but she was dressed and brushing her hair.

"Can you put my hair in a ponytail, please?" she asked, holding out the rubber band.

Ponytail-making was actually a point of pride for

Peter. When first faced with the task, he had botched it miserably. Now he was an old hand, although Caroline still did the braiding when Lacie wanted a more complicated hairstyle. Was that a job Donna could do instead? She did have an older daughter.

Did he want to diminish Lacie's relationship with Caroline when she was the one who had served as her mother-figure since Maisie's death? Had Maisie thought about how her plan would affect Caroline? Probably not, since Caroline's current role in their lives had not happened at that point. Would it be fair to supplant her with a new woman, or would it be a relief for her? There was no time to think about it now. "Done," he said, turning her around by the shoulders. "Let's go."

The game didn't start until eleven, but the boys were supposed to arrive at ten to warm up. The Hunters arrived late at the park because of passing through the drive-thru for Logan's breakfast. As soon as Peter pulled into a parking space, Logan flung open his door and dashed out.

"Can I go to the playground, Daddy?" Lacie chanted as she climbed out of the car. "Please, can I? I'll be really careful."

"I'm still thinking about it." Peter locked the car door and reached for Lacie's hand. He was only half-listening as she prattled on because he knew what she wanted, and he had other things on his mind. He was about to see Donna. What would she say? How would she act? Fangirl Donna was so different from Team Mom Donna. Was he supposed to act like something had changed between them?

"You can see me being careful from your seat,"

Lacie persisted. "Football is so boring. I hate football. Can I go to the playground? Can I, please? Please?" She built the crescendo up to her big finale, "Puh—leeze, Daddy! Puh-leeze!"

Peter closed his eyes and rubbed circles on his temples. What did he have to do to make the noise stop? Yield to her will. It was tempting, but if he let her go, there would be no buffer between him and Donna, no distraction to keep them off the topic of their date. He had decided a relationship with Donna had potential, but he was not eager to display that decision in front of all the other parents. "Lacie!" he snapped. "Give it a rest. You can't go down there unless someone is with you."

They arrived at the bleachers in time for everyone to hear Peter's last admonition. A couple of the other dads nodded in sympathy. The moms were too busy talking to each other to take any notice.

"How about Curtis?" Lacie suggested, undaunted. "Curtis can go with me."

At the mention of her son, Donna turned around and spotted them standing at the bottom of the bleachers. She jumped up and clambered down the seats. "Peter, hi! Thanks for last night," she said, loud enough for everyone to hear.

"Sure," he replied. "The band was great. But I didn't do much. You put it all together. I should be thanking you."

"It was my pleasure," she replied with a big grin. "Believe me, it was worth it." She winked at the ladies who had turned from their conversation to observe their interaction. "Now, what is this I hear about my son?"

Peter was not happy with Donna's implication that

they had been intimate, but he didn't want to humiliate her with a direct denial. If she kept it up, he would talk with her privately after the game. Instead, he focused on the issue with his relentless daughter. "Lacie wants to go to the playground during the game. I told her she can't go alone, and she said Curtis would go with her." He drew himself up to emphasize his authority and looked down at his daughter, who didn't appear impressed. "I didn't mean another child."

"I let Curtis do it all the time." Donna pointed across the distance at her son playing with his action figures at the foot of the slide. "They mostly play in the sand, anyway."

His impulse was to disagree just to prove she wasn't making decisions for him, but reason told him it was ridiculous. "Fine," he conceded. "But stay where I can see you."

"Okay." Lacie skipped off, humming.

Peter made a point of choosing a seat on the bleachers where he had a clear view of the children on the playground. Donna slid across the bench from her spot with the other moms and took a place next to him. He didn't move, but he put up a mental forcefield that didn't let her into his space. He answered when she addressed him directly, but he wasn't ready to give any signals that they were a couple. He looked for a way to move casually to sit with the other dads and still keep an eye on Lacie.

Donna never faltered. If she detected his distance, she gave no indication. "Peter saw a side of me last night that most people never see," she said to the other mothers with the mirth of a triumphant teenage girl. "When I'm at a concert, I'm like an eighteen-year-old. I even pulled out the old shirt I wore to all my concerts. Of course, it's a little tighter than it was then. I've nursed three babies, after all."

Peter felt the heat rising in his face. He needed away from her embarrassing commentary on their date, but he didn't want to humiliate her by making her look like a fool. He was saved between the first and second quarters when she got up to "keep the boys hydrated." He took the opportunity to move next to a man sitting alone at the bottom of the bleachers, making certain that he could keep Lacie in view.

Peter's new companion gave no indication of his arrival. His bowed head discouraged conversation. He was breaking open a peanut from a bag on the seat next to him and had created a pile of shells on the ground between his legs.

"Do you have a son playing?" Peter asked.

"Yep," the stranger replied.

He looked familiar, and Peter tried to place him. His red hair was thinning off a high, broad forehead, and from the side his nose was prominent with a slight downward curve at the end. What had he looked like when he was twelve years old?

"My son is Logan, number fifteen. Which one is yours?"

"Justin. Number one."

The red hair alone should have given it away, but he had never thought to wonder how dark brunette Donna had a red-headed child. Now that he knew, he could see that Justin's features more closely resembled his father than his mother. "Peter Hunter," he said, offering his hand. "Have we met before?"

"Wayne Lechleiter," he replied, shaking hands. "I

keep a low profile." He tipped his head to the right, where Donna had returned to her seat. "She's not exactly welcoming."

He thought about all of Donna's side comments about Wayne's failures as a father and husband, but one of her main complaints was that he didn't spend enough time with them. Surely, she wanted him to come to his son's games. He didn't want to ask any questions that would indicate he had ever talked to her outside of family duties, so he made sure to sound surprised. "Really?"

"You must not have known her long enough. I'm the guy who failed Her Majesty, the queen of the PTA." He popped a peanut in his mouth and kicked the pile of shells.

Stuck between a rock and a hard place, Peter was uncomfortable with Wayne's bitterness but curious to learn more about Donna from this different point of view. He opted to continue his exchange with the acrimonious ex, although, given her generosity toward the children, he felt compelled to defend Donna. "She does do a lot of good stuff for the kids."

Wayne's face drew up like he had tasted something rotten. "Of course, she does. It's her job to do everything because no one else can do it as well as she does."

"I don't know, Wayne. I'm glad she's willing to do it, because if I had to, it wouldn't get done. It's too much work."

"She's the martyr who doesn't get paid for working like a demon for the kids," he sneered. "She doesn't mention I pay her living expenses so she can do all of this "volunteer" work."

"Sounds rough." Peter made mental notes. He wanted to ask exactly what Wayne had done wrong, but he knew he was navigating a minefield.

Wayne sat up straight and brushed peanut shell flakes off his pants. "I know what people think, that I'm the bad guy, and she's the most amazing woman in the world. But the truth is, even before she kicked me out, I couldn't take it anymore." He turned to face Peter, his eyes intense and daring a challenge. "She micromanaged every aspect of our lives. How to dress. What to eat. What to say. Even when to have sex. I worked all the time just to get away from her nagging."

Peter shifted uncomfortably. That was too much information. Like a deer in the headlights, he knew he should get out of the way, but he had to take the hit. "She's bossy, huh?"

"I shouldn't say any more." Wayne stood up and stepped down to the ground. "For all I know, you want to date her or something."

Or something. Peter was torn. He had seen evidence of her domineering tendencies, but he had also seen her free spirit. There was more to Donna than met the eye, and evidently this guy hadn't brought out that side of her. It was time to leave the conversation, which had both confirmed his experience with Donna and caused him to rethink it. He stood up and turned in the other direction to climb back to where Donna sat with the other parents. "See ya 'round," he said, looking back over his shoulder.

"Yeah, see ya." Wayne walked away without looking back.

Peter had been so involved in Wayne Lechleiter's commentary, he forgot to keep an eye on Lacie. Peter looked at the playground, and there was his princess, hanging from the monkey bars. Her very carefully selected shirt was hiked up, exposing her stomach, and the gold sandals she couldn't live without had fallen onto the ground below her. Halfway along, she dropped, landing in the soft sand like a cat, while Curtis watched from the sideline. The little boy climbed the ladder and held on tight to the bars, trying to get up his courage to follow her. Ultimately, he just jumped down from the ladder and walked over to her as though he had done the same thing she had.

Lacie was fearless, just like her mother. Maisie was always the first one in the first seat on the biggest and fastest rollercoaster. Peter suspected Lacie would be exactly the same way. Sometimes that scared Peter, but it also made him proud.

Logan's team won again, on his touchdown. At the buzzer, the boys let out a war cry and mobbed the quarterback, shoving and banging chests. This was their tenth win in a row, an undefeated season, sending them to the playoffs.

Peter and the other dads slapped each other on their backs, sharing the joy every father feels when his son does something manly.

Out on the field, the coach reined in the players' ebullient celebration and instructed them to congratulate the other team on a game well-played, which they did with kindness and sincerity. Peter liked Coach Mike because he always reminded the boys that, with one bad play, they could be on the other side, and they had to treat the opposition with respect. Then they could celebrate.

Once the other team left the field, Coach shouted

joyfully, "I'm buying at Romano's!"

Peter whistled for Lacie, who obeyed immediately with Curtis hot on her heels. Curtis split off to run after Justin and Logan toward the parking lot. "You looked like you were having fun," he said as she took his hand.

"It was *so* fun," she effused. "Can I do it again at the next game? Will you come and watch me?"

"I could see you from where I was sitting," he said. "You are very strong and very brave."

Lacie looked up at him and shook her head. "Curtis is not brave."

Peter smiled and nodded. "He will be. You just have to give him time to work up to it."

"Okay," she replied, swinging their hands as she walked. "Where are we going now?"

"Coach Mike is taking the team for pizza."

"Can we go, too?" She hopped up and down, shaking his shoulder nearly out of its socket.

He felt happy. Happy enough to stop by Donna's car as they walked by. Somehow, his interaction with Wayne had made him like her more, not less.

"Logan can ride with me," she offered. "He needs to be with the boys."

"That's great. Thank you." He put a hand on her shoulder, and she looked up at him. Holding her gaze, he said, "And thank you for all you've done for the kids. You're a great team mom."

"Thanks. It's really nice to hear."

Her tone was warm but missing the earlier flirtation. Had she seen him talking to Wayne? She had to know her ex-husband would not be kind, and she probably expected Peter had no interest in her after talking with him. He found it very satisfying to surprise her, like there was a more equal balance of power in their relationship if she didn't know what he planned to do. "I owe you big time," he said. "How about I take you to dinner?"

"Do you mean the whole family?" she asked, searching his face.

Satisfying. "Nope. Just you and me."

"Sure." Her expression brightened. "When?"

"How about next Sunday?" He could see if any magic had developed between them now that he had her ex-husband's perspective. Wayne was bitter, but a father should understand that their children have to come first with his wife while they are young. All other animals defer to the success of the young, and there was no question Donna was devoted to the children. On one hand, there was no denying she was controlling and bossy. But on the other hand, she was also fun and free-spirited. The question was not if she would be a good choice as a mother for his kids. The question was, did he and Donna, with their individual strengths and weaknesses, make a good couple?

He mulled over that question on the drive home after pizza. Logan was quiet with his headphones in, and Lacie had fallen asleep. Suddenly, it hit him. Babysitter. He needed a babysitter to go out to dinner with Donna. He didn't think he could focus on Donna if he started the evening thinking about Caroline at his house, and knowing that he would be going home to her again. Of course, she might not be willing anymore. He had kissed her, and he had liked it. She knew him well-enough to read his mind, and she might not like what she found. He looked over at Logan and then in the rearview mirror at Lacie. How would he explain to them why their relationship with Caroline had changed?

Maybe he wouldn't have to. Maybe Caroline would act like it never happened, and they would go on just as they had since Maisie died. Maybe. But maybe he couldn't forget what it felt like to be so close to her, even for a few minutes. No, even a week was too soon to risk being alone with her.

Who then? He knew very few teenagers, and none he would trust. Who could he ask?

Donna had a teenage daughter. What was her name? Audra? She would probably know somebody who could do it, and if she didn't, Donna certainly would.

When they got home and his tired children were settled in front of the TV, he called. "Donna, it's Peter."

"Hi, Peter. What's up?"

A forced cheeriness ineffectively masked the expectation of disappointment. Had he been so transparent in his indecision that she didn't feel she could trust him? "Can you suggest a babysitter? The person I usually have is my office manager, and I don't feel like I can ask her again so soon."

"Absolutely." The relief was evident in her voice. "Let them come over here. Audra can watch them all. "

"Are you sure she doesn't mind? Four kids are a lot for anybody."

"We'll pay her extra. She's saving for spending money in college, and she'll be glad to have it."

"Great. Is 6:00 okay? I'll make us a 6:30 reservation at *Aquarium*. Do you like fish?"

"I do, and *Aquarium* sounds great. Six-thirty is a good idea, since it's a school night."

He hadn't thought about it being a school night, but

that was an added bonus. If things went well, they could easily make plans for another, longer night. If not, he would have a ready excuse for cutting it short. "Consider it done. See you then."

Chapter 13

When Peter got to work Monday morning, he walked in like a child who had muddied his good Sunday clothes, but the expected scolding didn't come. Caroline had obviously decided that ignoring it was the way to go. She was her typical upbeat self, and had even stopped for doughnuts on the way in. Doughnut shop coffee, infinitely better than the stuff from their office coffeemaker, sat steaming on his desk. The rest of the work day passed without incident, and he congratulated himself on dodging a bullet.

As the week progressed, however, he noticed that things had changed between them. Caroline was herself regarding work, but she didn't pop into his office unannounced or question him about following through with Donna. When he went out to the desk to have their usual end-of-day chat about the clients and the kids, she made an excuse and rushed out with her hoodie unzipped and her backpack open. He missed her company, but he knew it was his fault things had gone so wrong. He had no idea how to put them right without having the conversation they were both avoiding like the plague.

Sunday evening, Peter was tying his tie in the mirror. "What do you think?" he said to Buddy, lying at his feet. The dog looked up at him but had nothing helpful to say.

You look great, said Maisie's voice in his head.

I'm giving this thing with Donna another try. I don't hear symphonies or see fireworks when I'm with her, but she is good, solid company, and we have a lot in common.

Maisie's voice smiled. *Fireworks? The earth moved for us because we had our first kiss at seventeen. Our hormones were rocketing off in every direction.*

Not just hormones. I felt sparks when I kissed you all the way to the end.

Me, too.

"Everything just flowed when it was you," he said aloud. "I was lucky to find it the first time. I'll never find it again."

"Who are you talking to, Daddy?" Lacie strolled in unannounced, and Buddy rolled over for a belly rub.

"Just talking to myself." He turned around for her inspection. "What do you think?"

She tipped her head to the side and squinted. "I don't like the tie."

He took it off. "Not this tie, or no tie?"

She tilted her head the other way. "No tie. I like you better without it."

"No tie." He threw it on the bed.

"Curtis' sister is mean." She scratched an appreciative Buddy on his exposed underside. "She makes him be quiet while she talks to her friends on the phone, and she's on the phone *all* the time."

He remembered his older sister logging hours on the phone when she was in high school. She snapped his head off if he bothered her, which made him work that much harder to do it. He smiled at the memory. Little brothers could be a real pain in the neck. "Just stay out of her way. Only ask her if you really need something."

Lacie stood up and faced him with her hands on her hips. "Why can't Caroline stay with us?"

Peter had prepared for this. "Caroline has her own life, too, Little Bit. We can't have her with us at work all day and expect her to be with us at night, too. We can only do that every now and then."

Lacie spun around and stormed out.

Your daughter, he said to Maisie.

She didn't get that personality from me. She's like your mother.

Oh, God, don't say that. Say she's possessed by the devil or suffering from an extreme personality disorder, but don't compare her to my mother.

Just calling it like I see it.

As if on cue, the phone rang. Caller ID said "Hunter, R." Ruth, his mother. He knew she would deliver a verbal hand-slap since he hadn't called in two weeks. He deserved it, but he was short on time, so he decided to let it go to voicemail. He would call and grovel first thing tomorrow. At least, that was his plan.

"Hi, Grandma!" Lacie's voice carried all the way up from downstairs. "When are we going shopping?" A pause, then, "Can we go the next week?" Another pause. "Okay. Do you want to talk to Daddy?" Although she didn't need any more volume, she managed to take it up to a whole new level. "Dad-deee! It's Grandma!"

In the mirror, Peter saw a different man from the one who looked back at him moments before the call. This man looked rumpled and mismatched, in spite of Lacie's fashion advice. This man's mother would never have let him out the door in these clothes. According to his mother, this man was barely able to tie his own shoes, never mind have a successful veterinary practice. This was not a feeling he needed before going out on a date. Like a soldier going into battle, he steeled his resolve and picked up the phone. "Hello, Mother."

"I'm surprised you took my call." Her voice was almost a growl. "I thought you had forgotten I was alive."

"I've been busy. Since Maisie's gone, I'm picking up both sides of parenting, and it's hard."

"I was practically a single parent, your father worked so much. *I* still made time to call *my* mother."

"Sorry. I'll try to do better." He needed to move the conversation along. "What's up?"

"I understand you are dating again." Her disapproving tone made him feel like he was a teenager caught drinking in the park after curfew.

He focused on his thirty-seven-year-old self in the mirror to keep a firm grasp on his adulthood. He was a grown man and a father of his own children, not a little boy to be scolded for doing something without telling his mommy. "How do you know that?"

"Caroline told me when I called to see if you and my grandchildren were still alive. So, are you?"

Caroline may be a great kisser, but she was also a traitor. "Still alive?" he evaded.

"Dating."

He imagined her sitting in her armchair like a queen on a throne, looking down her nose as though he was a peasant on his knees before her. He sat on the bed, cradled the phone against his shoulder, and put on his shoes. "Yes, some. In fact, I have a date tonight, so I need to get off the phone." He knew that was too easy to work.

"How are you meeting these women?" she demanded.

He didn't have time to think of something she would find acceptable, so he went with the truth. "Some of them are people Maisie knew through the kids."

There was a pregnant silence that promised an unpleasant retort.

"Maisie was a wonderful person, God rest her soul, but she didn't always know what was best for you."

He bit his lip to keep from snapping. Maisie had tried hard to develop a warm relationship with her mother-in-law, but she never proved good enough for Ruth. His mother's slights toward his wife had been a constant source of friction between them, even more so since Maisie died. He didn't have time for a full-blown argument, but he couldn't let her comment stand. "She usually did pretty well. I had a happy life and two great kids with her."

She pressed on as though he had said nothing. "I know the perfect girl for you."

Here it came. "Of course, you do."

"She's a nurse at St. James Hospital." She paused for effect before announcing, "You have so much in common."

He looked down at Buddy, who watched his face intently, the spots over his eyes waggling sympathetically. The dog looked like he understood the conversation. "Mom, she treats humans. I work with animals. The only thing we have in common is that our patients can be uncooperative."

"A body is a body. How different can it be?"

Her tone had become lighter. She was playing matchmaker and trying to win him over to her point of view.

He rubbed his forehead and tried to seem interested, hoping to ease her off the phone. "How do you know her?"

"She helped at the hospital when I went in for my procedure."

"Procedure?" Another procedure? When was she going to run out of medical problems to test for? He knew a dutiful son would ask all the right questions and listen to the answers attentively, but he didn't have time for that.

"I had to have a colonoscopy." She punched every word to heighten the drama. "My doctor insisted I get one because of my grandmother's colon cancer. You should have one too, you know."

"I'm sorry, I didn't know. How did it go?" He looked at the clock on the bedside table. Five-fifty. He told Donna he'd pick her up at six. If the colonoscopy had revealed anything serious, his sister would have called him. How could he get out of this conversation?

"They found some polyps, but none of them were cancer, thank God. Ginny took me because you are always so busy."

Now they got to it. Guilt was the primary reason for her call. He made a mental note to thank his sister the first chance he got. He had to get off the phone. He stood up to leave like he would have if he was visiting at her house. "Mom, I've got to go."

"Who is this girl you're going out with?" she asked without a hint of urgency.

Peter felt his pulse pound in his head from the

stress of trying to end the conversation. "She's not a girl, Mom. Her name is Donna Lechleiter, and she is Logan's team mom."

"A team mom who's not married? What happened to her husband?"

"They're divorced, okay? I've really got to go."

"Fine. When are you going to call my nurse?"

She was relentless. Maybe Maisie was right. Lacie *was* just like his mother. He shuddered at the thought. "I don't know, Mom. I don't know anything about her. How do you know she wants go out with me?"

"That's the purpose of a date, isn't it? You'll ask her to a lovely dinner or something, and then you'll get to know her."

He was never going to win, and Donna was waiting. "Fine, I'll call her. Text me her name and number."

"You'll call her tomorrow?" she insisted.

"Yes, I'll call her tomorrow. Mom, I've got to go."

"Fine. I always want what's best for you, even if you don't ever call. Goodbye." Even her "goodbye" made him feel guilty.

"Come on, guys!" He flew down the stairs. "We're going to be late!"

If they said anything in reply, he didn't hear it. His full focus was on getting to the Lechleiter's house as fast as possible. He hated being late.

Justin and Curtis must have been watching for them, because they opened the door before Peter had the chance to ring the bell. The kids all ran up the stairs like a thundering herd of cattle as he stepped inside and closed the door.

"Hello, Peter." Donna walked in from the living

room. This was not College Days Donna or Team Mom Donna. This Donna wore a short black dress revealing very nice legs and a good figure she generally kept under school appropriate clothes. Her low-cut neckline hinted at the generous breasts that had stretched the concert T-shirt. He wondered if she ever looked like this for Wayne Lechleiter. She must have, at some point. Was her controlling nature enough to push him away even when she looked like this?

"Whew! You look great." He took a deep breath and blew it out slowly to calm his pounding heart. "Sorry we're a little late. My mother called right before we left, and I couldn't get her off the phone."

Donna nodded wisely. "I remember your mother. She came to one of the early games this season, didn't she? She was very sweet, but I can see she might be a handful."

"Sweet is not a word I would ever use to describe my mother," Peter said honestly, "but that doesn't matter. Are you ready?"

"Sure. Let me tell Audra we're leaving." She pushed open a swinging door Peter thought must go to the kitchen. "Audra," she called.

A sullen, younger version of Donna pushed through from the other side. "What do you want?" she snapped.

"We're leaving," Donna said cheerily, with a sideways look for Peter's reaction.

He said nothing about the girl's disrespectful demeanor, but made a mental note that she wasn't going to get quite as much extra money as he had planned. Peter never talked to his parents like Dalton and Audra, and he was pretty sure he would have been punished severely if he had. Were all teenagers today so disagreeable and difficult, or had he just had a bad sampling? Was this what he was in for with Logan and Lacie? He hoped they weren't like that to other adults when he was out of earshot.

"There's money on the counter for pizza, and frozen fruit pops in the freezer for dessert." Donna's sunny tone was noticeably forced.

"Fine," Audra said dismissively and disappeared back through the door.

The ride to the restaurant passed in uncomfortable silence as Donna composed herself from the unsettling exchange with her daughter. "Don't worry," she reassured him. "Audra is very responsible."

"I'm sure she is." Responsibility wasn't Peter's main concern. Lacie's complaints about Curtis' mean sister echoed in his head.

Peter pulled up to the restaurant valet station and handed off the keys. The last time he was here, there was no valet, but that had been at least ten years before. It was a barbeque place back then, styled to look like a rustic cabin in the woods. After that, it was painted yellow to represent a French country manor, and then blue to be a seafood shack. It seemed to be one of those cursed corners where whatever opened there rarely lasted more than a year. He and Maisie had often wondered about it when they drove by, until one day, shortly before she died, signs went up indicating new ownership and exciting plans. The renovations happened while he was still numb with grief, so it seemed like *Aquarium* had been completed with the wave of a wizard's wand. The parking lot was always full, so it appeared the magic spell had worked.

The maître d' led them to their table past an aquarium from the floor to six feet up that served as the divider between the bar and the restaurant and was so large that it seemed to be its own habitat. Colorful fish darted in and out of the man-made coral and hid in the swaying water plants, evading the attention of small but fierce-looking sharks.

The dim lighting and candle on the table set a romantic mood, but when the waiter came and asked for drink orders, Donna jumped in first. "Vodka and grapefruit juice, please."

Peter was amused. The perfect mother had a crack in her armor. "Gin and tonic," he ordered. When the waiter stepped away, Peter asked, "Feeling stressed?"

"A little." She blushed, hastening to add, "It's not you. It's Audra. She's a great student, and she has big plans for college. She has done nothing but make me proud, except that she is nearly impossible to deal with these days. I don't know what went wrong. Maybe I'm not doing it right." She picked up her napkin and focused hard as she unfolded it and spread it in her lap.

There was a question in her statement that Peter understood, being unsure of his own parenting skills, but he hoped he could respond in a way that would prevent tears. He never had done well with crying females, not even Maisie. "I think you're doing fine. I don't have much experience with teenagers, but what little I've seen makes me think they are all like that."

"All of her friends love me. They think I'm the cool mom, but she can't seem to stand the sight of me." She smoothed her napkin like she was petting a lap dog. "I'm hoping the boys will be easier." She dabbed at her eyes and looked up. "How is work going these days?"

Peter appreciated the smooth segue to a less emotional topic. "It's fine," he replied. "Always lots of sick pets needing attention."

She nodded. "Yes, I suppose there are. How did you come to be a veterinarian, Peter? I don't think you've ever told me."

"My father was a veterinarian. I worked in the office when I spent summers with him, and I liked it."

Donna braced her elbows on the table and rested her chin in her hand as though she was settling in for a long story. "Summers with him?"

He shrugged. "My parents were divorced."

She sighed. "My parents divorced, too."

Common ground. They were members of the same 'club.' "I was five," he said. "How old were you?"

"Old enough to be glad when he was gone." She smirked. "I was determined not to make my mother's same mistake, so I married the guy most unlike my father I could find. Dad could never hold down a job, and he was always begging money off different family members. So, what do I do? I marry a guy who works all the time. Great income, but no home life."

"Wayne doesn't seem like that bad of a guy."

"He's not," she admitted, "but I want a husband who's all in, everything fifty-fifty, or no husband at all."

Peter didn't know what to say. His father had worked ten to twelve hours a day, seven days a week, but that was what it took to establish a new business from the ground up. His mother had kicked him out for the same reason Donna did Wayne. No time for the folks at home.

He glanced at Donna, who appeared to be waiting

for his next comment. What did she want him to say? Was he supposed to agree with her? Was he supposed to assure her that he was not that kind of husband?

He opened his menu to have a place to direct his eyes. In his peripheral vision, he saw her open hers, though she still had her eyes on him. What could he say, honestly? Working with animals made him happy, but running a business did not. To be successful, he had to spend a lot of time doing things he did not want to do, things like marketing and budgeting and repairing the old clinic building. Occasionally he was more than a little grumpy when he got home at the end of the day. Maisie had not left him, but she had complained about it from time to time. Peter looked around at the other tables, the window, and the cart of desserts. Anywhere but at Donna.

When the waiter set their glasses in front of them, Donna sat up straighter and put on a happy face. "You said you're from Tennessee?"

Relieved, he latched onto the topic. "I am. I went to UT and everything. What about you?"

"I'm from a little town called Watkinsville. It's near Athens," she said, giving him a gentle punch on the shoulder. "And I'm a Bulldog, you old Volunteer."

He sighed out his tension. "Wish I could say Smokey is the better dog, but Uga usually gets the best of us." He hung his head but couldn't stop the corners of his mouth from twitching up.

She grinned. "Yes, he does."

The gap between them closed, and she slipped into her natural role of maintaining a constant stream of conversation.

"Is your father still working?"

Peter took a sip from his drink, but his throat was suddenly too tight let it go down. He had to gulp to swallow it. "I'm afraid not. He died from a heart attack five years ago." He shook his head. "After mom left him, he really didn't have anything to do but work, so he worked himself into an early grave, just like she predicted he would." He laughed a dry, mirthless laugh. "It gives her a lot of satisfaction."

Donna shook her head and straightened her napkin again. "I'm sure she isn't really glad about it. I've warned Wayne about the very same thing. Hopefully, he will do something about his work habits before he meets the same fate as your father. Whatever my feelings are, he is my children's father, and I don't want them to lose him." She tilted her head as though asking something that had suddenly occurred to her. "Does heart disease run in your family?"

He had expected her to say she was sorry for his loss, or ask if they had been close, or some other thing that a person usually says in such a circumstance. Was she asking to be sympathetic, or was she asking to find out about his genetic suitability as a husband? Her response reminded him of his mother, and he couldn't keep the edge out of his voice. "It does now."

"There's lots of heart disease in my family," she continued, either missing or dismissing his unhappy tone. "Both of my grandfathers died from heart attacks in their sixties. My dad has high blood pressure, but the doctor just told him to watch his diet and his stress. I get a stress test once a year, and I'm careful about what I eat. I know my blood pressure goes up during the holidays because I have the pharmacist check it every month or so. It gives me a good excuse for a weekend at a spa in January." She finished with a grin.

Peter relaxed. Donna could be entertaining and funny, two qualities his mother never had. The evening might be okay after all. If he asked few simple, well-placed questions, she would do all the work. "Where do you go to the spa?"

"There's a place in the north Georgia mountains called 'Peace Lily.' It's the best."

"Do you go alone?"

"Oh, no," she laughed. "My three best girlfriends come with me. One of them I've been friends with since I was two-years-old." Her can-you-believe-that tone seemed to surprise even her. "Do you have old friends like that?"

He nodded. "I do. I don't see them much because we knew each other when we were growing up, and almost everybody left after high school. When I go up for games, I see one or two of the guys who stayed in the area, but none live close to here."

The conversation continued along, rolling one topic right into the next like clouds moving across the sky. He enjoyed her company, but after her comments about Wayne, he noticed that many of the things she said sounded like his mother, who was certain she knew what was best for everyone. As a friend, it was easy to overlook, but he could imagine he wouldn't fare much better than Wayne as a love interest. Donna Lechleiter was not The One.

Either unaware or unwilling to acknowledge that his answers had become very, very short, Donna sustained her end of the conversation all the way home. "A man should be like you are, taking over responsibility when he is left alone. If I died, Wayne would give the children to his mother to raise." She stuck her finger down her throat like she was going to vomit.

He chuckled. "Not good, huh?"

"My ex-mother-in-law? No. Not good."

He walked her to her door, planning his next move. She might be a bossy chatterbox, but she deserved a little romance. On the other hand, he didn't want to lead her on. She deserved better than that, too. When they paused at her door, he leaned down and kissed her. It was a good kiss. Not too aggressive, but lingering and full.

When they parted, she sighed. "It's not terrific, is it?"

"I like you a lot, Donna. You're a great person, and I've never met a more devoted mother. But I'm not feeling it for you and me."

She smiled sadly. "It was comparing Wayne to your father, wasn't it? I could tell you didn't like that. But I didn't say anything that wasn't true."

Her comments affirmed his decision. "I think you and I are meant to be good friends. You've brought me back to the music, and I can never thank you enough for that."

She grinned, the mention of music lightening the mood. "It is good to know someone who gets the way I feel about Dreams of Home, and we have so many other bands to talk about."

"Absolutely. Plus, you know way more about being a mom than I ever will. Football parents united." He squeezed her arm. "We may not have made a love-match, but you will with somebody, and he will be a very lucky guy."

"Thanks so much for saying that. See you at the field?"

"At the field," he replied.

When they walked in, the house was eerily silent. How could there possibly be five children here? Had Audra bound and gagged the other four?

She sauntered out of the family room. "Hello, Mother. Did you have a nice time?" Condescension oozed from her tone.

"We did," Donna replied shortly. "What did you do to the other children? Lock them in the basement?"

Audra's haughty façade dissolved into mirth. "That's a good one," she laughed. "Wish I'd thought of it. The little insects are all upstairs. Haven't heard a peep from them since pizza."

There was a rumble over their heads, and then the stomping of feet. Lacie, Curtis, Logan, and Justin appeared at the top of the stairs, hesitating as though Audra was a dog that would bite them if they came down. She growled at them to enhance the effect.

Donna frowned, but Peter had to hide a smile behind his hand. The boys were at least twenty pounds heavier than Audra already, and they could have easily taken her down in a fight. But she was the top dog, and the boys knew where they fell in the food chain.

"Come on, guys," Peter said, sniggering. "Time to go."

Lacie and Logan came down the stairs and tried to scoot out behind Peter.

"What about 'Thank you, Ms. Lechleiter'?"

"Thank you, Ms. Lechleiter," they said to Donna and broke for the car.

"Goodnight, Audra," Peter said as he paid her.

"And thanks." He turned to Donna. "Goodnight, Donna. I had a great time."

"Me too, Peter. Thank you."

All the way home, Peter heard about how mean Audra Lechleiter was. They were still talking about it as they went up the stairs, trailed by an interested Buddy.

When the children were settled in, Peter plopped down on his bed. *Strike two, Maisie.*

That's why I gave you more than one.

How can anyone replace you?

I told you, I don't expect you to replace me. We shared all the firsts that no one else can ever share with you. I want you to be with someone who will make her own place.

There wasn't any magic.

No magic?

No fireworks. The earth didn't move, and the stars didn't sing.

Sorry.

She was closer than Suzanne Martin, though.

At least we're moving in the right direction.

You did okay. I can see why you chose each of them.

Maybe we'll hit it with the next one.

Maybe so. I still love you.

Loved you in that life and beyond, my precious husband. Kiss our babies for me.

Chapter 14

Peter always walked out of the exam room with Capt. Rogers and his German shepherd, Musket, and personally saw them to the door. There was no stopping at checkout, except to wave goodbye to Caroline. Retired together from a distinguished K-9 career in the Atlanta Police Department, they were two of his favorite visitors, and he saw them *gratis* to thank them for their service.

Turning back, Peter was jolted by the explosion of black and orange streamers, flying witches hanging from the ceiling, grinning paper pumpkins, and a bowl with an automated hand that grabbed at anyone who reached for its cache of candy, already half gone. He had not been a fan of Halloween since he grew too old for trick-or-treating, but Lacie and Logan had dragged him into their own frenzied anticipation of the day. Caroline was complicit in their celebrations, turning the clinic into a Halloween dream for every child who walked through its doors. Their most favorite decoration, and his least, was a string of photos hung corner to corner on the front of the reception desk. Each captured the likeness of an animal looking woebegone to be thrust into a costume its owners thought was either cute or hilarious. The cats looked particularly pissed off. Peter harrumphed and shook his head.

As he settled into his desk chair with his casually

thrown-together lunch, Caroline strolled through the streamers hanging from his doorjamb and sat in the opposite chair, spreading her lunch on his desk in front of her. Time had healed the breach between them and everything seemed back to normal.

"Didn't go so well with Donna, huh?" She put her napkin in her lap and picked up her fork.

Peter raised an eyebrow. "How do you know it didn't go well? Do you make a habit of discussing my personal life with everyone who calls?"

Caroline rolled her eyes and made a play of innocence. "Whoever do you mean?"

"You know exactly who I mean."

The corners of Caroline's mouth turned up slightly, but she bit her lip before it became a full-fledged grin. "I have not talked to your mother about anything personal. I merely confirmed her inquiries about your calendar, and I may have mentioned that one or two of the appointments were dates."

"Thanks a lot," he said, sarcasm dripping from every word. "Now she wants to be my matchmaker."

"Sorry about that. Her will is too strong to resist. But I have not talked to her since your evening with Donna. I figured it didn't go well because you're not walking around on Cloud Nine like I would expect if you had made a love connection."

"Cloud Nine? What am I, sixteen?"

The amusement disappeared. "You seemed pretty young when you got home from the concert that night."

Peter dropped back in his chair. It wasn't forgotten after all. She watched him intently while he thought carefully about what to say next. A boss did not compromise his relationship with his employees by making out with them. But to say Caroline was an employee was like saying Lacie was just a little girl he knew. She had been with him from the days when she watched toddler Logan while Maisie covered the reception desk. She had taken on the office manager job at twenty-two when they had Lacie, and Maisie needed to stay home. And then, through the worst of Maisie's illness, she was always there, helping out in any way she could.

There was one memory he worked hard to repress, though sometimes, when he was alone with her, it floated into his consciousness unbidden like the answers of a Magic 8 Ball. As he looked at her across the desk it came, and as hard as he tried to block it, there was no mental wall strong enough to hold it back.

Caroline had taken the children home from the hospital so they wouldn't have to be haunted by the memory of getting no response from the person who had loved them most in all the world. He moved his chair until the legs scraped against the metal frame of her bed and held her limp hand to his cheek, its warmth the last tenuous thread of proof she was still with him. They had removed life-support when it was clear there was no brain function, so the only sound in the room was her labored breathing. He watched the rise and fall of her chest, knowing he should pray for her release, but instead praying God would bring her back. Don't leave me, don't leave me, his soul chanted to hers, but there was no answer. Finally, her chest fell and never rose again. He sat a bit longer, holding her hand, unwilling to let the nurses take her away where he could never see or touch her again.

He made his way home on autopilot. He needed to

be with his children with an all-consuming desperation unlike anything he had ever known. He found them all in Lacie's bedroom, dimly lit with the nightlight. Lacie was cuddled in the crook of Caroline's arm on the bed, sucking on her bottom lip as she had since she was a baby. Logan had brought the pillow and blanket off his bed to lie on the floor by his sister's bed, Buddy curled protectively against his back. The beagle lifted his head when Peter entered but did not leave his post. Peter stood for a few minutes, taking in the scene, and then dropped to his knees and laid his head on the bed. Caroline stirred, loosened herself from Lacie, and slid down on the floor next to him. She put her arm over him, and her tears wet the back of his shirt as his soaked into Lacie's bedspread.

He shook off the memory and looked at her across the desk. Caroline sat still as a statue, watching him. Could she see the tears pooling in his eyes? Did she ever think of that night? He hoped she might let him off the hook by filling the silence with her own conversation, but no such luck. She was set to wait however long it took for him to speak.

The truth? Those kisses were not simple at all. They were the crack in the dam of his deepest feelings, a breach in the barrier that contained the reservoir of memories that he shared only with her. He shook his head to clear his mind. "I was caught up in the moment." Honest but ambiguous. "It was crazy. Kissing the babysitter is the dream of every teenage boy, and you were the fulfillment of that fantasy." He cringed. Calling her a "fantasy" was making things worse. *Shut up before you dig a deeper hole.*

She nodded, but seemed a little disappointed. "I

understand. Good music does that to me, too."

Hopeful that was the end of that conversation, Peter leaned forward to finish his lunch. He noticed the microwave container on her side of the desk. "What are you eating? That looks pretty good." He was grasping for conversation that would eliminate the elephant in the room.

"It's a baked potato," she said wryly. "I'll be happy to make you one, if you'd like."

"Mine don't look like that," he observed. They eased back into friendly banter, but a vague tension hung in the air. He knew it would grow if he allowed the conversation to lag. "You know, I still owe you dinner for babysitting."

"I told you, you don't owe me anything. I'm happy to do it."

"You may think it's no big deal, but it is a huge deal to me." He sank his teeth into the safe topic and held on like a dog with a bone. "You have to let me buy you dinner."

"Okay," she agreed, "if you feel that strongly about it."

He had never done anything to thank her properly, and not just for babysitting. He wanted to give her an evening that would make her feel as special as she was. "I do."

A puff of air disturbed the orange streamers. "I'm hungry," said a little voice from the doorway. "Can I have something to eat?"

The streamers parted, and Lacie stepped through. Peter stared for a moment, certain his daughter was a hallucination. "Lacie!" He jumped out of his chair, his dad-fear kicking in. Had she walked the block from the bus stop alone? Had she crossed the busy street by herself? "What are you doing here?"

"It's early release," she said. "The parents are coming to talk to the teachers."

He knelt in front of her and cupped her face. "So, you came home on the bus and walked all the way to the clinic by yourself?"

"Yes, I did." She beamed.

Peter willed his heart to stop pounding. She was here. She was okay

For once, Caroline looked just as surprised as he was. "I forgot all about parent-teacher conferences." She stood and took Lacie's hand. "Yours is tomorrow."

Peter followed them into the breakroom. "Does Logan have one, too?"

"His is Friday. Don't worry, I cleared your schedule."

Caroline came into sharp focus. Her thick, curly hair pushing the limits of the band holding it neatly out of the way. Her kind sapphire eyes always reflecting what he was feeling back to him. Her small, compact body stretching to pull down the food she had so lovingly stocked for his children that was now mysteriously out of her reach. He leaned over her, her back against his chest, and pulled down the box of peanut butter crackers. She looked up to thank him, her face inches from his, and the words rushed out before he could temper the emotion in his voice. "You know, Caroline, I couldn't do any of this without you."

A beautiful smile lit up her face. "I'm happy to do it."

With a last meaningful glance at Peter, Caroline put the crackers on the table in front of Lacie and fetched a juice box from the refrigerator.

Lacie sighed and kicked her legs. "We're supposed to wear our costumes to school on Monday, and I don't have one yet." She took a delicate bite of cracker and sip from her juice box and looked at Peter for a response.

"Halloween is Monday," he remembered out loud, putting the pieces together. "You need a costume for Halloween." Trick-or-treating. A treasured rite of childhood. Mobs of children running from house to house, little ones with plastic pumpkins, older ones with pillowcases. Last Halloween, Lacie had gone with Kimmie Archemann, but the Archemanns had moved to Missouri earlier this year. He needed a new plan.

With her uncanny ability to read his mind, Caroline offered, "I can help. Josh has gone to Gainesville for a football weekend, and he won't be back until Tuesday."

"So, Josh is staying in the picture?" He tried not to sound disappointed. He had no right to the myriad feelings he felt. Not to disappointment. Not to disapproval. Not to jealousy.

A cloud passed over Caroline's face. "He's trying to be better. I broke up with him because he was drinking too much, and he promised he would stop. He is drinking a lot less."

Going on a football weekend with the guys was not a way to drink less. Peter wanted to see glowing Caroline return, so anything negative he had to say about Josh needed to be saved for another time. "I'll take you up on your offer for help."

"First, we need to make my costume," Lacie interjected, reclaiming Peter's attention.

He laughed. "All right, Little Bit. Do you know

what you want to be?" He realized how ridiculous the question was as soon as it was out of his mouth. Did she know what she wanted? Was the sky blue? "I'm guessing the Ice Queen."

"Everyone is being the Ice Queen," she said scornfully. "I want to be a movie star."

Every time he thought he had something figured out, she pulled the rug out from under him. "A movie star?"

"With a beautiful dress and lots of makeup."

"Beautiful dress and makeup?" What did that look like on a six-year-old?

"I've got the perfect thing," Caroline jumped in. "I was Marilyn Monroe at a costume party last year, and I still have the wig. I can do your makeup, and we'll find you something glamorous to wear." She looked at Peter. "Don't worry, Dad. It will be age and school appropriate."

"Thanks," Peter answered. "This time, you must let me take you out to dinner, Josh or not."

"How about I come over to answer your door for Halloween, and you can buy me pizza?"

Peter made a face. "You know that's not what I mean."

"What *do* you mean?" she said coyly.

"I mean a real dinner at a restaurant."

"Only if we can take Logan and Lacie, too."

"I want to go," Lacie chimed in.

Good idea. Not exactly what he had in mind, but it didn't seem so much like a date. "That sounds like a plan. How about Sunday night?"

"There's a Falcons' game."

"It starts at eight," he answered. "We can go early.

What do you say? You can come back to the house after and watch the game."

"And we can make Halloween costumes before," she concluded, prize-winning smile back on her face. "Count me in."

"Excellent," he said. "Any preference for restaurants?"

Before Caroline could answer, Lacie stood up on her chair and put her hands on her hips. "I want to go to *Hofu*," she said, referring to the local Japanese restaurant. "The cookers make the food right in front of you. I like the onion volcanos."

"*Hofu* is good for me." Caroline gave two thumbs up.

"We're going to *Hofu*? When?" Logan appeared in the doorway.

"Sunday night," Peter answered. "We're taking Caroline out to dinner."

"'Bout time." Logan took crackers off Lacie's napkin. "Caroline should always go with us, Dad. She's like a member of the family."

"Thanks, Logan. That's a nice thing to say." Caroline did not linger on the loaded statement. "We're going to do Halloween costumes before we go."

"No problem for me," Logan replied. "I'm going as a football player. Totally easy."

"Easy or lazy?" Peter asked then thought better of it. There was something to be said for easy. "Actually, that sounds good."

Chapter 15

Sunday afternoon, Caroline arrived and let herself in. She wasn't dressed for dinner, but she was carrying a hanging bag. "Nice pumpkin," she said, indicating the freshly carved jack-o-lantern on the table by the door.

Peter looked fondly at the product of a new, happy memory with his children. "Thanks. We did it this morning. I'm still not brave enough to give Logan the knife, but they scooped out the innards and drew the design on its face. All I had to do was cut on the lines. Logan wanted to lodge a butcher knife in its head, but Lacie wouldn't have it."

Lacie came running down the stairs. "Is that for me?" She danced around Caroline and the hanging bag.

"Yes, it is," Caroline replied, smiling. "We're going to have some fun."

Lacie jumped up and down, clapping her hands. "Yay! Yay! I'm going to be beautiful!"

"Yes, you are." Caroline patted the bag. "I cut down an old prom dress so it would fit her. Wait until you see."

Lacie grabbed Caroline and pulled her toward the stairs. "You made a dress for me? What color is it? Is it purple? I love purple."

"Hey, Lacie," Peter reprimanded. "Let Caroline put down her stuff first, how about it? Maybe get something to drink?"

Lacie looked at Caroline to see if she wanted either of those things and decided she didn't. "No, Daddy, she wants to make my costume. Don't you, Caroline?"

"It's okay," Caroline laughed. "I'm actually looking forward to it." They disappeared up the stairs.

Peter joined Logan watching football in the family room. Logan rarely talked about losing Maisie, although Peter suspected she was often on his mind, a thought confirmed by Logan's homework assignment on "being resilient." He had tried to reach out many times in the months after she died, but they only had real conversations about sports and school. Peter figured that, at least, was keeping the lines of communication open. "What's the score?"

Logan shook his head. "Twenty-eight-twelve, Cowboys. The Broncos stink."

"Maybe, but they beat the Dolphins and the Dolphins beat us."

"Won't happen again," Logan answered firmly. "Falcons are on fire."

Peter enjoyed the back and forth. "Yeah, but they play the Eagles tonight, and the Eagles are undefeated."

Logan punched his fist into his palm. "It's about time someone taught the Eagles some humility, and we're absolutely the team to do it."

Just as Peter became absorbed in the game, the period ended and the cameras were diverted to the half-time show.

Logan went into the kitchen for a drink.

Peter heard popping and smelled the aroma of microwave popcorn. He channel-surfed, looking for another game. When Logan returned, drink in his right hand, bowl of popcorn cradled in his left, Peter asked,

"Are you sure about your costume?" He wanted to keep the conversation going, hoping Logan would reveal anything about what was going on in his mind.

Logan trained his attention to the television. "I told you, I'm going as a football player. I don't need to do anything but put on my uniform."

Peter reached over and took a handful of popcorn out of the bowl. "Who are you trick-or-treating with?"

Logan continued to chew as he spoke. "Michael is coming over here because his neighborhood is lame. He's going as a superhero disguised as a regular person."

"So, he's just wearing street clothes?"

"Yep, they mask his secret identity. Smart, huh?"

Peter disapproved. If they were going to be trick-or-treaters at their age, they needed to put some effort into their costumes. "Sounds lazy to me."

"Naw. He's wearing a T-shirt with a big 'S' on the front that you can see through his button-down."

"That's better, I guess."

Logan nodded at the TV. "New England's got no defense. Go back to the Cowboys."

Peter changed the channel and enjoyed watching the game with Logan's running commentary. The re-energized Broncos surged and stunned the Cowboys into a frantic scramble to hold on to their lead. Sometime during the fourth quarter, he heard footsteps on the stairs and realized Lacie and Caroline had been upstairs over an hour. When they walked into the family room, he saw why.

Lacie wore a shiny, slinky purple gown that fell to her ankles. She'd finally found the right outfit for the light-up purple shoes with heels that she had begged for until he'd been broken by the sheer strength of her will. Her hair was tightly curled like the pictures he had seen of his grandmother at some formal dance in the 1950s. She had on a thick layer of bright red lipstick, and her eyes were lined with dark mascara and eye liner.

She pirouetted into the room to stand right in front of the television.

"Move," Logan growled. "I'm watching the game."

Peter was speechless, the game forgotten.

"Am I beautiful, Daddy? I think Caroline made me beautiful," Lacie asked, knowing the answer.

"Yes, yes, you are," Peter stammered. *Halloween*, he reminded himself. *It's for Halloween*. He eased into a smile. "You look very glamorous. I bet yours will be the best costume."

"I know," she said brightly, twirling so he could see her from every side. "I want Caroline to make all of my Halloween costumes."

"That looks like a lot of work for a kid's costume," Peter observed to Caroline, who stood beaming in the doorway.

"I told you, it's one of my old prom dresses. I just cut it off and took a couple of darts to pull it in. It didn't take any time at all."

"You do look great, Little Bit. I'm sorry that you have to take it off to go to dinner."

"I want to go like this." She pouted, her hands on her hips again.

Peter was having a good day. He didn't want to ruin his mood by having a battle of wills with Lacie. He looked to Caroline for help.

She twirled one of Lacie's curls on her finger. "You don't want everyone to see you before tomorrow.

Movie stars never let people see what they are going to wear to the Oscars before they get there."

Lacie dropped her hands and looked up at Caroline with teary eyes. "But how will I look like this tomorrow if I take it off now?"

Caroline squatted down to be eye-to-eye. "You have to get ready on time so your dad can bring you to the office early." She winked at Peter. "I'll be waiting with all of this to help you get dressed."

Lacie put her hand on Caroline's shoulder in a gesture so adult Peter almost laughed out loud. "Promise?"

Caroline stood up and took Lacie's hand. "I promise. Let's go up and get changed for dinner. You'll look beautiful in your regular clothes, too."

Peter relaxed. "We'll go when the game is over," he called after them. "There's only five minutes left on the clock." He and Logan would only require a few minutes to get ready, so they could all be out the door by five-thirty, plenty of time to eat and get back before the Falcons' kick-off at eight.

In fact, the game ended, he and Logan dressed, and they were waiting impatiently in the foyer with no sign of the women. Peter looked at his watch. Five-forty. "C'mon, girls," he called. "Time to go."

"Coming," Lacie sang as she bounced down the stairs, a little girl once again.

Peter's response stuck in his throat. Caroline had stopped on the landing to let Lacie dance down the stairs. The midnight blue dress perfectly matched her eyes and set off an unbelievably tiny waist. Had this stunning young woman been hiding right in front of him all along?

"You look nice," he said, afraid anything more accurate would embarrass them both.

"Thanks." She stepped down next to him. "I'm sorry you had to wait. It took a while to get the makeup off Lacie's face." She reached up to fasten his button-down collar.

"She looks better," he said, locking the door behind them. He put his hand on her back as he followed her around the car and opened the door for her.

"Yes, she does. Don't worry. By the time she's ready for makeup, she'll realize she's a natural beauty."

Even though *Hofu* was filled to overflowing, they honored Peter's six o'clock reservation and ushered them directly to their seats around a large, flat griddle. Their chef was a comedian, addressing most of his comments to Logan and Lacie, whom he instructed to make the menu selections for the adults, as well.

"This is fun." Caroline leaned forward to look more closely at the griddle and chef's workspace. "I didn't realize it would be like this."

"You've never been to a Japanese restaurant?" asked Peter, taking a swallow of beer.

"Nope," she replied. "My experience with restaurants is pretty limited."

"You and Josh don't go out?" He tried to imply a casual attitude with another swig from his bottle.

"No." She shook her head. "Neither of us is a successful veterinarian. Actually, neither of us is a successful anything."

"I wouldn't say that." Peter shook his head. "I'm not sure I'd be a successful veterinarian if you didn't keep me on track. You're the one who makes the office run smoothly."

"Thanks," she said with a mischievous smile. "Can I have a raise?"

Peter snorted. "I'm not that successful. Have you had better offers?"

"What would you do if I said yes?"

He knew she was kidding, but still, his heart gave a little flip. "I'd say tell me who they are so I can size up my competition."

"Sorry. I signed a confidentiality agreement," she teased. "Look, here he comes with our meat."

The chef's antics with knives and fire entertained Caroline and the children, but Peter's mind was occupied with their conversation. He'd barely held it together for much of the time since Maisie died, and Caroline had made sure he covered everything that needed to be done. Whether she really had another offer or not, he ought to pay her more just to be sure he priced her out of the market for anyone else.

She looked good. He had never thought about her looking good on top of everything else. He wouldn't ever be able to look at her at work again without thinking of her chestnut brown hair pulled back to show off her graceful neck or the hourglass figure hidden under her office clothes. He remembered how that figure had felt in his arms after the concert, and he struggled to keep his hand from covering hers where it lay on the table. She had grown up right under his nose, and now she was another man's woman.

What was it with Josh? Peter didn't want to beat a dead horse, but she was a good friend. More than a good friend. Jealousy aside, Josh was a loser with a capital "L," and she deserved better.

Once the chef stepped away, their primary

entertainment was watching Lacie sneak her food onto Logan's plate as though she was fooling them into thinking she had eaten.

"I see you." Peter struggled to cover his amusement with a firm tone. "You need to eat your own food, Lacie."

"I want ice cream," she proclaimed, sneaking another shrimp to Logan under the table.

He popped it in his mouth and sat without chewing, looking at them with big, innocent eyes.

Caroline muffled a laugh behind her hand.

Peter made a valiant attempt to keep his face expressionless, but the corners of his mouth turned up in spite of his best effort. "Logan, stop eating her food. Lacie, you have to eat more dinner before you can have dessert." Negotiation was his best strategy. "One piece of steak, one piece of chicken, and one shrimp. Then ice cream."

"Dad," Logan said, ignoring Peter's directive and relieving Lacie of another shrimp. "The game starts in half an hour."

"But I want ice cream. It's just an old football game. I hate football," Lacie pouted.

Peter was having none of that. She might be a princess, but no child of his would be a whiner. "Don't give me that attitude, Lacie. The game is as important to Logan as ice cream is to you."

"But Logan likes ice cream, too," she said, changing demand to negotiation.

"Yeah, but this is a big game, Lace. If the Falcons beat the Eagles then they move into playoff contention," Logan pleaded. Even he was out-maneuvered by the strength of Lacie's will.

"Why don't we get ice cream at the store and take it home?" Caroline offered. "I can run in and go through the self-checkout. It'll take five minutes. "

"That's a good plan." Peter signaled for the check. "Let's do it. Thanks."

Caroline turned an eagle-eye on Lacie to make sure she kept her promise to eat what Logan had left on her plate.

Logan wanted expensive "Moose Tracks" ice cream, and Lacie wanted pink peppermint. Peter pulled up to the front of the store and handed off the money. Caroline hopped out and dashed inside while Peter turned the car around to head out of the parking lot. She was back almost instantaneously with two bags and jumped back into the car, dropping the groceries at her feet. As she buckled her seatbelt they were already back on the road.

In the backseat, Logan sat forward and beat a drumroll on the back of Caroline's seat. "That was awesome! Caroline, you're the bomb!"

"Thank you, thank you." She smiled, accepting her accolades. "I know my boss. When he wants something fast, I'll be chasing the car through the parking lot if I'm not back when he's ready to go."

"C'mon," Peter teased. "I would have gone slow enough for you to catch us and jump on. You could ride home hanging off the back like a garbage man." He could see Logan laughing in the rearview mirror.

"Garbage man! Good one, Dad."

Next to Logan, Lacie looked upset. "What if she fell off?"

Caroline reached down to pull one of the ice cream containers from the bags. She took off her seatbelt and turned in her seat to show the label. "Look, Lacie. He would never leave me when I have his favorite, Double Chocolate Delight."

"That's right." Peter shared a look of parental unity with Caroline as she faced forward and put on her seatbelt. For a few minutes, he felt content. It had been a good night.

His contentment lasted until he saw the strange car parked in his driveway.

"Josh," Caroline whispered.

"What is he doing here?" Peter asked darkly.

"I don't know. He's supposed to be in Florida with his buddies."

He watched her consciously change her expression from disagreeably disturbed to pleasantly surprised, but he could still sense the wary tension in her body.

For his part, he did not bother to feign pleasantness. This man was an unwelcome intruder into their happy family night. "Stay in the car," he instructed the children. Body tense as a wound spring, he got out and walked around to open her door, but she was out before he could get there. He kept his distance to allow Caroline to control the situation, but he was ready to pounce before Josh could do any damage.

"Hi," she said brightly. "I thought you were in Gainesville. How did you know I was here?"

Josh leaned casually against a car that had seen better days. "Jed has to be at work tomorrow so we came home early. You're always talking about your great Dr. Hunter, so I figured you would run straight to him as soon as I was gone." His voice was tight. "Nice place, Dr. Hunter. Guess the vet business must be pretty good."

"Guess so," Peter replied. "I'm surprised to see you, Josh." Even from a distance, he reeked of beer.

"I imagine you are," Josh retorted. "Are you paying her for these extra hours she's working for you?"

Caroline put a calming hand on the arms folded across his chest. "It's not like that," she soothed. "I came over to help the kids with their Halloween costumes. Dr. Hunter took me out to dinner to say thank you."

Josh looked her over like he was sizing up a new car. "And these are your 'playing with the kids' clothes?"

"Of course not. Dr. Hunter told me ahead of time that we'd go out so I came prepared."

He glared daggers that bounced off Peter's equally fierce glare. He obviously was not used to having his belligerent posturing challenged, and he shifted uncomfortably around his car to open the passenger-side door. With the car between them, he reasserted some of his swagger. "Fine, but now I'm back. Let's go."

Peter balled his fist and clenched his jaw in an involuntary reflex. He wanted to stride around the car and let Josh be the threatened one. He couldn't make her leave him, but he could make sure Josh knew what would happen if he hurt her.

When he glanced at Caroline, she nodded at the wide-eyed children in the car and pleaded with him silently to let it go. "I'm coming," she surrendered.

Peter had no authority to stop her. "I'll see you in the morning. Remember, we've got an early start to get Lacie's costume on," he called after her as a warning to

Josh. He was watching.

As Josh's car skidded out of the driveway, Peter got a glimpse of Caroline's unhappy face through the windshield, and he wondered again why someone like her would put up with someone like Josh.

"Boy, Dad, Josh sucks," Logan offered as he got out of the car.

Peter had to agree.

Chapter 16

Their Monday morning routine was unusually uneventful because both kids were excited about Halloween, but Peter couldn't enjoy his success. All of his senses were set to maximum sensitivity, ready to pick up the least catch in Caroline's voice or miniscule sign of soreness in her movement. The night before, Josh had morphed from a pesky insect to a venomous snake. Peter realized he had been so focused on his own situation he hadn't been paying close enough attention to what was really going on with her.

The smooth morning made it one of the rare days when they beat Caroline to work.

Lacie immediately panicked. "Where is she, Daddy? I need my costume on, and the bus is coming."

He grasped her shoulders and turned her toward the wall. "Look at the clock, Little Bit." He pointed at the cat clock with the ticking tail on the wall behind the desk. "Can you tell what time it is?"

She pointed at the numbers and counted out loud. "The little hand is on the six and the big hand is on the four. Five, ten, fifteen, twenty. It's twenty minutes after six o'clock."

Peter was proud. Most kids couldn't read an analog clock, but Lacie was smart, and she paid attention in school. "That's right, and Caroline is meeting us at six-thirty. She's not late. We're early."

Lacie looked doubtful. "We're never early."

Peter couldn't decide if he was amused or irritated by her grown-up observation. "We are today."

Someone kicked the outer door as though their hands were too full to knock. Peter opened it to see Caroline heavy-laden with the pieces of Lacie's costume and other assorted grocery bags. She was smiling, and her cheeks were flushed pink. How could she look so good so early in the morning? "Do you need some help?"

"Nope," she laughed. "If you take anything the rest is going to fall like a house of cards. Just hold the door and let me in." She waddled awkwardly across the room and dropped the packages on the desk. "Whew. I didn't realize how much stuff I had."

"What is it? What is it?" Lacie jumped up and down.

"Not everything is exciting, sweetie, but I do have some very cool Halloween candy."

Peter took the opportunity of Caroline's attention on Lacie to take stock of her well-being. There were no bruises that he could see or any heavy makeup a woman would use to hide the signs of abuse. She appeared to be moving fine as she bustled around, putting away all of her purchases, and then put her hands on Lacie's shoulders to physically turn her around and head to the bathroom for costume assembly.

"Don't worry, Dad," she called over her shoulder. "Now that I know what I'm doing it will go much faster."

The "movie star" wasn't quite ready for her "appearance" when the bus came, so Peter had to fly out the door to drive her through the carpool line. His heart was pounding when he dashed back into the clinic, but he allowed himself a deep breath when he found Lynn, the technician, had stepped up to take care of the boarders. From that moment on, his whole team was busy all day, even working through lunch, and, although he thought it was ridiculous, Peter was appropriately appreciative of the "creative" costumes many of his patients wore.

As they went through the work day everything seemed normal, but he couldn't ignore the nagging pinch of worry where his skull met his neck. He knew Caroline would never do anything to disappoint the children, but between the stolen kiss and the conflict over Josh, the air around them was constantly charged with an unfamiliar tension. He had to know for sure that their plans were still on. During one of the times they passed in the hallway, he stopped her with a touch on her shoulder.

She cupped her hand over his. "What's up?"

"Are you still coming tonight?" He examined her face closely to gauge the truth of her reply.

"Why wouldn't I?"

"Josh won't be upset? I don't want to make you feel bad, but I also don't want him showing up at the house again."

A cloud passed over Caroline's happy face. She turned away and walked back to her desk. "I'm sorry about that. Since he came home early from Florida, he took an extra shift tonight. He thinks there'll be great tips on a holiday. He'll be working late, and I promised to come after trick-or-treating with candy for the whole shift."

"You're taking my kids' candy for Josh?" he

teased.

She laughed. "No, I'm not taking your kids' candy." She pointed to grocery bags under the desk. "I bought more than enough on clearance over the weekend."

This was his chance. "What happened after you left last night? Was he okay?"

Her mouth was still smiling, but the light had gone out of her eyes.

"He's all bark and no bite. Once we got home, he fell asleep. Too much beer."

"Is that right?" Peter scanned her face, assessing the truth of her words. "I thought he was going to stop drinking."

She averted her eyes and pushed the files on her desk into a pile. "I had a great time at dinner, Doc. Thanks so much." When she looked up, her face was calm. "Tonight is going to be a lot of fun. I love Halloween."

Peter wanted to pursue the "Josh" topic further, but the after-lunch crowd was filling the waiting area. Once again, he shifted it to the back burner to simmer for later.

Lacie came in, glowing, and ran straight to wrap her arms around Caroline. "My costume was voted favorite in the class! I was on the morning announcements as one of the best in the whole school! Thank you for making it for me!" she gushed. "I love you!"

"I love you, too, sweetie." Caroline laughed and kissed the top of her head.

He felt like an outsider looking through a window at a precious moment between a little girl and her beloved...beloved what? Friend? Sister? Aunt? He choked on the word that came hard, even in his silent thoughts. Mother?

Caroline took Lacie's hand. "Let's go look in your backpack. You shouldn't have any homework, but we need to make sure." She turned her attention to the waiting room, which still had a handful of occupants. "I'll be right back."

Peter followed them as far as the exam room with his next patient and paused to watch them walk down the hall. If he had to make Lacie's costume, it would never have won any prizes. Who was he kidding? He wouldn't have *made* a costume at all.

Caroline had been the real mother figure in his children's lives for the last year and a half. Maisie's list had him looking for someone to fill the empty place she had left, but was it already taken? No, it was not. To fully occupy that place, she'd live with them, and that meant being a wife to him, as well. To be his wife, she would have to...

The memory dislodged itself from his gut and rose to settle in his chest like a bowling ball. The impulse to hold her and kiss her that night had been beyond his ability to resist. She had fit to his body like they were two halves of a single figure, and she had answered his every kiss with unspoken permission for the next.

He leaned his head against the door. What had Maisie said? *We shared all the firsts that no one else can ever share with you.* Caroline had not experienced those "firsts" yet. Engagement. Wedding. House. Child. She deserved to be with someone who would share those milestones with her as they happened, not someone who had already lived through them all with the love of his life. She should be the love of someone's life, not second best.

He turned the doorknob and went in.

****

Since the neighborhood plan was to begin trick-or-treating with the younger children as soon as it was dark, Caroline followed the Hunters home when the office closed at five. Peter called ahead and picked up pizza on the way, enough for his family and a small army of Logan's friends. Logan had only mentioned Michael, but Peter knew that group would swell to at least five or six by the time their pillowcases were full.

Caroline and Lacie dashed immediately upstairs to freshen her costume, and Peter took advantage of being alone to grab a bite of pizza. The doorbell rang before Peter had finished his first slice. He dumped three, super-sized bags of assorted candy into the largest mixing bowl they owned and answered the door. A toddler dressed as a bumblebee held up a small plastic pumpkin and mumbled something close to "Twick-or-Tweat!" Peter's Halloween Grinch heart melted, and he squatted to eye-level, holding out the bowl to his visitor. "What would you like?"

The little boy took a cherry Tootsie-Pop. "T'ank you," he said, at the prompting of the protective parent standing right behind him.

Peter and the man nodded at each other, the communally accepted greeting between fathers.

Lacie and Caroline appeared just as the enthusiastic group of Lacie's friends arrived. They took generous offerings of candy from Peter's bowl, which he handed off to Caroline with a sigh of resignation.

"It's all good," she said, patting him on the back.

"Relax and have a good time."

Peter was surprised to actually enjoy himself. Yes, the "holiday" was a media driven exploitation by the candy companies. Yes, the sugar wound the children up like watch springs and rotted their teeth. Yes, it demolished routines and made for cranky early-risers the next morning. But everywhere he looked, happy people were having fun. Friends and neighbors sat around portable fire pits as they handed out their candy. Cars moved slowly and respectfully past the mobs of frenzied, absent-minded children. A police car made a welcome pass through the neighborhood, its window down and the friendly officer waving as he rode by. Logan even stopped to greet his little sister when his gang of rambunctious preteen boys stampeded through the crowd of younger children.

By then, however, Lacie and her friends were done, and she complained that her dressy shoes hurt her feet.

Warmed by his camaraderie with the other parents, Peter yielded his usual insistence that she pay the price for her own decisions and allowed her to ride home on his back. As soon as they walked in the door she perked up, eager to show Caroline her spoils.

"How were the trick-or-treaters?" Peter asked as they followed Lacie into the family room, where she dumped the entire contents of her bag on the floor and began sorting her candy by type. Buddy lay nearby, tail wagging, his eyes following each movement of her hand.

"Great!" Caroline enthused. "It was so fun. I had to back off a bit on the candy dispersal, though. I'm afraid we are going to run out."

"Are you kidding? With all the candy I bought?"

He took the seat next to her on the sofa and propped his feet on the coffee table.

"Logan and his friends took healthy handfuls before they left. But that's okay, I just opened one of the bags I brought for Josh."

"Then Logan and his friends can give you some of their candy to replace it."

"That'll work." She smiled. "So, Lacie, what is the candy of the year?"

Lacie surveyed her piles. "Lots of people had these little candy bars." She pointed to two similar stacks of bite-size candy, one in white wrappers and one in brown. She took one off the white pile and popped it in her mouth. "I like the white chocolate best."

"Only one more piece, Little Bit."

"But, Daddy," she pleaded. "It's Halloween."

"No reason to get sick," he said firmly.

She looked at Caroline for support, but found the adults united against her. "I'll share," she offered with a coy tilt of the head.

"Nice try." Peter smirked. "Go up and get ready for bed, but don't brush your teeth yet. I'll let you have one more piece."

"Okay." She hopped up and waited for Caroline, who followed to help her take off the heavy makeup. After Lacie stomped up the stairs with Caroline trailing behind her, Peter's thoughts turned back to Josh. Before last night's incident, Peter had just thought Josh was irritating and full of himself. But now, he was afraid there might be real danger lurking behind his angry words.

Caroline returned before Lacie, and Peter felt compelled to broach the subject. "I know it's not any of my business, but does Josh get like that a lot?"

Caroline's smile disappeared instantly. "You're right. It's none of your business," she said without elaboration. She squatted down and poked through Lacie's piles.

He wasn't offended, but Caroline never talked to him like that, and the curtness of her reply only strengthened his resolve. "I'm concerned for you," he persisted, his eyes following her every move. "Does he ever hurt you? Did he hurt you last night?"

"I already told you he didn't." She held up a bite-sized piece. "My favorite is caramel. Do you think she'll miss this one?"

Like a dog with a bone, Peter had his teeth in the subject, and he wasn't letting go. "You told me you let him back because he had stopped drinking."

"He's not drinking as much. It was just a bad night." She held up the candy like she was examining a piece of art. "I don't think she'll mind just one." She took off the wrapper and popped the candy in her mouth.

Peter continued looking at her intently. He wasn't budging until he was satisfied she was safe. "You need to tell me the truth. If he is threatening you, we've got to do something to stop him."

She rocked back on her heels and looked him straight in the eyes. "He got mad because he's jealous of you, but it passed."

He fell back against the couch as though she had punched him in the chest. He didn't want to bear any responsibility for unleashing the monster. He thought he was the one who was jealous. "Jealous of me? Why?"

"Because he sees that I'm happy around you, and I don't act the same way when I'm with him." She picked up a red-wrapped piece. "What do you suppose this is?" She looked at Peter and realized he wasn't going to drop the topic until he was satisfied. "He's right. I give my best all day at work, and sometimes I don't have much energy left when I see him at night."

"He gets mad because you come home tired? Does he have any idea what you do all day?" Alarms were going off like air raid sirens in his head. The situation was worse than he'd feared. How had this gotten by him so long?

She waved away his interrogation. "It's okay. It means a lot for you to be concerned, but I have it under control. I'm actually flattered he cares enough to be jealous."

She rolled forward on her knees and visibly focused on the piles of candy to put an end to their conversation, but Peter had been put on high alert. Josh was big enough to intimidate Caroline, but Peter was sure he could take him if the need arose. He was at least four inches taller, and a good bit more fit. He was ready to step in uninvited if he saw signs that he was hurting her in any way.

"I'm going to steal another piece of Lacie's candy," she confided slyly, as though the previous conversation had never happened. "Want one?"

"Sure," he replied with a smile, but he couldn't force the unease out of his voice. "I'll take the coconut one. She'll never miss it."

"Here ya go."

He peeled the candy and popped it into his mouth. He wanted to keep going, but what was he actually hoping to accomplish? Did he want her to admit she was afraid? Did he want her to end things with Josh once and for all? Did he want her to stay with him forever so he could protect her from a menacing boyfriend and anyone else who threatened to harm her?

He watched her on the floor, picking through Lacie's candy. She'd take a piece, then redo the pile so the little girl wouldn't notice it was gone. Stay with him forever? Where did that come from? How much protection could he be? He wasn't able to save Maisie.

His reverie was shattered when Logan and his friends thundered in like a rampaging herd of buffalo. As Peter expected, the group had grown from just Logan and Michael to a total of six, but the four extras left as soon as they saw the empty candy bowl. Logan and Michael lifted their bulging pillowcases like laborers on a railroad chain-gang and dumped the contents on the kitchen table with a thud. The piles of empty wrappers mixed in with the impressive spoils of the evening's activities explained their frenzied behavior. There would be a serious energy crash by morning.

"Dad, can you take Michael home?" Logan asked through a mouthful of candy. "He texted his mom, but she didn't answer. He thinks she fell asleep on the couch."

"Can you stay a few more minutes?" Peter asked Caroline, hoping his interrogation hadn't chased her away.

She settled into her seat on the sofa and picked up the remote. "Absolutely."

"Only one more piece of candy for Lacie," he instructed.

"Of course."

Her answer lacked conviction, and he suspected she was going to let Lacie slide in an extra piece or two. "You're going to give in to her, aren't you?"

Caroline slapped her hand over her heart. "You don't trust me? I'm wounded."

Peter made an unhappy face. "You're not the one who has to get her up in the morning."

Caroline nodded. "That's true. I can stay over if you want, as penance for my crime." As soon as the words came out, her body went rigid, and she looked at him with saucer-eyes. "I mean…I just mean…I could sleep here on the sofa…I could set the alarm on my phone…" she stammered.

Peter could not block the mental image of kneeling by the sofa and waking her with a tender kiss. He squeezed his eyes shut and willed away the vision. It didn't work. With his eyes closed, he saw her. With his eyes open, he saw her. He had to get out. "Be right back," he said, following Logan and Michael out the door.

When he returned, Caroline was in the kitchen adding her share of Logan's candy to her bag. She was already wearing her jacket like she was ready to dash out. Was she running to avoid Josh's anger? Or running away from his efforts to protect her? He had no choice but to let her go with many thanks and no mention of Josh. He didn't want to send her off with bad feelings after they had such a good night.

Once he saw the kids to bed, Peter assumed his usual place in his bedroom, Buddy stretched out against his leg. He absentmindedly scratched the dog between the ears while he talked to Maisie.

Halloween was better than I thought it would be, he admitted.

I always said you were missing all the fun.

Could you see the kids in their costumes?

Yes, I am always watching our babies.

Lacie looked so grown-up in hers. It scared me a little.

He heard her chuckle. *I told you she's going to give you a run for your money. Tonight was a vision of the future.*

He shuddered. *I like her better as a little girl. I wish she could stay that way forever.*

Her tone became sad. *And I wish I could have seen her grow up.*

Me too. Peter had to head off the grief with a change of subject. *I'm afraid Josh is not treating Caroline right.*

He never has.

Why does she put up with him?

Because she doesn't want to be alone.

Do you know? Can you see? Do I need to step in?

Be alert. If you go after him before she is ready, you'll just make things worse.

But what if he does her some real damage?

She needs a champion, but she won't ask.

All right, then. I'll pay a visit to his work tomorrow and let him know I'm watching. How could I figure things out without you?

I'm happy to help.

He sighed and rubbed her empty space on the bed. *What about when I need to touch you? What about when I need to pull you against me and use you as a human shield against the world?*

I can't do that anymore. That's why I want you to find a living woman to hold.

No one can replace you.

I told you, sweetheart, this is not to replace me. This is to start fresh.

You want me to date, take care of the children, and make sure Josh doesn't hurt Caroline?

It's called multi-tasking, my darling. You can do it.

Even without you?

Even without me.

I never wanted to do any of this without you.

I know. Loved you in that life and beyond. Kiss our babies for me.

Chapter 17

What a difference a day made. Peter had been so proud of their punctuality on Halloween morning, but as he anticipated, the post-candy crash made it nearly impossible to get Logan and Lacie up for school. He stormed into the office with his children dragging behind him like zombies. His irritation was compounded by Caroline's good humor. She had been at the clinic long enough to take down the Halloween decorations, which were piled on her desk to be put in the box on the floor and stored away for next year.

"It isn't worth it," Peter snarled, reneging on his change of heart about Halloween.

"Sure, it is," Caroline countered, handing each of the children a breakfast bar. "All that fun, and just one morning of pain. In twenty years, they won't remember the bad stuff, only that Halloween was terrific." She smiled. "And so will you."

"Humph." Peter retreated into his office and took a quick sip of the coffee she had left for him before dashing out the door to get Lacie to the bus. On his way back, he waved at Donna, who was sitting in the parking lot, motor running, waiting for Logan. His son pushed past him with a barely audible, "See ya," and jumped into the car which promptly sped away.

Once they were gone, he returned to his office to finish his now-cold coffee. He took a long gulp and puckered his face at the bitter taste. He could have taken the cup to the microwave, but that required too much effort in the little time he had. It was just the first swallow that was so terrible anyway, and after the initial shock, he rocked back in his big leather chair and nursed the rest while he organized his thoughts.

First, he couldn't wait another day to put Josh on alert. He'd have to be sneaky to get his schedule from Caroline without her suspecting his motivation. Would she be mad? Better mad than maimed. Josh, warned, today.

Two...he opened the drawer where Maisie's package had sat since he'd started going out with Donna. He shook the last two envelopes out onto his desk and picked up "3."

Dearest husband,

Here you are, looking for contestant number three. Suzanne offers a gracious, peaceful environment, and Donna offers great organization and lots of help with the children. For whatever reason, neither is a good fit. I'm actually kind of happy, in a weird, posthumously jealous way, that these women I knew so well were never any competition. Still, this isn't about me, it's about you, and the next woman is definitely all for you.

Hillary Hoffman is, without question, the most interesting person I have ever met. I haven't introduced you, or even talked about her to you, because I am afraid she will make you dissatisfied with your schlumpy housewife. She's not really beautiful in the conventional sense, and she certainly never seeks the spotlight, but when she walks into a room people take notice. She's a freelance photographer, and her work has taken her all over the world. The places she's seen and the people she's met stagger the mind, and yet, in spite of it all, she is a great listener and makes you feel like you are the one with the fascinating life. She will do for you what I have not done in many years—free you from the constant burdens of job, house, and children, and give you an engagement with the world outside of our small community that you have not had for a very long time.

I know her from the gym. She and I always plan to take the same classes, even though she misses a lot of time, traveling for her jobs. Start there to find her.

Enjoy her, my love. You are in for a great ride.

Love you in this life and beyond. Kiss our babies for me.

Maisie

Peter dropped the letter in his lap. This was an altogether different animal from the others. Both Suzanne and Donna had been part of their lives when Maisie was alive, and they had something in common going into their relationships. He didn't know this woman from Eve, aside from the fact that she was a photographer who traveled and Maisie considered her interesting. How did he walk up to a strange woman and start a conversation without getting pepper sprayed?

I know her from the gym. Where had Maisie belonged? It was close, he remembered, because she used to stop by the office on her way home. He should have paid better attention when she told him about it.

He had no choice but to ask the one person who knew everything. He cleared his throat with a sip of coffee. "Caroline?"

"Yessir?" she called back.

"Do you remember where Maisie worked out?"

"She went to *Tough Tony's*. Why do you ask?"

"I just…wondered." He held his breath, hoping she would accept his weak response.

"Just wondered?" She materialized in his doorway. "Does it have anything to do with the third envelope on your desk?"

"Maybe."

She leaned against the doorframe and crossed her arms. "Someone I know?"

He hadn't kept her out of the loop with the others, so he understood why she felt so free to ask, but something about this one felt different. Was it that Hillary was from outside the usual sphere of their daily routine? Was it because he felt selfish and guilty seeing someone just to please himself, even if she was on Maisie's list? Maisie had said she wanted someone to help him with the children, but Hillary Hoffman didn't seem a good candidate for that job. Was it that this time, unlike the others, he couldn't get rid of the vision of kissing Caroline awake on the couch? "Somebody she knew from the gym," he replied, shuffling the papers on his desk into a pile. "Is my first patient here yet?"

She squinted at him and said slowly, "The Meyers just walked in."

He breathed a sigh of relief. "Go on and take them back to the exam room, please."

With a last look, she turned away from him and walked back to the desk. "You got it."

Tough Tony's was close enough to walk on a nice, leisurely day, but given he only had half an hour for lunch, he would have to make the five-minute drive. To do that, however, he wouldn't be able to work through lunch. So, again, he had to involve Caroline. With the waiting room full of pet parents, he walked out to the desk instead of calling to her. "I need to keep my lunch time open today. Don't schedule any walk-ins, okay? Ask them to come later or, if it's an emergency, call me."

She swiveled to face him with a smirk on her face. "Planning to get in a workout?"

"Not exactly." He expected her to pry further, but instead he got the feeling she had the whole thing worked out already.

She turned back to the desk. "I can clear you for a whole hour."

"Great," he replied, trying, and failing, to sound nonchalant. He strode quickly back to the exam room, a place where he felt comfortable and in control.

His first three patients were routine vaccinations, although the Newparts' Doberman puppy jumped off the exam table and led them on a chase around the room, necessitating two full-grown men, Peter and Greg, to corral him and hold him down. Peter forgot all about Hillary Hoffman when Ashley Watterman showed up with a kitten she found under a bush in her backyard. After a full exam, shots, and treatment for ear mites, Ashley was happy to say that the kitten, which she named Dakota during the exam, would be a surprise pet for her children when they got home from school.

Peter walked Ashley out to tell Caroline there would be no charge for the little rescue, and when he saw the empty waiting room, he looked at his watch. Noon. He went back to wash his hands, and then tried to appear casual as he walked out the door. "I'll be back."

The five-minute drive didn't give him enough time to think of what to say other than, "Maisie wanted me to meet you." From the parking lot, he peered through the big picture window at the cycle class in progress. Cycling had been Maisie's favorite workout. She'd boasted that she burned up machines in class, and proved it by charging ahead of him whenever they rode along the Greenway together.

He was surprised that, instead of overwhelming him with crippling grief, some of his memories of Maisie were starting to make him happy. Like the concerts of their youth that Donna brought back, riding bikes with her was one of the good ones. His chest hurt from the realization that he hadn't gone riding with the kids since she'd passed away. He would have to do something about that as soon as possible. His kids needed to make some new, happy memories.

If cycling class had been Maisie's favorite, and Hillary had worked out with her at this gym, then Hillary might be in this class. Could he possibly be that lucky? Suzanne had been in the waiting room, and Donna had been in the parking lot. Why wouldn't Hillary be at the gym?

He pushed through the front door.

The face of the young man behind the desk lit up as though he was seeing a favorite uncle. "Dr. Hunter! Hi!"

Peter scanned the greeter's face for anything familiar, but found no clue. "I'm sorry, do I know you?"

"You probably don't remember me. I'm Robbie Abernathy." He came out from behind the desk and held out his hand. "My folks have been bringing our boxer to you for a really long time."

He might not remember all the humans who passed through his clinic, but he never forgot an animal. Abernathy. Boxer…got it. He cupped the boy's hand in both of his to shake it. "Of course. Bruiser. Bruiser Abernathy."

"That's right! It's pretty awesome you remember. You've got to have a boatload of patients."

"Bruiser is a pretty cool dog. It's great to see you, Robbie. You're all grown up."

"Thanks." He beamed. "What can I do for you today, Doc?"

"I'm looking for someone." Peter took a moment before pressing on. He cleared his throat to maintain his air of authority. "Do you know Hillary Hoffman?"

"Sure. She's been out for a long time, but she came back today. Lucky for you, huh?"

"I guess so." *Lucky, Maisie?* "I've never met her. Can you point her out to me?" Good, now he'd have the kid to verify his identity and make him seem less of a stalker.

"Sure," Robbie replied. "They're coming out now." The large, chatty group of cyclists was exiting the classroom. "There she is." Robbie indicated a woman at the back of the group.

What had Maisie said? *She's not really beautiful, but when she walks into a room, people take notice.* She was perfectly assembled with no leftover parts or waste, and she moved with efficient assurance, never doubting where to place her next step. Her skin was tan, and her curly, brown hair was streaked with gold, not with the temporary dazzle of a visit to the hair salon, but permanently, like she spent most of her life in the sun. Even in this relaxed setting, as she smiled kindly at the woman prattling in her ear, she was scanning the environment like she was setting up her next shot.

With a nod at Robbie Abernathy, Peter called to her. "Hillary?" he said. "Hillary Hoffman?"

"Who's calling my name?" she asked, searching the faces of the bustling crowd.

"I am," said Peter, swimming against the current to get to her side. "I'm Peter Hunter. My wife was—"

Her face relaxed, and she gave him a sad smile. "Maisie Hunter, my good friend."

Peter was relieved he wouldn't have to sell himself, but at the same time, he wondered how Maisie could have been so close to a woman she had never mentioned to him. "Yes, that's right."

"How can I help you, Dr. Hunter?"

Peter was thrown a little off-guard by her directness and blurted out his answer without measuring his words. "Maisie thought we should meet. She said you were the most interesting person she had ever known."

"Maisie." She looked away and whispered, "Your wife was the kindest person I've ever known." When she turned back to him, tears were welling in her eyes.

He felt an immediate connection with this woman who had thought so much of Maisie. They'd just met, but they were members of the same club. The brotherhood/sisterhood of people who had been touched by Maisie. "Do you have a few minutes? Can we grab a cup of coffee?"

She wiped away a tear rolling down her cheek, and he could see her visibly will her face into a more playful expression. "No coffee after working out, but there is a juice bar next door. Why don't we grab a juice and chat?" She held the door for him and then pushed in front to lead the way three stores down to Java Juice.

Once they were seated with their drinks, her serious tone returned. "I knew she was sick. She didn't want to talk about it, but I'd seen that her hair was gone. It'd come back the last time I saw her, and all she would say was she was doing better."

"It came in curly. She never thought she'd have curly hair," Peter murmured.

Hillary focused on her cup, pumping her straw up and down. "I was gone a long time photographing newly discovered Viking ruins in Greenland. When I got back, she was gone." She looked up at him. "What happened?"

"It was her liver." The memory of Maisie's last days flooded in. He tried to avoid it, dismiss it, and ignore it, but his grief always lurked inside him like a coiled snake, ready to strike. "One day, she was there, cheering at Logan's baseball game and putting puzzles together with Lacie. That same night, I noticed her eyes had turned yellow. We went to the emergency room, and she never came home. It was just that fast."

Her eyes misted again. "Did you know she was the best friend I ever had?"

"No, I didn't." Why didn't he pay more attention to Maisie's chattering while he still could?

"She was." Hillary smiled. "When I would come back to class after being out a long time, she would stop whatever she was doing and run to throw her arms around me. She was the only person who ever did that.

Ever. Anywhere."

The memories were painful, but precious. "She was a great hugger. She used to lock me in a bear hug, and she wouldn't let go until I hugged her back."

"Maisie was crazy about you. She often apologized because she thought her conversation was so one-sided, always talking about you and Logan and Lacie. But I enjoyed it. It was like setting up for a shoot at a place I had never been." She sat up straight, as though she had been hit in the back by an arrow. "I can't believe I didn't ever think of it. I should have taken pictures of your family. She would have loved that."

He rolled his glass in his hands. "Too late now."

She reached across the table and squeezed his arm. "No, it's not. You're still a family, even if she's not in the picture. Let me come and shoot you and the kids."

Peter wasn't sure he was ready for a family picture that didn't include Maisie. "I don't know…"

"She would have loved it." Hillary sat forward as though perched to spring into action. "How about I take some photos of your staff for the clinic, like promotional images for your website and advertising? We can casually include portraits of you and the kids, and it won't feel like you are intentionally cutting her out. If you don't like them, we won't have wasted our time."

He couldn't think fast enough to know what to do, but she seemed so certain. "Okay, I guess."

"I'll need to do it sometime when you are all clean." She was almost giddy. "No dog poop or blood on your clothes."

Peter sniggered. "That's almost never."

"I bet we could do it with a little bit of warning.

Today is Tuesday. How about Thursday?"

"Two days? I thought it took longer to set up a photo session."

"It does if I'm trying to capture a cheetah chasing an antelope, but human subjects are usually willing to sit on command."

Hillary was more than merely interesting. She was a force of nature, and he was powerless against her momentum now that she was on a roll. He tried to stall. "It'll have to be after the kids get off the bus. That's pretty late in the day."

She waved off his hesitation. "I'm between jobs, so what else have I got to do? Thursday, five o'clock? Five-thirty?"

Peter scratched his head. "Five-thirty, I guess. But I have to ask my staff."

"No problem. I'll call your office and speak to Caroline."

He startled like she had doused him with cold water. "You know Caroline?"

"Maisie said you wouldn't be able to run the clinic without her." She pulled a business card out of her gym bag. "This is how to reach me." Looking at her phone, she asked, "What time do you have to be back?"

Peter's watch showed 12:45. "Now." He stood and held out his hand. "It was great to meet you, Hillary."

She rose and clasped his hand with a grip so strong, he would never have expected it from a woman. "I'm so glad you came looking for me. I've missed Maisie, and I'm happy to have a new friend."

In a hazy state of confusion, Peter returned to the office. Seeing Caroline behind the desk reminded him he had one more task to accomplish that day. Josh.

Caroline had mentioned Josh was working at *Jilly Joe's* restaurant that night. That made him easy to find, but Peter knew he needed a well-thought out plan before he approached him. A wrong move could make things a lot worse for Caroline.

****

"Hey guys, I feel like going to *Jilly Joe's* tonight. What d'ya say?" Peter decided taking Lacie and Logan would make his visit seem innocent and keep Josh off his guard. It was crowded and brightly lit, so he knew they would be safe, and he would take care of his business with Josh out of view so they would never know.

Lacie grabbed Peter's hand and swung it hard. "Oh, Daddy! Oh yes, please!"

Logan spun around and looked down his nose at Peter. "What's the punchline, Dad? What terrible thing do you want us to do? Clean out the refrigerator? Identify the parts of speech in a hundred sentences? Eat raw vegetables instead of potato chips?"

Peter stifled a laugh. "Why so suspicious, Logan?"

Logan ticked off the reasons on his fingers. "A-it's a school night. B-you are always complaining that we never have a night at home because of football. C-we don't go to sit-down restaurants except for special occasions."

Peter used his fingers the same way. "A-it's also a work night, and I'm too tired to cook. B-we finally have a night off football, and I don't want to spend it in the kitchen. C-you guys are older now, and I can trust you to behave in a good restaurant."

Logan grinned. "I'm convinced, and I'm starving. Let's go."

219

Jilly Joe's was a sports bar with a reputation for excellent food and unusual menu items. The owner, Jill London, trained at the prestigious International Culinary Institute in New York City. They were also known for their remarkably pleasant employees, which made Peter wonder if there might actually be a side to Josh he had never seen.

The restaurant was much busier than Peter expected on a weeknight, and he was afraid they'd have to wait for a table. "Can we sit in Josh's section?" he asked the young woman at the desk. "He's a friend of a friend." In his peripheral vision, he could see Logan looking at him with his mouth hanging open, but he concentrated on the hostess and pretended not to notice.

She ran her finger over the seating grid displayed on the podium and stopped when she found what she wanted. She looked at him with a smile that made the whole room seem brighter. "We're in luck. A table just opened." She grabbed three menus. "Right this way."

Josh arrived before they had finished taking off their jackets. When he recognized them, his smile became forced, and he spoke through it so anyone looking would think he was saying something nice. "Why are you here?"

Peter kept his voice even to hide his ulterior motive. "Caroline mentioned you work here, and I thought we'd give it a try. Some days after work, I don't feel like cooking. Beer and pizza would be fine for me, but I have to do better than that for the kids." Peter would never actually have beer and pizza if he was eating alone, but he wanted to ease the tension by appealing to their common manhood.

"Okay. Sure. What can I get you to drink?"

He wasn't cheery, but at least they were moving forward. He brought their drinks and took their food order, visibly relaxing with each interaction. When Lacie couldn't decide between chicken fingers and macaroni and cheese, he actually smiled. "Why don't you order both? I bet that guy," he pointed at Logan with his pen, "can finish whatever you don't eat."

Logan rubbed his hands together and licked his lips.

Josh was so accommodating and fast, Peter almost forgot why he had come. Almost. This was not the man he saw interacting with Caroline on Sunday night, and he suspected that, after a few drinks, he would become that man again. When Josh came to check on them, Peter remembered the dangerous predator instead of the pleasant waiter, and he resolved to follow through on his plan. His shoulders and neck tensed, and he couldn't keep the tightness out of his voice. He needed a distraction to occupy his kids while he talked to him alone. "Logan, Lacie, what do you say to dessert?"

Josh seemed to pick up on Peter's body language instantly. He took a step backwards and shifted his weight to his front leg so he could make a quick getaway. The fake smile returned. "Do you need to see a menu?"

Seemingly unaware of the drama playing out between the two men, Logan shook his head. "I looked when we ordered dinner. I'll take a chocolate shake."

"Do you have a scoop of vanilla ice cream?" Lacie asked delicately.

"You got it. What about you, Dr. Hunter?"

Peter was certain the strain showed on his face. "None for me, thanks. Just the check."

"Coming right up." He charged away at a pace only slightly less than a run and was back in a flash with the bill before Peter could get his credit card out of his wallet. With the credit card in hand, he dashed off and returned with the desserts and the charge slip. "It's been great serving you," he said, body half-turned to dash away again.

"Hold on a second, I'll give it right back to you." Peter made a show of adding a sizeable tip. As he handed off the tray and pen, he asked, "Before we leave, can I talk to you for a minute outside?" He pushed himself up with both hands on the table. "You guys wait here and finish your desserts," he said to the children. "Logan, keep things under control. I'll be right back."

Outside, Josh reverted to his suspicious, contentious demeanor. His arms were rigid by his sides, and he flexed his hands. "I knew that nicety-nice stuff was just an act," he snarled. "What do you want? Did Caroline put you up to something? I've got customers waiting, and I don't have time for female drama."

"No," Peter replied, keeping his voice low and emotionless. "Caroline doesn't know I'm here."

Josh squinted as though he could physically see through to Peter's motives. "What, then?"

Peter mentally counted to three, looking directly into Josh's eyes. "The way you treat Caroline concerns me." He enunciated each word.

"Oh, it does, does it?" Josh sneered. "I always knew you wanted her for yourself. Even before your wife died."

Peter's fist clenched, but he willed it to stay at his side. After their first kiss he couldn't deny he wanted more of Caroline, but that only made him more determined to prove to himself his actions were only a momentary lapse in judgement. "No," he said. "That is not the case. I am talking to you because she is my friend, and I think you might do her harm."

Instead of the denial Peter expected, Josh's lips curled up to reveal his teeth like a snarling dog. "How is that any of your business?"

Peter widened his stance to hold his ground if the other man threw a punch. "It is everybody's business to protect a friend from abuse."

Josh stepped up nose-to-nose, his jaw set and his eyes wide. "You think I abuse her? Did she tell you that?"

Peter didn't back down. "No. I am going on my own observations."

"I have no intention of 'abusing' her," he spat. "Leave us alone." He turned to walk away.

Peter grabbed Josh by the shoulder and spun him around. "I'm afraid I haven't been clear," he growled, squeezing so tight it seemed his fingers would push through the skin. "Caroline is a very important member of our family. I will not have her hurt by you, or anyone else. I want you to know that I am watching. If I see any sign, any at all, that she has been treated badly, I will do what is necessary to protect her. No warnings, no second chances. And should I be required to 'defend' myself against her assailant," he straightened to his full height and glowered menacingly, "I believe the police would take my side."

Josh yanked his shoulder free and disappeared without another word. Peter followed slowly, shaking his head. He had tried hard to stay calm, but his anger overwhelmed his good intensions. He hoped he hadn't made things worse.

Chapter 18

Peter was ready to defend his confrontation with Josh, but Caroline never showed any awareness of it. Instead, she and everyone else were almost giddy with excitement over the upcoming photoshoot with Hilary Hoffman. Especially Lacie.

"I'm going to wear the new sweater Grandma bought me," she declared, as confident of her choice as a full-grown woman. "She said it is the perfect color for me."

"I do like that cinnamon color on you," Caroline agreed. She turned to Peter. "Hillary wants you to decide whether we wear scrubs or street clothes."

Peter couldn't keep the irritation out of his voice. What difference did it make? "You wear scrubs in the office. Do that."

"But it wouldn't hurt for people to see that we are real people with lives outside of the clinic," she countered.

"Then wear street clothes," Peter said brusquely.

Logan walked in to find everyone standing around the reception desk.

Lacie pirouetted like a ballerina. "We're having our pictures made!"

"Why do *we* have to do it?" Logan complained. "I don't want to be in pictures for the clinic."

Seconds before, Peter didn't care, but he was tired

Beth Warstadt

of Logan's grumbling and determined to stop him from becoming as rude as Dalton or as surly as Audra. "The photographer was a friend of Mom's, and she is doing us a favor."

"Fine," Logan conceded. "But I'm not dressing up."

"Nobody is dressing up," Peter said, less forcefully. "What you wear to school will do, as long as you don't get your lunch all over the front of it."

"I'll do it because Mom wanted it," he replied. "What's to eat?"

****

Thursday morning, Hillary called and asked them to meet her at Five Forks Park after work.

"That takes care of the scrubs or not dilemma," Caroline commented.

"How's that?" Peter asked.

"These are not typical office pictures," she replied. "I should have realized. Hillary Hoffman is an artist."

"She's good, huh?" Peter had never heard of her before Maisie's letter.

"Yes, she's good. I went to one of her exhibits at the High Museum." She sighed like a teenager with a celebrity crush. "She is amazing. And she's taking pictures of *us*."

"I guess so." He still felt like Hillary had rushed him into the project without giving him a chance to prepare himself for family portraits without Maisie. Sure, she was cushioning those pictures within the framework of office shots, but when the time came, they would still be a family with a missing mom.

Most of the leaves had fallen, but the park in November was still beautiful. Hillary had chosen a spot

226

under a solid, old oak tree with low-hanging limbs that begged to be climbed. There was a bench nestled between two of its exposed, gnarled roots, and Hillary directed Dr. Park and Caroline to sit, with Greg and Lynn leaning against the tree branch behind them. Peter kneeled next to Caroline on the right, and Savannah propped on the bench arm next to Dr. Park on the left. Hillary snapped away, mimicking a high fashion photographer to make them laugh and put them at ease. She reorganized them multiple times to get a variety of shots from which they could choose. She made the whole process so much fun that Peter forgot to be stressed.

"Okay, now," she said casually, "Let's get a picture or two of Dr. Hunter and the children before we lose the light."

Peter tucked the giggling Lacie into his customary football hold and grabbed Logan playfully around the neck.

"Kids, climb the tree," Hillary instructed. "Logan, you'll have to help Lacie."

Peter almost laughed out loud. Climb? Tree? "Lacie won't need help. The princess persona is just an act." Proving his point Lacie was sitting on the limb with her legs dangling before Logan could crawl into place next to her.

Hilary tilted her head, considering their placement. "Now, Peter, crook your arm up on the branch next to the kids and lean back." Her camera fired a barrage of clicks.

"Next, sit on the bench with Lacie standing between your legs. Logan, you squat down in front. "

They complied as instructed.

"Excellent. Now," she paused for effect, "tickle Lacie, just a little bit."

Peter grinned and poked Lacie until she squirmed and giggled, which made Logan laugh, too.

"Look at me," Hillary said from behind the camera.

They did, and she snapped away.

With the light almost gone, Hillary stood up and put her camera in the bag. "Outstanding, everybody. I'll bring them in for you to see on Monday."

"Hey, Doc," Greg spoke up, "don't you want to take us all to dinner?"

Peter made a face. "To dinner where?"

"*Shelley's.*" He poked his thumb over his shoulder. "It's right here."

Morris Shelstein ran a diner next to the park entrance that was always packed with families after games and practices. Peter reflected that Thursday nights in November the only sporting events were rec league and junior varsity high school football games, and the fans wouldn't descend on the restaurant until much later. Buoyed by the good spirits of the photo session, he smiled and nodded. "Okay, I'm game."

"Yay, yay, yay!" Lacie grabbed Peter's hand and pulled him toward the parking lot.

"Hillary, this includes you, too, if you're free," Peter offered.

She looked up from her camera bag. "I'd love to."

As their jovial group walked out to the cars, Peter noticed Caroline trailing behind. Her shoulders were hunched and her head hung like a beaten dog. His stomach clinched. Had his encounter with Josh caused problems after all? "What's wrong?" he asked, falling into step with her.

"I can't go." She didn't look up.

"Why not?" he asked, pretty sure he knew the answer.

"Josh has the night off, and he wants me to hang with him and watch television."

"You still have to eat." He wanted her with him. Since Maisie died, he always felt most at ease with Caroline by his side, the same way he wanted to be with the children. Even if his talk with Josh hadn't done any harm, it hadn't done any good, either.

"So does he. Do you want me to call and invite him?" she asked, looking at him sideways.

"No," Peter admitted. "That wouldn't be my first choice. In fact, it wouldn't be any of my choices."

"Exactly," she said sadly. "You know, you haven't seen him at his best."

"I guess not, but I'm not optimistic." He couldn't tell her about his secret visit to the restaurant. He had seen a pleasant side to Josh that night, but when Peter confronted him, it fell away like he had taken off a mask.

She didn't respond or try to defend him. She knew Peter had good reason to be unhappy about Josh's behavior, and she couldn't offer him any proof to expect better.

As they reached her car, Peter tried one last time. "You are the glue that holds the whole office together. It's not the same without you."

"Thanks for saying so, Doc. I'll take you up on it another time." She got in, waved at him with a weak smile, and pulled away.

He walked slowly to the SUV, where Logan and Lacie had their noses pressed against the windows, mouthing to him to hurry up. He picked up his pace. He knew there was nothing he could do, but he could not undo the knot of uneasiness that was pulled tight in his middle.

The rest of the staff made a merry group sitting at four tables they had pushed together.

"Where's Caroline?" Lynn asked, looking over Peter's shoulder at the door.

Peter glanced out the window at an empty place where her car should have been parked. "She went home. Says Josh is waiting for her."

Greg frowned and shook his head. "That Josh is a piece of work. She needs to dump him."

"He sucks," Logan added.

"That's not our call," Peter replied, though he couldn't agree more. He took the remaining open chair, which happened to be next to Hillary.

She put her hand over his as he sat down. "Josh is her husband?"

"Boyfriend," Peter said. "He's not a very nice person when he drinks, and he tends to drink a lot."

"You're worried for her."

"Yes." He cleared his throat and glanced at his children to be sure they had not overheard. This was supposed to be fun, and Caroline's decision was hers to make. "I think some of Shelley's meatloaf and mashed potatoes will cure what ails me." He raised his voice so the whole table would hear. "I may not be able to pay for anyone else when Logan gets done. Has anyone added up the cost of the entire left side of the menu?"

Logan grinned. "You got that right, but I'm getting everything on both sides."

Greg slapped him on the back, and the party

atmosphere was restored.

Once their orders were placed, Peter turned his full attention on Hillary. "I hear you are a world-famous photographer."

She chuckled. "I manage to make a living."

"And you travel a lot?"

"I do." She swept her hand around to indicate the whole world. "I've been lucky to see lots of amazing things, and I try to share them with people who may never get there."

"That's very altruistic of you," Peter teased.

"I do get a fair bit of enjoyment from it for myself. And I am well-paid."

"Any surprises?" he asked.

"People surprise me, always," she answered. "The news would have you believe the world is filled with tension and animosity, but the truth is you would find you have a lot in common with fathers in Vietnam, China, Greenland, or Peru. If it weren't for the language barrier, you could easily compare notes with veterinarians in Paraguay or Morocco, or the Philippines. We are all far more alike than we are different."

"That's kind of comforting. Based on the television and the internet, I've been nervous about what kind of world I am sending my children into."

"It's not nearly as bad as everyone thinks it is."

Peter took a drink out of the water glass that had miraculously appeared in front of him. "I did a semester abroad in college, but I was too young and unaware for that kind of deep reflection. The beautiful rivers and forests in Germany have stayed with me, but I bet you've seen a lot more."

Hillary put her hand over her heart. "Oh my God!" she exclaimed. "I wish everyone could see what I have seen. That's why I take pictures."

"Like what?" Before he was just making conversation, but now he was intrigued.

"Sunrise from the porch of a Japanese temple. The excavated ruins of a forgotten village in Africa. A wolf mother nursing her cubs in a Canadian forest. Even things I see that other people walk by every day without noticing. Street musicians as good as those in Carnegie Hall. Artists who draw museum-quality portraits of tourists for twenty-five dollars. Service animals calmly keeping their people safe while humanity churns all around them. The world is a remarkable place, and it is my job to see it all. How lucky am I?"

"I'd like to see the world through your eyes," Peter said, swept up in her passion.

"I'd love to show you my pictures," she replied, "but there is something beautiful right here and right now that you shouldn't miss."

"What's that?" he asked.

She nodded at the children and whispered, "Those two, right there."

Peter looked where Logan and Lacie sat leaning their heads together. They were engrossed on a napkin drawing Logan was making with the restaurant-provided crayons. He felt a swell of love and happiness that was always accompanied by an ache for their mother to share it with him. *Can you see this from Heaven, Maisie?* "Yes," he said, "I'm a lucky man."

"You certainly are." She discreetly aimed her cell phone and captured the moment.

Peter took another drink to clear the emotion out of

his throat. "Where were you last? And where are you going next?"

Hillary smiled. "Last month, I photographed Diwali celebrations in India. I have a little break now, but in December I'm travelling around the country to cover Ugly Sweater Runs."

"What?"

"It's the latest rage. Wear an ugly Christmas sweater and run for charity. Funny *and* heartwarming."

"Seems a little mundane compared with Japanese temples and African ruins."

She grinned. "Not at all. People having fun when we are inundated with bad news on every front is definitely worth some serious attention. There's one in Decatur. You can bring the kids to watch." She paused and looked him up and down. "Even better, you look like a runner, why don't you give it a try?"

Peter smirked. "I don't do races. Too much pressure. And I don't do ugly sweaters. I'm afraid I'll see someone in a sweater I wear all the time."

Hillary laughed out loud. "The doctor has a sense of humor."

Greg overheard her comment and joined in. "Yeah, how about that? Although we don't see it much, right guys?"

Dr. Park, sitting on Peter's other side, leaned forward so she could see Hillary. "Sometimes, when he says funny things, he keeps such a straight face that I'm not sure whether to laugh or not."

"Dad makes people laugh?" Logan asked, shaking his head. "No way."

"That's because you don't give me any reason," Peter replied, the corners of his mouth threatening to turn up. "When you're not around, I'm hilarious."

Logan looked doubtful. "I don't think so. Say something funny."

All eyes turned on Peter. He was under the gun. He was only funny by accident, and he had no idea what to say on demand. "You need to ask the animals. I say funny things to them all the time."

"Speaking of the animals," Dr. Park drew his attention, "I need to ask you about the Hollands' collie."

"Sure," Peter replied, glad to be back in familiar territory.

After a brief conversation about behavioral training alternatives, Peter turned his attention back to Hillary. "I would like to see your pictures. Can we get together sometime?" Maisie had wanted him to do this. He had tried with Suzanne and Donna and come out unscathed, so there was no reason to put off the inevitable. He enjoyed listening to Hillary talk about her adventures, and he genuinely wanted to see the world through her lens.

Hillary was as enthusiastic about his suggestion as she was about everything else. "Sure. Do you have plans for tomorrow after work?"

Tomorrow? That was soon. Her 'seize the day' attitude was appealing, but unsettling. "Uh, yeah," he stammered. "Tomorrow works. As long as I can find someone to stay with my kids."

"You should probably come to my place. That will be easier than trying to bring the pictures to you."

"Can I take you to dinner after?" he proposed, trying to regain control of the situation.

"Are you asking me out on a date?"

"Maybe I am," Peter admitted, lowering his voice to be sure he wasn't overheard. "Do you mind?"

"No, I don't." She matched his secretive tone. "You don't think Maisie would mind?"

Could she see through him? Could she tell this was Maisie's idea? "I don't," he replied. "After all, she wanted us to meet."

"Okay then. Six o'clock?"

"Sure." He had backed himself into a corner again. Where would he find a babysitter on such short notice? He didn't feel like he should ask Caroline, not given what was going on with Josh. He could call the teenagers he knew, but he wasn't optimistic about finding one who wasn't already committed for a Friday night.

Driving home, the most undesirable solution came to him. He shuddered.

He'd have to call his mother.

****

As he expected, there were no teenagers to be found on short notice, so he had no choice but to implement plan B. Peter dialed the phone and braced himself for the necessary groveling.

"Hello?"

Her voice was pitiful because she knew it was him, and he silently cursed the inventor of caller ID. "Hello, Mother." Peter forced enthusiasm. "How are you?" A big mistake, but it was out of his mouth before he could stop it.

"So, you care about how I am? Since when do you care how I am?"

He had expected this. They'd had this conversation dozens of times. "I always care about you, Mom. You know I do. I've told you how overwhelmed I am since Maisie died." Here came the brilliant *coup de grace.* "I'm just not as good at taking care of a family as you were."

"Of course, a mother really holds the family together. Fathers are too preoccupied with work. They can't help it. It's just the way they are. I was practically a single mother even when we were still married because your father worked all the time."

Groveling was working. "Now that I am in the middle of it, I can see you are right."

"Speaking of which, did you call the nurse?"

He felt her thumb in his back. "Not yet. I'm sorry. Nobody knows me better than you do, Mom, so I'm sure she is perfect. I've just been too busy to follow through."

"What a surprise," she snipped. "I'm sure you've found time to see others." She paused to let the guilt sink in. "You never call unless you want something," she continued in her accusatory tone. "What is it?"

Peter took a breath. And she wondered why he didn't call. "How would you feel about entertaining your grandchildren tomorrow?"

"I assume so you can go out with someone other than the person I recommended." A statement, not a question.

"She was a friend of Maisie's, Mom," he offered. "It's no big deal."

"I suppose I shouldn't pass up an opportunity to see my grandchildren, since you so seldom bring them around. I am happy to have them, whatever it takes to get them here. Bring them early enough that I can take them out to dinner. You know I don't like to drive after dark."

"Will do. And thanks, truly."

"You're welcome."

Click.

Peter didn't drink much, but he needed a beer. He took one out of the refrigerator and strolled into the TV room. Lacie had fallen asleep with her head in Logan's lap. He was oblivious to her as he ran through channels looking for something interesting. Peter sat to nurse his beer before carrying her up to bed.

"Been talking to Grandma?" Logan asked without looking away from the TV.

"How'd you know?"

"The beer."

"Humph." Logan was very predictable, until he wasn't. There was a lot more going on in his head than he showed. "You and Lacie are spending the night with her tomorrow."

"Why?"

"Because I'm going to get together with Hillary Hoffman."

"Why?"

"Because I asked to see some of the pictures she's taken."

"Why?"

"Because she is a famous photographer who has been all over the world, but I never heard of her before this week."

"Why did you hear of her this week?" Logan had asked all the other questions while still focused on the television, but now he turned his full attention on Peter.

Peter paused. He hadn't been ready for that one. Truth was always best, at least as much as he could.

"She was a friend of Mom's, and Mom wanted me to meet her, so I did."

"Would Mom want you to have a date with her?"

"I'm not sure you can call it a date," he responded, picking his words carefully. "But, yes, I think Mom would be okay with it."

"Okay," Logan said, and settled into the sofa to watch *Field of Dreams*.

By the time Kevin Costner had kidnapped James Earl Jones, Peter was too tired to finish the movie. He carried Lacie up the stairs, laid her gently in bed with her bear, turned on the nightlight, and headed down the hall to his room.

He assumed his customary position on the bed, beagle by his side, and began his conversation with Maisie.

Why did you pick Hillary Hoffman?

Why not Hillary Hoffman?

For one thing, we have absolutely nothing in common.

You found nothing to talk about?

Actually, we did.

So, what's the problem?

She doesn't have children. She doesn't have a business. She doesn't have a mortgage. Why would she be interested in me?

You are anything but boring, sweetheart. Maybe she needs someone to share things with, just like you do. Maybe the old things don't matter as much as discovering new things together.

New things? Without you? We were supposed to do all new things together.

I know, but that point is moot now, isn't it?

Everything I do in this world, our world, you are there. Patients knew you, parents knew you, and kids knew you. How can I step into a world that has never known you?

Most of the world has never known me, and I certainly don't expect you to confine yourself to the little corner that has. Try it.

Because you wanted me to.

Because I wanted you to.

I miss you.

I miss you, too.

I love you.

I loved you in that life and beyond. Kiss our babies for me.

Chapter 19

Peter and his sister had worked together for over a year to find the perfect place for their mother when she gave up the large suburban home where they grew up. The generously-sized apartment was one side of a duplex in a well-maintained retirement community, and all the living space was on a single-level to accommodate the ever-increasing pain in her knees. It was large enough to fit all of her important possessions, but small enough that they had been able to downsize from the overwhelming accumulation of thirty years in the same house.

He should have felt satisfaction at the happy resolution to their efforts, and his mother should have been pleased. That was not the case. She complained constantly about the location or the neighbors or the maintenance, any problem that resulted in his coming over to see about things. She was not the kind of mother who met him at the door with freshly baked cookies or iced tea, but she received him most often with a tapping foot and puckered mouth. Seeing his mother was usually not a pleasant experience.

But now, as he arrived with Lacie and Logan, she welcomed them with arms thrown open for loving hugs and showers of kisses on cheeks and heads. It reminded him of the mother she had been, teaching him and Ginny to play Monopoly and making forts with blankets on the living room furniture. Looking past her, he could see blankets piled on the sofa with flashlights on top, ready for the evening's construction. She didn't cook anymore, but tonight she would take Logan and Lacie to her favorite Italian restaurant where Mr. Nicoletti let them make their own pizza. There were always boxes of pastries for dessert and for breakfast. They actually liked visiting Grandma, although Logan was beginning to catch on as she nagged him about his too-long hair and his messy clothes. Logan had also realized she was Dr. Jekyll when she talked to them and Mr. Hyde when she spoke to Peter.

With a quick kiss from Lacie and a very manly handshake from Logan, the children left him standing in the foyer with her. As soon as they were out of sight, Ruth's demeanor went through a radical change.

Arms crossed and chin set, she asked, "So who is this woman you are going out with?"

Powerless to resist, Peter answered meekly like he was an acne-stricken high-schooler. "Her name is Hillary Hoffman."

Ruth's eyes opened wide. "Hillary Hoffman, the photographer?"

"Yes?" he responded, uncertain about the meaning of her sudden change in mood.

"She is wonderful. How in the world do you know her?"

"She was a friend of Maisie's." Was this a trick?

"Really?" She tucked her hand in the crook of his arm and steered him toward the door. "I would love to meet her. Her photographs are beyond artistry, and she has been so many interesting places. She must be fascinating to talk to."

"I don't know her well yet, but so far she's good," he stammered.

"Have a wonderful time." She patted him on the back as she ushered him out the door.

As he drove to the address Hillary had texted him, he thought about her as contestant number three. She was a very different animal from the other two. First of all, she was evidently famous to everybody but him. Second, while Suzanne Martin was obviously good at what she did, it appeared Hillary Hoffman had a talent that exceeded anyone he had ever known. Third, Donna had the same responsibilities he did now, but she also shared similar, more liberating, experiences in her pre-parenting days. Hillary Hoffman lived in a world he had never inhabited, a place with few responsibilities and fewer boundaries. How could he possibly have anything to say that she would find interesting? He imagined sitting in uncomfortable silence at dinner, with her pushing her food around on her plate, bored out of her mind and counting the seconds until she could go home.

He reached the address on the GPS, and checked to make sure he had the right place. This was no pricy loft with an expensive city view or bohemian flat in the artsy part of town. It was a small, ranch-style house straight out of the 1960s with big maple trees in the front yard and ribbons of ivy trailing up the red brick. Her copper SUV was parked in an old-fashioned carport. The fallen leaves in the front had been raked into piles but not yet bagged for disposal.

He stepped onto the concrete stoop, and the door opened before he rang the bell.

"Welcome, welcome!" Hillary ushered him in with a grand sweep of her arm.

She was wearing comfortable-looking jeans and a white sweater with the sleeves pushed up to her elbows. Her casual ponytail and the minimal makeup on her cheery face stirred a sense of familiarity. This woman could definitely be one of Maisie's friends, and in fact, was probably more like her than either Suzanne or Donna. There was no pretense, no posturing, no sign that she was a world-famous anything.

"You can hang your jacket on the coatrack," she said, pointing to the hooks on the wall by the door. "How about some wine? Or maybe a beer?"

"A beer would be great," he replied, glancing around as he followed her into the kitchen. The upholstered, sectional sofa and beach-pink walls reminded him of his house growing up, but his mother had updated that 80s style long ago. He wondered what Suzanne might say about it.

The small kitchen appeared minimally used. When she opened the refrigerator, Peter saw just wine, beer, and an assortment of take-out containers from a variety of restaurants. She handed him a bottle of Becker Lite. He examined the label to make sure he was seeing it right. How was it possible that someone with such an exotic life drank the most common beer in America? He popped the top off with the opener mounted on the cabinet.

Peter followed her back into the living room, but instead of joining her on the sofa, he slowly perused the eclectic collection of souvenirs scattered across glass and brass side tables and bookshelves. He recognized dancing figurines from southeast Asia and pottery from South America, but he couldn't identify the source of the heavy brass bells. He was surprised how much of the collection was also from places not so far away.

"Most of those are not mine," she commented with a smile. "This was my parents' house, and most of those souvenirs are theirs. A few belong to my brother, too."

Peter sat down at the opposite end of the sofa. "Does your brother live close by?" It was interesting that she had a brother. He had assumed she lived in a bubble untouched by relationships and responsibilities. Did they have other things in common after all?

"My brother lives here, too."

"You both live in this house?" Peter looked around for places another person could be hiding. Was someone about to materialize from the shadow of the hallway? "Is he here?"

"Nope." She shook her head. "He also travels for work, so we aren't usually here at the same time."

Relieved that he was not about to be jolted by someone jumping out from behind a door, he relaxed into the sofa cushions. "What does he do? Is he a photographer also?"

She reached below the side table closest to her and pulled up a photo album of 8x10 color photos. "He does a different kind of art. He is an architect. But he doesn't design buildings you have heard of. He designs low-income housing in different parts of the world and works with government agencies and global charities to secure funding. He's a busy guy." She scooted close to him and held the album between them.

Sitting up put him right next to her, and he got a whiff of her perfume. It was different from the floral fragrances he was used to. It was spicy, like cinnamon and ginger, and it conjured up visions of exotic

Moroccan markets and Indian bazaars.

He shifted his focus to the album. Most of the pictures were of the same man, sometimes standing in front of clusters of buildings scarcely bigger than sheds, sometimes surrounded by groups of native peoples. He scrutinized the man's image for a resemblance between brother and sister. They shared the tanned skin of people who work outside for a living, but his hair was lighter and his build bulkier. The eyes looking out of the photos, however, were the same eyes looking at him from Hillary's face. "Both of you are too busy for a family?"

"Yep, our branch of the family line stops with us. Our legacy is our work." She scanned the contents of the room. "Our parents loved to travel and took us all over the world. We saw amazing things, some good and some bad, that gave us a different perspective on the world than other kids. It made it a little hard to fit in." She sighed deeply.

Peter had never worried about fitting in until he became the lone father in a group of mothers. Before Maisie died, he would have given little thought to Hillary's confession. Now, he had a different frame of reference. "So, you were closer to your family than the average kid."

"I suppose that's true." She snapped the album shut. "It's all history now, and you know what, if I hadn't been free from all the fetters of friendship and teenage angst, I probably wouldn't have been so eager to leave and pursue this career. I do love my job." She got up and walked around the room, running her fingers lightly over books and boxes and figurines. She turned to face him and opened her arms wide. "No matter where we go, this has always been our home base. It doesn't make sense to pay rent on two apartments when neither of us is home more than half the year."

Hillary was very matter-of-fact in the statement, but Peter suspected there was deeper emotion behind it. "Do you ever get to see him?"

"Not here. At home, we're ships that pass in the night, but I am lucky to have enough flexibility with my travel that I can visit him wherever he is once or twice a year. Every now and then, he catches up with me, as well." She picked up a snow globe with a beach scene and shook it. She held it up to the light and watched the sand fall. "Sometimes, we catch a perfect beach day in Spain or Greece, or Thailand." She chuckled. "Or Florida. I love Florida. All the shells you see in here are from Sanibel. Amazing things are not always far from home." She returned to her place on the sofa. "So, Peter, how are you finding being a single dad?"

Peter was taken off-guard by the conversation's sudden change in direction. She did that a lot. "Lots of men do it for lots of different reasons," he stammered.

"Yes, but I am not talking to *lots* of men. I am talking to you." She sat back, waiting for him to answer.

He paused to gather his thoughts. How *was* it being a single dad? "Surprising." He smiled, repeating her answer to him at the diner after the photo session in the park.

Hillary tucked her legs under her. "Surprising how?"

"It's a lot more work than I expected, harder to coordinate schedules and remember to feed, clothe, and bathe them. Non-human animals are much easier. Put food in a dish, bathe them once a month or so, either take them out or clean the litter box. No worries about the variety of foods or clothes. Of course, the cleaning out the litter box part is better with humans," he said with a straight face.

She laughed. "I suppose that is true. I haven't spent much time with children since I was one."

"I am surprised at what good company they can be, depending on their attitude. Sometimes, the things they say stop me cold in my tracks. They can be very insightful."

Her expression softened, and her eyes were misty. "When they remind you of Maisie, does it make you sad or glad?"

That was a question, wasn't it? For a long time, when he noticed her in them, he pushed the thought away immediately. Somehow, it seemed appropriate for Hillary to ask, and somehow, he didn't mind giving her the answer. He smiled. "I've been fighting it since she died, but now I am starting to look for it. They are polite because of her. They hold pencils and forks properly because of her. They are honest because of her. Because of her, they don't say "like" after every other word, or a dumbfounded "uh" when they respond to a question." He paused and looked away. "The way Lacie cocks her head to the side when she's thinking. The way Logan hugs a pillow when he's watching TV. Those were her mannerisms." He sighed. "They take my breath away."

"That's wonderful. This is the perfect time to look at the pictures I took on Thursday." Hillary pushed herself up. "Then we can go to dinner. I have the perfect place in mind. *Nicoletti's* Italian restaurant.

Their pasta is some of the best on the planet, and that includes Italy."

He chuckled and shook his head. "My mother is taking my kids there."

"Maybe we'll see them." She held out her hand to pull him off the sofa. "I'd love that."

He took her hand and stood up. "Maybe. My mom is a fan of yours, and she can be pretty annoying when she gets fixated on something." He wasn't sure he was ready to handle his date, his children, and his mother all in the same place.

"It'll be fun." She led him through a short hall with doors open into each of the three bedrooms. At the end was a door onto a porch with waist-to-ceiling windows on three sides. Several of the crank-style windows had been rolled open to fill the room with cool, fresh air. Arrangements of pictures covered two long tables. A tilt-top drafting table looked out on the shaded backyard surrounded by a privacy fence. Bird feeders were scattered throughout the yard.

"This is nice," he observed, "but I'm surprised to see so many actual photographs. Isn't everything digital these days?"

She nodded. "For submissions, yes. But I am a very tactile person. I like to hold the actual image in my hand, and remember what it felt like in the moment."

He picked up a picture of children playing soccer in front of an army base. "That intensity of feeling is why you are so good." He pointed toward the windows. "I would think all this light would be bad for photographs. "

She shook her head. "It's pretty well filtered by the trees." She stood back and let him peruse the collection at his leisure, waiting to see what caught his eye.

His mouth fell open at the sight before him. He could feel the spray from the waves crashing against the boulders on a pristine, uninhabited beach. He could hear the joyous laughter of the children dancing in the gushing water of an open fire hydrant. He could sense the eyes of the snow leopard looking through him as though they were standing inches from each other. He felt small and humbled by the green and blue folds of light against a midnight sky. "Is that the aurora borealis?"

"Yes." She leaned against the wall with her arms folded, watching him with eyes like the snow leopard. "It is one of the most stunning sights in the world."

"It's on my bucket list. Someday." Hillary's pictures reminded him there was more of the world to see than the confines of his house, clinic, and park. Everyone was right. Her view of life was a symphony, and she was a virtuoso.

He continued his slow progression around the room until he got to the drafting table. There, in the center, was the picture of Logan and Lacie at the diner looking at Logan's napkin artwork. He ran his fingertips lightly over their bowed heads before looking up. "This is beautiful," he whispered. "May I have it?"

"It's yours," she said. "I told you, sometimes the most magnificent shots pop up close to home." She didn't say anything else or move from her post, allowing him the space and time to continue his review without interruption.

He appreciated her respectful silence. Peter had never been much of a talker himself, and he found it was a rare person who could refrain from a constant, running commentary on the subject of their attention. It was an understanding Maisie had acquired as their relationship matured, and it was one of the things he missed most about her.

On a side table next to a chaise were the pictures of his staff. They were excellent, of course, and he knew everyone would love them. His gaze lighted on a picture of Caroline. She was looking with great intensity at a fallen leaf, tracing the patterns with her fingertips. He didn't want to discuss their ever-more complicated relationship, so he didn't comment or touch it. From the corner of his eye he could see Hillary watching him, and he wondered if she knew.

He did pick up the picture of him and the children in the tree. "No Maisie," he said sadly.

"All Maisie," she contradicted, moving to his side. "Look at her smiling through Logan's blue eyes. Look at the bow she loved putting in Lacie's hair. She is not in the picture. She *is* the picture. You and the kids are what filled her up and made her alive. In some ways, you will never take a picture without her."

Peter held it as though it would disappear if he put it down. Looking past it, he saw an image he wasn't expecting. It was a close up of his face. He picked it up to look at it more closely. "When did you take that?"

"When you weren't watching," she replied, smiling. "You are a great subject."

"I don't think that's true." He made a face.

Her cheek brushed his arm as she stepped closer. "That's because you're not the photographer. You are a very attractive man. You have a very handsome face."

Peter's body tensed at her nearness. He didn't know what to say.

Hillary cleared her throat. "C'mon. Let's go see if we can catch your offspring eating pizza."

He relaxed. "With Logan's appetite, that shouldn't be too hard."

****

Ruth, Logan, and Lacie were already waiting for their food when Peter and Hillary arrived, and Ruth nearly tripped over her own feet moving them to a table big enough for five. So much for a date.

Ruth orchestrated their seating so Peter was on Hillary's left and she was on her right. "I'm so pleased to meet you," she gushed. "I'm a huge fan."

Hillary pulled a pad and pencil out of her bag and handed it to Logan and Lacie for drawing. "Thank you, Ruth. It's very satisfying to have someone appreciate your work."

Ruth puffed up. "I love fine art. I'm trying to educate my grandchildren about art and music. If I could have more time with them, I could make them great connoisseurs."

Peter caught the implication that she was filling in a deficit in his parenting, and the little dig that he neglected bringing his children to visit. He rubbed the back of his neck hard to hold back his sharp retort.

Under the table, Hillary squeezed his hand. "Logan and Lacie are at an age where they don't have a lot of extra time for such things. With your appreciation for great art and music, I'm sure they will pick it up along the way."

"I hoped that would work with Peter and his sister, and Ginny did pick it up, to some degree. From Peter I got nothing."

"I wouldn't say that," Hillary replied. "Before we

came to dinner, Peter was at my house looking at some of my work. He has a very good eye."

"It's good to know I wore off on him at least a little bit." She leaned in so she could look across Hillary at Peter. "Perhaps we can go to the High Museum sometime so you can share your fine appreciation with me."

"Sure." Time to change the subject before she pinned him down on a date. "What do you have planned for Logan and Lacie tonight after dinner?"

At the mention of their names, Logan and Lacie looked up. "What are we going to do, Grandma?" Lacie asked. "Can we build a fort in the living room?"

The lines around Ruth's pursed lips softened. "Of course, sweetheart. I already have the blankets ready on the sofa." She turned her attention back to Hillary. "Did you make blanket forts when you were a child, Hillary?"

"I never did. It sounds like a lot of fun." Hillary did a good job of making her voice sound jealous.

"It is," Lacie enthused. "Daddy did it, too, with Aunt Ginny, didn't you, Daddy?"

Peter relaxed and nodded, catching his mother's eye. "We did. We loved sitting inside and playing games with our flashlights."

The change in Ruth's attitude was astonishing. The mother he had known and loved growing up was still in there. "Afterward, we'll turn out all the lights and watch *Pride of the Yankees*. Since Logan loves sports so much, it's a movie he must see. Lacie will probably fall asleep, so she and I can watch the old Rogers and Hammerstein *Cinderella* in the morning, when Logan is sleeping in."

Hillary sighed. "It sounds wonderful, Ruth. I never knew my grandparents. Logan and Lacie are very lucky."

Mr. Nicoletti himself brought their pizzas to the table and sat down to chat with them. "Mrs. Hunter is one of our best customers," he explained in a thick Italian accent. "I am so happy to see her here with her family."

Peter shook his head and smiled at the surprising turn the evening had taken. The stress was gone. Ruth introduced their new friend, and Mr. Nicoletti was thrilled to discover that Hillary had visited his small town outside of Genoa. She promised to bring her pictures the next time they came to his restaurant.

Peter had just taken the last bite of his third slice when Lacie's patience expired. She pushed her plate away. "Grandma, if we don't go soon it will be too late to do anything fun."

Ruth stood and picked up both checks, waving away Peter's protests. "It has been a wonderful evening. It is so nice to get to know you, Hillary."

Hillary hugged her. "Thank you, Ruth. I can't wait to do it again."

Ruth went to the counter to pay.

Peter picked up Lacie to hug and kiss goodnight. He gave Logan a much more manly squeeze around his shoulders. "See you guys in the morning."

"Not too early, Daddy," Lacie said, taking Ruth's hand. "Grandma and I are watching *Cinderella*."

"I'll call before I come to make sure you're done." Peter winked at his mother and followed Hillary out to the car. The evening had gone much better than he expected.

On their way back to her house, Hillary looked at the pictures the children had drawn. "Logan is really very good. Are there other artists in your family?"

"My mom is pretty talented," he commented, accessing an old memory of his mother occupying him and Ginny with doodles on demand.

"Did she do anything with it?"

He shook his head. "Just entertained us kids."

She held up the notepad so he could glance at it. "I can't tell you how to parent, but if I were you, I would encourage Logan to develop this talent as well as his athletics. After all, he is more likely to be a graphic designer than a professional athlete."

"True, but maybe he'll be a veterinarian."

"Either way, a little art wouldn't hurt." She put away the tablet. "Hey," she said suddenly, "I have a show in the Roderick Gallery on Thursday night. There'll be beverages and some kind of *hors d'oeuvres*. Why don't you bring the kids?"

He tried to imagine Logan and Lacie in an art gallery. "Sounds pretty adult to me. And it's a school night."

"I think you're selling your children short. They are much more perceptive than you give them credit for." She paused. "I'll make you a deal. You come to my show, and I'll go to Logan's game on Saturday." She added, "Ruth said she was going to the game, and I can run interference for you."

Peter laughed. "An offer I can't refuse."

"Excellent."

They pulled into her driveway, and she allowed Peter to play the gentleman by opening her car door. She led him to the carport, which was dark and secluded from the street. She put her arms around his neck and pulled him down to kiss her.

He pushed in and deepened their kiss. It felt good, and he wanted to do it some more. It didn't have the fireworks he had felt with Maisie, but she had been right when she wrote it wasn't necessary to recapture the passion of their first time.

Of course, kissing Caroline after the concert had set off its own little explosions in his brain, but that had been a mistake he couldn't repeat.

"Come in?" she whispered.

A tempting offer, but intimacy with another woman still felt like a betrayal of his wife. Oddly, it felt like a betrayal of Caroline, too, but he pushed the thought away as quickly as it came. It was no more appropriate to think of betraying her than being jealous of her boyfriend. "I don't think that's a good idea," he whispered back.

"Too soon?"

He dropped his forehead to hers. "Too soon."

"I understand," she murmured as she pulled away. "Goodnight, Peter. Thank you for a great time."

"You, too," he replied, retreating slowly to his car.

No music on the way home. No music, no talk radio, and no kids. Just solitude and thoughts of the night's surprises. She was not at all what he expected. He had always thought photographers kept a lens between themselves and real life. For Hillary Hoffman, photography was a window for everyone else to experience the world as she saw it.

The emptiness of his house overwhelmed him. The ache eased somewhat when Buddy bounded out of the dark to welcome him. He squatted down to scratch the dog behind the ears, and then proceeded through the house without turning on the lights, past the eerily quiet children's rooms, to his own bedroom where the bedside light created a shield against his solitude. Was this what it would be like when Logan and Lacie were grown and out of the house?

Maisie loved him, and she knew he would be no good alone.

No one will ever make me stop missing you, he thought to her.

That doesn't mean you can't be happy again.

I am happy with Logan and Lacie.

I know, but they won't stay forever. You need someone else just for you.

Not Suzanne. Not Donna.

No, but maybe Hillary. You like her, don't you?

I do. You were right about how interesting she is.

I told you to trust me. Give her a chance.

Okay. Maybe Hillary.

Loved you in that life and beyond. Kiss our babies for me.

Chapter 20

The next morning, after he picked up the children at his mother's, he told them about Hillary's exhibition. "I wasn't sure you would like it, but she thinks you guys are great art appreciators." As he expected, Lacie was excited about going to such an adult function, but Logan's enthusiasm surprised him.

"It's not like boring old paintings and stuff," Logan explained. "Her pictures are actual photographs of cool places and real people. I looked her up online."

"Okay then," Peter responded, putting away his verbal weapons. He had been ready for a fight.

When Thursday night came, Logan not only went along without complaint, but he came downstairs in the khaki pants and button-down shirt Peter had forgotten he owned. He was even wearing a clip-on tie that Maisie must have bought, because he had never seen it before.

The Roderick Gallery was open and airy, but intimate. Peter didn't immediately see Hillary, but he knew she would be mingling around with all of the guests and didn't expect her to have much time for them. He focused instead on the collection, and his appreciation for her talent grew with every set of pictures.

Logan was uncharacteristically reflective and strolled slowly past the pictures, while Lacie raced from each one to the next that caught her eye. Peter moved quickly to keep his daughter from bothering the other adults, but she was not disruptive, and they seemed to enjoy her enthusiasm.

A detailed study of Neuschwanstein Castle stopped Lacie dead in her tracks. The sumptuous murals and tapestries, as well as the golden chandeliers and hand-crafted furniture, were her dream come true. Enthralled, she moved no further, giving Peter a chance to relax on a nearby bench.

Logan caught up and sat next to him, stretching out his long legs and crossing them at his ankles just like his dad.

"You surprise me," Peter said. "I had no idea you liked this stuff."

"Mom took us to museums a lot. We went to the zoo and the botanical gardens, too."

"I vaguely remember that."

"I think you wanted her to do it, but once it was done, you didn't think about it anymore," Logan observed.

He thought again that Logan was a more complicated creature than he acted most of the time. "You miss Mom."

"Yeah."

"You don't usually say so."

He crossed his arms across his chest. "What difference does it make? It won't bring her back."

Peter put a hand on his shoulder so Logan would look at him. "We need to share her, you and I. Lacie doesn't remember her in the same way."

"It's hard. The other guys don't understand, and they don't know what to say if I mention her. So, I don't."

Peter nodded. No one would ever share their grief. He thought of Maisie's devotion to their children and felt the lump in his throat that was never far gone. "More's the reason why it's just you and me."

"I guess."

"We remember her together, and then we go on to be happy without her, because that is what she wanted."

"Is that why you went out with Ms. Martin and Ms. Lechleiter? Because Mom wanted you to?"

"Yep."

"Don't pick Ms. Martin. Dalton is an idiot." Twelve-year old Logan was back. "Ms. Lechleiter is okay. I like hanging out with Justin."

The corner of Peter's mouth twitched. "I'll keep that in mind."

"Hillary is cool, too."

"Good to know." He'd considered Suzanne and Donna in terms of being a mother to his children, but it hadn't crossed his mind with Hillary. He had a hard time picturing her as team mom or room mom, but that wasn't all there was to being a parent.

"What's to eat?" Logan said, standing up. "I think I saw a guy walking around with little hot dogs."

Peter found a high table with barstool-type seats where Lacie could sit with Logan while he searched out appetizers and drink to satisfy her finicky tastes. Little quiches and Chinese dumplings did the trick, and she was very happy and grown up with her Shirley Temple from the open bar. As soon as he returned, Logan took off in search of his own food. They were discussing the contents of Lacie's drink and the joys of maraschino cherries when Hillary found them.

"I'm glad to see you," she said, taking the seat next to Peter. "How do you like the show?"

Logan returned with a plate remarkably piled considering everything available was light finger-food. "They're cool," said Logan, swallowing a dumpling whole. "I think I'd like to try taking pictures."

"I'd love to work with you, Logan," Hillary responded. "I already mentioned to your dad that you have an eye for art."

"I need a camera." Logan turned his gaze pointedly at Peter.

Peter nodded. "Sure. Christmas is coming. Why don't you ask Santa for a camera?"

Logan made a face at the mention of Santa, then glanced at Lacie and changed his attitude. "Sure. I bet Santa will do it."

"I love the pictures of the castles," Lacie said. "I wish I could have a castle for Christmas."

"Wouldn't fit under the tree." Logan dismissed her, sliding uneaten food off her plate.

"I know that," Lacie replied, kicking him under the table for emphasis. "I just said I wish."

"Maybe you can visit a castle, instead." Hillary turned to Peter. "You know, I can get us decent seats on a flight to Germany."

"Germany?" Peter asked as if he had never heard of it. In fact, he had done a semester abroad in Germany and still understood a little German, but that was a lifetime ago.

Hillary laughed. "Yes, Germany. You know, Germany? Mountains, forests, Heidi, Wienerschnitzel?"

Peter looked at her face for a sign that she was joking. There was none. She meant what she said. He was struck by how truly different their lives were. "We can't go to Germany. My kids don't have passports."

She folded her arms and leaned them on the table. "Why not? Isn't getting a passport something you do for your kids, like getting a social security number?"

Peter was flabbergasted. "Uh, no," he stammered. "I think most of the children around here do not have passports. That's a get-it-when-you-need-it thing."

"So, now you need it." She said it as though passports would magically appear.

Peter's commonsense regained control and cleared his mind. "That's not happening," he said firmly.

"Okay then," she said cheerily, ignoring his mood change. "How about just you and I go?"

Peter looked at his children, who were watching him intently. His days of impulsive decisions had ended when Logan was born. "My passport expired ten years ago. I haven't used it since I went to Germany for a semester abroad in college."

"If I'm going to show you the world, you're going to need one, wouldn't you say?"

He couldn't deny that part of him would love to jump a plane and head off on a whim. But that was not his reality. "I appreciate the offer, Hillary, but I can't take a trip to Europe without more planning. The kids have school, and I already have a full schedule of patients."

Hillary was unfazed. "How about a German restaurant then? Have you ever been to Heidelberg Haus?"

It was better than a trip across the ocean, but still hard for a father of two on short notice. "Tonight? It's getting late, and the kids have school tomorrow."

"But I want to go," Lacie stated firmly, swinging her legs.

Logan stopped mid-chew. "What is German food like?"

Peter narrowed the entirety of German cuisine down to what he knew his son would find enticing. "Sausage and potatoes."

Logan swallowed. "Count me in."

Hillary shook her head. "It'll just be adults, okay, guys? I don't think you'll like German food, anyway. Lots of stinky cabbage and beer." Hillary glanced sideways at Peter with a smile. "Besides that, we're going to talk about things that are boring to children. How about we plan a trip to an American castle for everybody another time? The Biltmore House is beautiful at Christmastime, and I think they put up their decorations around the first of November. That was two weeks ago."

Lacie's legs stilled, and her eyes lit up like they were reflecting the Christmas tree lights. "Is it really a castle?" She turned her attention fully on Peter. "Can we go, Daddy? Please? Please?" She used her best I'm-so-cute-you'll-do-anything-I-want voice.

Peter opened his mouth to say his standard, "We'll see."

"Absolutely," Hillary jumped in. "In fact, I can combine work with play and do a photo essay on the Biltmore House at Christmas through the eyes of a child. I can even squat down to see the whole thing from a small person's point of view. It'd be good practice for you, too, Logan. I'll let you use my camera until Santa can bring you one. How does that sound to everybody?"

Logan sat forward and leaned on the table like the adults. "I could get into visiting the Biltmore." His voice quivered a little from his effort to control his excitement.

"Yeah!" Lacie slid out of her chair and danced around. "I want to do that. Can we, Daddy?"

"Maybe," he said as she flung herself into his arms.

"I love you, Daddy," she whispered, burying her face in his neck.

He hugged her tight. This alone made the trip worth the effort.

With Lacie mollified, Hillary resumed planning their night out. "I have to work late here tonight, but how about tomorrow night?"

"I'd like that. I have to find another babysitter, though."

"Can I have a friend spend the night?" Logan asked.

"I want Caroline to stay with us," Lacie chimed in.

Peter sighed. "I have to ask her, and if she says yes, she gets to approve the friend."

"Cool." Logan seemed confident in Caroline's approval.

Peter looked at Hillary and smiled. "I guess I'm good to go, as long as Caroline can babysit."

"Excellent." Hillary stood up to leave. "Seven o'clock okay?"

"It all depends on Caroline."

"I'll make reservations, and you let me know if it doesn't work out."

****

Friday morning, after Logan and Lacie got off to their respective schools, Caroline popped in to Peter's office. "Hillary called for me to babysit and schedule you for dinner. Is that okay?"

"She already called? That was fast." He hadn't even had a chance to bring it up himself.

"Yep. Lucky for you, I am free. Heidelberg Haus is closed for renovations, so she's changed the plans to French. She says they always make room for her at Chez Picard."

Hillary brought out a range of emotions that left him feeling out of control of his life. Her attention was flattering, but she had to accept him as he was. And he was anything but impulsive. "I'm sorry she assumed you would be able to stay with the kids." Peter had tried to steer clear of creating problems between her and Josh since he'd realized she wasn't going to leave him. "Are you sure it's not a problem?"

"Not at all." She was smiling, but there was no shine to her eyes, and the tone of her voice was flat. "You know how I love to be with Logan and Lacie." She was obviously trying to be enthusiastic, but he knew her too well to be fooled. He moved closer to her and sat on the front of his desk. "There's something you're not saying."

"There's nothing wrong, I promise. Having a night with the kids is exactly what I need for a little attitude adjustment."

If she didn't want to talk, he had to let it go. "All right. French it is. Tell her thanks."

****

Driving to pick up Hillary for their date, Peter couldn't shake the uneasy feeling leftover from his exchange with Caroline. He wished she had arrived at his house with the same joy she'd had on Halloween night, but she was much more subdued, almost depressed. "Hi, Doc. Have a good time" was all she said. When he asked again if everything was all right, she just said, "Sure" and went to find Lacie. Was she upset about his date with Hillary? Had she found out about his encounter with Josh? Worst of all, had Josh taken it out on her? Whatever was bothering her, she wasn't saying, and that worried him. He couldn't lose Caroline. She was the glue that held him together.

Hillary got in the car with an exuberance that drove all his concerns from his mind.

She turned in her seat to face him. "I can't wait to share Chez Picard with you. I love French food!"

"I don't know much about French food except bread and cheese," Peter admitted. "You'll have to tell me what's good."

"No problem with that. It's all good."

The restaurant was not snobby Parisian French as Peter expected, but provincial French with country stews and potatoes. For appetizers, they had hearty breads, baked on site, and slabs of locally made cheese.

Hillary picked the wine, and Peter was surprised when it was pink. "Rosé has become very popular in Provence," she explained. "I like it because it is a little more robust than white, but not as bold as a red."

"You could tell me almost anything about wines, and I'd believe you," Peter said. "I know nothing at all."

She held up her glass and let the light shine through it, then took a sip and rolled it around in her mouth before swallowing. "Umm," she purred. "I'd love to go with you to the wine country in the south of France. Then you could not only appreciate the taste, but also picture the beautiful vineyards."

Peter shook his head. "The south of France. German castles. The aurora borealis. You talk about these places as easily as I describe the produce section at the grocery store."

"It's my job to go to these places like it's yours to care for animals. I can't imagine doing what you do. In fact, I can't imagine doing anything that would be the same day after day." She took a sip and rolled the glass between her palms.

Peter swallowed. "Of course, it's not really the same every day. In fact, it's not really the same every hour. All of the animals present with different problems, and believe it or not, they all have different personalities. I never know what's going to happen."

Hillary propped her chin on her hands. "Do you ever think of doing anything else?"

"Like what?"

"Traveling, for example. You said you did a semester in Germany. Didn't you ever want to go back?"

"Truly, I haven't thought about it. Marriage, vet school, the clinic, the kids—my life has been pretty full the last fifteen years."

"You said the aurora borealis is on your bucket list. Where else? Or what else?"

A question no one had asked in a long time. "I'd like to go fly-fishing in Montana." He shook his head. "When I told Maisie that, she said she'd be happy to bring a book to read while I got that out of my system. Wading up to her waist in freezing cold water was not her idea of a good time."

Hillary slapped her hand on the table. "I love fly-fishing. We can go tomorrow, if you want." She paused. "Wait. I'm sorry. I forget that other people have responsibilities. I think my impulsiveness would have prevented me from being a good mother."

"I don't know about that. I think you'd have your kids' passports all up to date and jet around the world to see firsthand the things they study about in school. That would make you a pretty remarkable mother."

"Thanks for saying so, but considering what I do for a living, it's kind of a non-issue at this point. Unless, of course, I am able to take up with someone else's."

He sat back and looked at her to see if she meant what he thought she meant. She was willing to be involved in the raising of his children? They *did* like her. "Are you saying you'd do that for Logan and Lacie?"

She rolled her eyes. "I'm just saying that I don't want to have babies, but I don't mind the thought of children that are already housebroken. And, yes, the first thing I would do is get them passports."

He laughed. "That would certainly qualify you as a good mother in Lacie's book."

Her eyes darkened seductively. "Seriously, do you ever think of doing things without the children? You're a father, but it's not all you are."

"Not for a long time." He paused. "Not until I met you."

She smiled. "That's funny, because I haven't thought about sharing it all with someone until I met you."

He swirled his wine. "I would like to see things with you, Hillary. I would like to run off to Timbuktu on a whim and see the pictures you take for my own eyes. But I will always be a father first. My children need me, and I need them."

"Of course, you are, Peter. That is one of the most endearing things about you. But do you think there might be a little room in there for me, too?"

How did he answer? Was there room for her? He wanted there to be. This woman with the striking green eyes and sun-streaked hair wanted him, just him, regardless of how good a father or son or veterinarian he was. She wanted to spend time with him and share things, just the two of them, shutting out the rest of the world and all of its demands. Was there a place for that in his life? He loved his children and loved his job, but a little freedom every now and then could be a wonderful thing.

It was hard to say no to her hopeful, inviting eyes. "You're a temptation, no doubt about it."

She winked. "That was my plan. Now I have something *really* tempting to dangle in front of you. I have tickets to the National Coalition for Arts Education gala in Washington next weekend, and I need a date. It's black tie, and I have a killer gown. What do you say? You don't need a passport," she teased.

"It's quite a leap from cabbage and beer to black tie in DC." He shouldn't have been surprised, given their conversations about kids and spontaneous vacations, but he still couldn't wrap his mind around travelling several hundred miles for dinner. "It's got to be at least an eight-hour drive. When do you plan to leave? Are we staying overnight? Because that's a whole different level of babysitting." He paused. "And I haven't danced in a really long time."

Obviously, Hillary's brain was not clouded with as many obligations as his. Her response required no thought at all. "No problem on all fronts. *World* magazine is flying me up there on their private jet. As far as staying overnight, that can be negotiated. And I'm not expecting you to waltz. The usual rocking back and forth is fine."

"Black tie?"

"Yep. When was the last time you wore a tux?"

"It's been a while. Wedding, probably."

"I know you have things you have to do, but you deserve a little fun, too. What do you say we try the gala in DC and see how that goes?"

He sighed. "It does sound like fun."

"It will be," she answered with a big grin. "You're going to love it."

"'I'll try' is the best I can offer."

"That's all I'm asking." She seemed completely confident he would go, and with good reason. He couldn't imagine a man who would turn her down.

Driving home after dinner, Hillary reached across and took his hand where it rested on the seat next to him.

Peter intertwined their fingers. "I guess I can let the kids stay with my mom. You're on her approved list, so she probably won't complain."

"Why not Caroline?'

How could he answer? He could never admit out loud that he was fighting his feelings for Caroline. The mention of her brought back his uneasiness at her distant demeanor when she arrived that night. Had Josh finally driven home the wedge between them? Or was

Hillary causing stress in a way Suzanne and Donna never had? Either way, thoughts of Caroline had no place between him and Hillary tonight. "I've abused Caroline's good will way too many times to ask her again so soon. Besides, you heard my mother say she doesn't see her grandchildren enough."

"I did."

Peter pulled his car into her driveway and killed the motor. He turned in his seat to face her. "I had a great time tonight."

"So did I." Her voice was low and husky, her eyes dark and heavy-lidded.

He leaned across the space between them, slid his hand behind her neck, and pulled her to him. Their kiss was long and slow. When they broke apart, he leaned his forehead against hers. He remembered Donna's car, and her scooting across the seat to reach him. "These cars were a lot better for making out when the front seat was a bench."

She chuckled. "Must be trying to keep people on the straight and narrow." She took a deep breath. "You could come in."

He wanted to go in with her. He wanted to continue kissing her, and pull her closer, and hold her for a long time. But he still wasn't ready for where that would lead. "I want to, Hillary. You can't imagine how I want to, but I need to get home. Caroline wasn't feeling well when I left. I'm lucky she stayed anyway so we could go out."

"Okay," she said, "but one of these days you are going to stay. Soon."

Chapter 21

In the short time he had known her, Peter had learned that Hillary was a person who would be true to her word. He knew that she would be at Logan's game on Saturday, because she said she would. As he sat at the park, waiting for her, he watched Logan's team warming up on the field and Lacie playing on the playground. This place and these people were a fundamental part of his life and defined who he was. His was a life filled with home and kids and work. Hillary had shown him a world beyond this one, and he wanted to go with her to see it, but he wouldn't give up ballparks and backpacks and Teacher Appreciation Weeks. Would Hillary fit into his world as she was asking him to come into hers?

If he pursued his interest in Hillary, where did Caroline belong? When he got home after the French restaurant, Caroline was more like her old self, smiling and teasing him about his date, but she didn't hang around for details. There was still a little tickle on the back of his neck that things had changed between them, and not for the better.

Hillary showed up at the field precisely at kickoff time, camera bag over her shoulder. She was doing this for him, and he owed her his undivided attention. Undivided except for the game, of course. And for his daughter on the loose. And for the interactions with the other parents. Undivided attention? That didn't exist in the life of a single father, no matter how interesting his companion.

She took her place on the bleachers next to him. "Whew! There's enough traffic in this parking lot for it to be the Super Bowl. I had to park over the curb in the grass."

Peter chuckled. "It's the last day of the season and ours isn't the only game today. Thanks for coming."

"Absolutely," she replied, unpacking her camera. "Wouldn't have missed it for the world."

She turned the camera on him first and took a shot that was a little more candid than Peter would have liked. When she showed him the digital picture, he had to admit it wasn't awful.

"Does that camera come with a feature that makes everybody look good?"

She squeezed his leg. "Nope. My cameras only show the truth." She scanned the crowd. "Where's Ruth?"

Peter huffed a little laugh. "I hope you're not really here for her. I could have told you after our evening at *Nicoletti's* that she would cancel. She's always too tired. Or she doesn't feel well. Or she's too busy."

Hillary shook her head and squeezed his leg again. "No surprise there."

She dropped her hand from his leg when Donna Lechleiter clomped up the bleachers to take position on his other side. "Hello, Peter. Great day for a game, isn't it?" She faced forward, but Peter could see her eyes shift sideways to check out Hillary in her peripheral vision. He thought they had left things pretty clear, but Donna still gave off vibes of ownership.

Peter made a show of taking Hillary's left hand to leave no doubt that he was here with her. "Donna, this is Hillary Hoffman."

She reached across Peter to offer her hand to Hillary. "Hi," she said. "I'm Donna Lechleiter. I'm team mom."

Hillary kept her grip on Peter's hand, but extended her right one to shake Donna's. "Hi, Donna," she said warmly. "I was friends with Peter's wife."

"How about that?" Donna's smile looked like someone was pulling her cheeks tight from behind. "So was I. How did you know her?"

"We worked out at the same gym." Hillary's smile was much more natural and sincere than Donna's.

Donna pushed a little harder. "Then I'm surprised you knew her so well. Working out isn't really conducive to conversation, is it? Maisie and I spent hours chatting at these football games, and baseball too, for that matter. And then, of course, I was also Lacie's room mother." Donna radiated tension, jockeying for the top position in the who-knew-Maisie-better competition.

Hillary was up to the challenge. "I imagine you did know the "mom" side of her really well. We did a fair amount of talking while we were on the treadmills and bicycles about Peter and the kids, but also other stuff. We would always go out after class to the juice bar, and we could talk for hours."

"What did you talk about, Hillary? Do you have children?"

"No, I don't, Donna, but I like children, and I enjoyed Maisie's stories. We found lots of other interesting topics, too."

"Perhaps, but nothing more important than the kids."

Peter squirmed. Now he knew how a ping-pong net felt. "That's true, Donna, but I know that you also like music. Hillary, what kind of music do you like?"

"Actually, I went to the Dreams of Home concert in October," Hillary answered.

Fangirl Donna took over. "Peter and I were at that concert," she squealed. "Could you believe it? Donnie hasn't lost a beat."

"No, he hasn't. When was your first concert?"

He stood up to stretch, and Donna scooted behind him to get closer to Hillary. "I think I'll go down to the sidelines for a minute. See how the boys are feeling." He congratulated himself on diverting Donna's aggression, but he hadn't been prepared for the interaction with her, and he needed time to come up with a plan.

Keeping Lacie on the playground in his peripheral vision, he stepped up to the fence around the field for a closer view of the game. He found himself standing next to Wayne Lechleiter. Knowing how Wayne felt about Donna, it wasn't a position he would have chosen, but it was too late to pretend he didn't see him.

"Told you," Wayne smirked. "Once she gets her claws in you, you're sunk. She never lets go."

"She let go of you," Peter countered, not appreciating this man's attempt to bash his ex-wife. Donna was bossy and controlling, but she also got a lot of things done that other people weren't willing to do. At the very least, she deserved their respect.

"Humpf," Wayne grunted. "No, she hasn't. Thanks to the courts, she has me all tied up with a pretty little bow."

Peter kept his eyes on the field. "I don't understand."

"As long as she has the kids, she has all the power. If I want to see them, even for my regular visits, I have to work around the schedules she sets up. Then there's the money. Anything they need comes straight from me because she isn't working, but I have no say on what is necessary or not."

Once again, Peter was caught in a topic he didn't want to discuss with Wayne. He had stepped from the frying pan into the fire, and he was desperate to find a way out.

His salvation came from Caroline, who appeared suddenly by his side. She started talking as though she had no awareness of his conversation with Wayne.

"Hey, Doc, I came to see Logan play, but I didn't bring any money. Would you get me a hot dog and a Coke?"

Peter was grateful to see her because it rescued him from Wayne, but more important, it was a crack in the wall that had grown between them. He glanced up at Hillary and Donna, whose expressions and gestures were still excited and effusive. "Sure," he said with an exaggerated sigh. "Sorry, man. Gotta go. You know how these employees are. Give, give, give."

Wayne waved them away.

When they were out of earshot, Peter said, "Thanks a lot. When did you get here?"

"It was my pleasure," Caroline answered as though there had never been anything wrong between them. "I got here about twenty minutes ago, long enough to see you being tossed back and forth like a hot potato. Who knew there could be so much drama at a middle school football game?"

Peter stopped walking so he could look her fully in the face. "Are you making fun of me?"

"Not at all, Doc," she replied, her eyes sparkling. "I didn't realize you had become such a stud."

"Very funny."

Her teasing tone gone, she said, "Sincerely, it's Logan's last game, and I didn't want to miss it."

"I hope it doesn't cause you problems elsewhere." He didn't want to start an argument, but his issues with her boyfriend were never far from his mind.

"Never mind Josh." She shooed like she was brushing away a pesky fly. "It's football."

Lacie came running up behind them and grabbed their hands. She expressed no surprise seeing Caroline with Peter, even though she knew he had been expecting to watch the game with Hillary. "Daddy, I want a Ring Pop."

He dropped her hand. "No Ring Pop. You always ask, and I always say no."

"You know what I want, sweetie?" Caroline asked, dropping down on one knee to be eye level with Lacie.

"What?" Lacie pouted.

"I love ballpark hot dogs with catsup and mustard and relish. Yum, yum." She rubbed her stomach with her free hand.

"I don't like mustard," Lacie whined.

Caroline nodded wisely and stood up, still holding Lacie's hand. "I understand. Catsup and relish then."

"One hot dog with catsup and relish," Peter confirmed, nodding his thanks to Caroline.

She winked at him and asked, "Lacie, do you ever

watch the games?"

"What games?" Lacie had recovered from the Ring Pop disappointment to swing between them once more.

Caroline and Peter shared a smile. "The football games."

"Yes, but they get boring. I only watch when Logan is doing something good."

"Like now!" Caroline exclaimed, dropping Lacie's hand and pointing to where Logan ran at top speed from his team's twenty-yard line toward the goal, until their opponents finally brought him down on their own 10-yard line. The boys hopped up and got in formation so fast, it seemed like they were in a film set on fast forward.

Peter's vision tunneled to his son, the ball, and the white lines on the field. The ball snapped, the quarterback stepped back, took aim, and threw the football like a missile to Logan's outstretched arms in the end zone. "Yeah!" Peter jumped and pumped his fist in the air. "Way to go, Logan!"

Logan yanked off his helmet and waved to his dad before being jumped and pulled to the ground by his celebrating teammates. It was one of those milestone moments they would never forget.

Caroline's face was flushed from the excitement, and she threw her arms around Peter. "How 'bout that!" she exclaimed, squeezing him tight. "Our boy went all the way!"

He looked down into her happy face, and everything else became fuzzy and out of focus. "It will mean a lot to Logan that you were here to see his big moment." His voice was low so only she could hear. He brushed a stray hair from her eyes. "It means a lot to me."

Caroline scanned his face, stopping on his mouth. "It is the most important thing in the world to me, right now." She glanced past his right side, and whatever she saw made her pull away from him and step back. "Never mind the hot dog," she said, making a hasty exit. "The game is too exciting." She was gone before he had a chance to reply. He was staring at her receding back when Hillary stepped beside him. "Is that Caroline?"

Had Caroline run away because Hillary was coming? "Yep. She wanted to see Logan's last game. She's like a favorite aunt, or even an older sister."

"Of course, she would want to be here, although we should go with the favorite aunt. There is no way she could ever pass for your daughter." Hillary slid her hand through the space between his body and his elbow. "I've decided I want a hot dog. Let's sit with her when we go back."

Peter looked to see if they were casting Donna aside, but she had moved from their original place and was intensely involved in a conversation with one of the other moms.

Lacie skipped to where Caroline sat, leaving Peter to carry her food. Caroline moved over to make room, greeting them all, including Hillary, with a happy face. Peter reconsidered his concern about Caroline and Hillary. It must have been something else that caused her to leave so suddenly.

Lacie claimed her spot on Caroline's left. There was no competition for ownership between Caroline and Hillary as there had been with Donna. Sitting on opposite sides of him, they talked like old friends. Peter listened to their conversation but kept his eyes on the field as Logan's team battled the other one in a tug-o-war up the field and back. Their boys were good players, but the other side had good boys, too, and as the game grew near the end, Logan's team was down by five.

With thirty seconds left on the clock, Logan's quarterback had one good play left. The stands went silent like someone had turned off the sound, and every single person was on their feet, sending brainwaves for success out to their players.

The center snapped the ball, and the quarterback handed it off to the player running by him. Suddenly, Logan had the ball and dashed at top speed toward the end zone, away from the players chasing the other receiver. The crowd in the stands went wild, jumping and cheering, high-fiving and hugging. Hillary and Caroline captured Peter in a bear hug sandwich, and he grabbed them each in turn.

Lacie pulled on his belt. "What happened, Daddy? What happened?" she shouted at him over the raucous crowd.

He swung her up into his arms and kissed her cheek. "Logan and the other players did something amazing! They won the game!"

Lacie jumped up and down, cheering and clapping with the rest of the fans.

After the boys peeled out of their dogpile, Coach Mike went to congratulate the other coach and have his players shake hands with their opponents to acknowledge an incredible game, well-played. Peter joined the other parents on the field with Caroline by his side. Hillary circled the celebration, snapping pictures from every angle.

Finally, the jubilant crowd trailed out to the parking lot.

Peter opened the hatch of the car so Logan could take off his pads before the ride home.

Caroline hugged Logan, disregarding his excessively sweaty body, and said, "I'm so proud of you."

Logan, the undemonstrative pre-teen boy, squeezed her hard. "Thanks, Caroline."

Hillary captured the moment through her lens.

Peter was surprised. "He's not exactly photographic material right now."

"He absolutely is." Hillary let her camera drop on its cord around her neck. "He's the victorious gladiator."

Caroline nodded. "I like that. Logan the gladiator."

Donna walked up with Justin and Curtis in tow. "Hi, everybody. Hillary, it was great to meet you." She focused her attention fully on Peter. "Justin wants Logan to spend the night. Would that be okay with you?"

All eyes were on Peter for the answer. On one hand, he wanted to sustain his pride-swollen heart by keeping his son close for frequent high-fives as they walked through the house. On the other hand, it was Logan's happy moment. "Logan, do you want to go?"

Logan exchanged a nod of understanding with Justin. "Sure. Can I go home and take a shower first?"

Another sign Logan was growing up. "Absolutely. Mrs. Lechleiter doesn't need two reeking football players in her car."

Donna scrunched her nose. "Thanks for that. Give

me a call as soon as he's done, and I'll run by and pick him up."

Peter didn't want to impose on her when she was the one hosting the sleepover. "You don't have to do that. I'll bring him to you."

"No need. I'll run them out for dinner after I pick him up. Bye everyone." Donna pivoted on her heel and strode away.

Hillary chuckled. "Is she always like that?"

Peter watched Donna arrive at her car, direct Curtis to get in, and instruct Justin to remove his pads. "What do you mean?"

"Orchestrating every situation."

Caroline took the reply. "Yep. I can always count on a call from Donna to update Peter's calendar." She sighed and gave Logan another hug. "Love you, buddy, but football is over. Time to go home."

Peter's happy heart gave a little miserable beat. "Josh is waiting?"

She forced a smile. "He'll be off work soon."

Hillary hugged her. "It was great spending time with you."

"Me, too. See you Monday, Doc."

Peter's gaze followed her as she walked away.

Hillary waited until the children were in the car. "I have a bad feeling about Caroline and her boyfriend."

"So do I, but she doesn't want me to get involved. I offered." He walked her to her car and opened the door for her. "Thanks for coming. I'm glad we gave you a good game."

She turned to Peter before she got in, close enough that he could feel her breath on his face as she talked. "I'd never been to a kid's game before. It was a great time. Too bad the season is over."

"There's always baseball." He looked around to see who was watching. There were no prying eyes, so he leaned in and kissed her. "Nothing as romantic as a bunch of sweaty pre-teenagers."

She kissed him again. "I'm not always looking for romance. Sometimes I'm looking for life, and you've got that in spades. Goodbye, Peter. See you soon."

"Bye." Peter was still smiling when he got in his car.

"Hey, Dad, you and Hillary, huh?"

Seemed their kisses were not as private as he thought. Peter looked in the rearview mirror to see if Lacie was paying attention, but she was already nodding off. "Maybe. Do you mind?"

"Nope." He sat forward, grinning. "How about that "hook and ladder" play? Were you surprised?"

Peter took the change of subject gladly. "I've never even seen the pros pull that one."

Their conversation continued on the drive home. Logan raced into the house to shower and change, but Lacie didn't stir when Peter picked her up and carried her in. Peter was glad for Donna's insistence so he didn't have to drag Lacie out when Logan was ready to go.

When he walked Logan out to the car, Donna rolled down her window. "I'm a little jealous," he said, only half teasing.

She gave a Cheshire cat grin. "You could come."

"'Fraid not. Lacie is sound asleep." He wondered at Curtis, laughing with the bigger boys. "How is Curtis still so wide awake?"

Donna looked back. "He never wants to miss any

of the action with his big brother."

Peter patted her door as she rolled up her window and watched her van drive away until it was out of sight. He walked in the house slowly, a little deflated to have the party gone without him. He climbed the stairs and did a quick check on Lacie before heading to his room.

Buddy was already on the bed and rolled over for a belly rub when Peter came in and stretched out.

I wish you could have seen Logan tonight. He was amazing. He ran a "hook and ladder" play. Even the pros don't try it.

It makes a dad proud.

Yes, it does. Hillary was with us.

How is that going?

I like her. She reminds me of another life.

Times when you had fun.

Yes. A lot of them with you.

But some of them were without me. You can do that again.

This was what you wanted.

Yes. It is time for you to rejoin the world.

Caroline knew that, too. That's why she gave me your letters.

She did, and she was right. Loved you in that life and beyond. Kiss our babies for me.

Chapter 22

Peter didn't feel like he could ask Caroline to stay with Logan and Lacie overnight while he was out of the city. What if Josh showed up and caused trouble without him there to protect them? He was already afraid Josh might do something to Caroline. He didn't want to see his family on the nightly news.

As she had from the beginning, his mother was happy to take the children in support of him going out with Hillary, especially to something as prestigious as the Gala that she could brag about to her friends. He rented the first tux he had worn since his wedding and passed Lacie's inspection before dropping them off at their grandmother's house.

He knocked on Hillary's door and heard a muffled, "Come in." He stepped in and closed the door behind him.

"I want to make an entrance," she called gaily from her bedroom.

Familiar, casual, lying-on-the-ground-to-take-a-picture Hillary had been replaced with stunning, cover-of-a-magazine Hillary. Her hair was swept up with feathery tendrils framing her face, perfectly made up to highlight her jade-green eyes. Diamond earrings dripped from her ears, sparkling in the fading sunlight through the windows. The sleeveless bodice of her black dress, tapered to emphasize her waist, opened to a full skirt that made her seem to float as she walked.

"Wow," Peter said, awestruck. "You look great."

Obviously, that was the reaction she wanted, because she smiled and twirled like a little girl. "You don't look so bad yourself," she said suggestively. "I thought you were handsome before, but this takes it to a whole new level."

"Thanks," he said.

They were interrupted by a knock on the door, and she opened it to a man in a nondescript black suit. "I believe you called for a limousine?"

"Thank you. We'll be right out."

When the driver was out of sight, Peter chuckled. This event was feeling more and more like a princess ball Lacie had orchestrated. "A limo?"

"We want to do it in style, right?" She patted his chest. "Besides, that way we can get the party started."

"Right." Peter's stomach clenched. What kind of party? Hillary had lived an uninhibited lifestyle. What was she expecting to happen?

His face must have reflected his fear. She straightened his tie, and looked up at him with misty eyes. "You are the only man I've ever been with who panicked at the word 'party.' I just mean chatting over a glass of wine. No one should ever drink and drive."

Peter let out the breath he didn't realize he was holding.

The limousine was obviously meant for executives. It had a bar, satellite television, and, for this occasion, atmospheric jazz.

Hillary offered him a glass of red wine with a color so deep, it was almost black.

Peter accepted it and sipped, even though he wasn't

really a wine guy.

"Would you rather have a beer?" she asked with a sly smile.

Peter was caught. "I would, if you have one," he said with relief.

She opened an expensive import, which he didn't enjoy as much as his usual Becker Lite, but it was better than wine. Her calm confidence dissipated his anxiety and eased the tension in his shoulders. He relaxed into comfortable conversation about the exotic animals she had photographed, and her elegant posture gave way to enthusiasm when she discovered he had done an internship at a zoo in veterinary school, and actually touched animals she had only seen from a distance.

When they drove right onto the tarmac of a local airport to a small, gleaming white jet, Peter felt like a celebrity. The captain, co-captain, and steward greeted them at the top of the stairs and ushered them into an interior more elegant than any room in his house. While Hillary talked with the crew, he took a seat, scanning the cabin to take in every detail of polished wood and upholstered chairs. Lacie and Logan would want to know everything he could remember about flying on a private plane.

As soon as they were in the air, the steward presented Peter with an unidentified beer in an elegant glass etched with the company logo. Although the taste was as unfamiliar as the one from the trip to the airport, it was much more appealing, and he leaned back, stretching to let its warmth spread through his body. He wasn't surprised when another limo waited at the airport in Washington to whisk them away to the five-star resort.

The buildings of the hotel encircled a restored cathedral converted into spectacular event space. Shimmering gold fabric had been draped from the soaring ceiling and matched the tablecloths. The ornate overhead chandeliers gave off a soft, romantic light, and the ambiance was enhanced by candles in hurricane lanterns on the tables. An ensemble of string and brass musicians played, and a few couples swirled around on the dance floor.

Hillary made countless rapid-fire introductions, and his brain became too overloaded to remember all their names. After another couple of beers, however, he found that even rich, important people could be easy to talk to if you hit on the right subject, and many of them had pets. He and Hillary danced, they drank, they talked, and Peter enjoyed himself far more than he expected.

He'd lost track of time when Hillary took his hand and pulled him into a quiet alcove in the shadows where they were totally blocked from prying eyes. She leaned coyly against the stone wall, seducing him with sultry eyes.

He braced himself with one hand propped over her shoulder, and lowered his mouth to hers.

She pressed her hands flat against his chest, returning and deepening the kiss. She untied his bow tie and unbuttoned the top buttons of his shirt. "I have a room upstairs," she whispered.

A room. With Hillary. Raw desire flowed into his body from her hands on his chest. It would be so easy. He knew she didn't want anything else from him. She didn't want a home, or children, or a mortgage, or minivans. She just wanted a night of passion. There was no reason to resist.

But something didn't feel right. He leaned his forehead against hers. "I can't," he said finally.

"Why not?" She untucked his shirt so she could rub her hands over his bare back.

He stood up and pulled away, but reached back to tenderly tuck a stray hair behind her ear. "If I was twenty years old, I would have had you right here, hell with who could see. But I'm not. Sex is not enough anymore, Hillary." He paused to cushion the blow. "I want to make love, and as much as I like you, I don't love you."

She wrapped her arms around his neck and tried to pull him back to her. "I don't love you, either, but we can still share something very special. We're talking one night of passion here, Peter, not a lifetime of love."

He gently removed her arms. "I can't do that. Not anymore." The part of his brain controlled by his libido screamed, *Are you out of your mind?*

She leaned back against the wall. "A man turning down free, no-obligation sex? No way."

"Way." He tucked in his shirt. He felt better when he saw Hillary's smile. It wasn't what she wanted, but she wasn't crushed. "Are you ready to go?"

"I'm not done here yet," she said with a wink. "I have a few more hands to press and a few more patrons to schmooze. I'm always looking for the next interesting job. I'll use the room myself and head back tomorrow or the next day."

"I'm sorry," he said sincerely. "I like being with you, and God knows you are incredibly sexy, but it's just not in the cards for us."

"Perhaps not." She smoothed her dress and hair. "I

think it's in the cards for you and someone, though."

"What do you mean?"

"I mean I've seen something through my lens that you haven't seen yet." She kissed him on the cheek. "You are gorgeous, Peter Hunter. See you around."

In the quiet of the limousine taking him to the airport, he thought, *I'm sorry, Maisie. Strike three.*

There was no answering voice. Maisie had gone silent.

Though he continued to reach out to her, she never did speak to him as he tried to sort through the alcohol-induced muddle in his head. Maisie had made her list with the intention of getting him back in the saddle. She had loved him and the kids, and she didn't want them to have a home without a mother. The women she had suggested had been good choices, and he had enjoyed them all, each more than the one before, but as Caroline had said, there were no fireworks. No magic. No love connection.

As Caroline had said.

She knew, she could tell before he even spoke, how his dates had gone. She had said what he couldn't put into words. With Suzanne, Donna, and Hillary there had been desire, but no fireworks, no magic.

But Caroline had set him on fire with her kiss, so that he wanted more and more. Even now, the memory of her fitting so perfectly in his arms took his breath away. He had been certain he would never find that again, that he would have to settle for a love that was a mere shadow of what he had known with Maisie. Instead, the thrill of a brief encounter with Caroline had become a standard none of the others could reach.

Maisie hadn't included Caroline in his list. She had

been too much of a sister to them, too much a part of both of their lives to consider her for filling Maisie's place. But he wasn't the man he had been when his precious wife had made her heartfelt list, and Caroline was no longer the little sister they had known. She had grown into a woman more beautiful and wiser than they could ever have imagined when she entered their lives so many years ago. When she entered their lives at sixteen, and he was twenty-seven-year-old veterinarian passionately in love with his wife, it never occurred to him to think of her as a woman. But, at twenty-six, she had become the only person a thirty-seven-year-old widower with two children could imagine spending the rest of his life with.

"I'm sorry, Maisie," he said in a low voice, hoping wherever she was she could hear him. "I will always love you, but you knew better than anyone that someday I would have to move on, and you wanted me to have a partner on that journey. You tried to find that person for me, and I love you for that. But I have found my own number four."

Chapter 23

By the time the plane landed and the limo took him to Hillary's house to retrieve his car, it was after three am. He got in behind the steering wheel and sat, staring at bare tree limbs swaying in and out of the light of the streetlamp.

Now what?

Every reason he had dismissed Caroline as a love interest was still there. She had been a little sister to both Maisie and him since she was sixteen, but she wasn't sixteen anymore. She was still on his payroll, but she worked more *with* him than *for* him, just like Maisie had. She had been there for them during Maisie's end times, and she had pulled together the shattered pieces of their family when he barely had the strength to hold up his head. She didn't only maintain the calendar of clinic appointments. She kept track of every school function, every team function, and every other kind of function for him and his kids with love and patience and humor. She put bows in Lacie's hair and kept Logan's voracious appetite appeased.

Now there was something new, something that wouldn't leave him alone. He closed his eyes and focused on the memory of holding her close. She fit in his arms perfectly, and the warmth and life in her made him feel whole again in a way he never thought he would.

Whether or not she returned his romantic affections, Caroline was one of the most important people in his life, and there was someone close to her who posed a real danger. Peter had to save her from Josh. But would she let him?

Therein lay the problem. Peter had always thought Josh was a stupid, delusional drunk, and now he thought he was a dangerous, stupid, delusional drunk. Did that give him the right to go barreling in and thrust himself between them uninvited? Crazy as it was, Josh had the right to come out swinging if Peter fulfilled his previously unfounded assertions that he wanted Caroline for himself.

He banged his head against the steering wheel, paralyzed by his indecision. Finally, he came up with one small action. He would drive over to Caroline's apartment and sit in her parking lot while he mulled over his options. Perhaps being close to her would help him see more clearly what to do.

When he got there, he was surprised to see her lights on. If she was up, he might be able to talk to her. But how would she feel if he just showed up in pre-dawn hours without warning? What if she had fallen asleep with the lights on, and woke up too irritated to let him in? She was the person who helped him come up with a solution to his problems, but this time she was the problem. At best, she would think he was completely nuts. At worst, she would tell him to leave and never mention it again. Would that end the relationship he had just realized was the only one he wanted for the rest of his life? Whichever was going to be true, he was drawn irresistibly to be where she was, so he got out of the car to go in.

He could hear Josh's angry voice from the bottom of the stairwell. Instead of creeping meekly up the stairs, he took them two at a time to reach Caroline's door. It was cracked open, and without giving himself away he could see Caroline cowering in an armchair, her legs pulled up against her chest as a shield.

Out of sight, Josh screamed at her, slurring his words in a drunken rage. "You have never supported my dreams, never cared what I want."

Peter heard a crash that sounded like a table being thrust over. Caroline had not been hit by the debris, but he lifted his arm into position to burst through the door. He waited, tight as a wound spring, to give Josh enough time to push her beyond the point of no return.

"You think Dr. Hunter is the greatest person that ever lived, that he has done it all right. That's a lie! Do you hear me! It's a lie! He's just another one of those spoiled mama's boys who's had everything handed to him! What does he know about real work? Nothing! Do you hear me? Nothing!"

From behind the door, Josh came into view and braced his hands on the arms of Caroline's chair, trapping her. He pushed his face into hers so close their noses touched. "If you cared about me half as much as you do about him and those brats, you'd hand over the money without a word. This man I met at the restaurant recognized that I am too good to be a server. He says he will help my idea happen, and he can tell I am exactly the kind of person to make a huge success out of a business like this. All I need is the capital to invest. He can see it, and he doesn't even know me. I have spoiled and coddled you for five years, but you have no faith in me. No faith!"

Peter couldn't listen anymore. He thrust open the door and stepped in. "That's enough. Back off."

Caroline had pulled so deeply into herself that she didn't even look up.

Josh was briefly stunned to silence, but quickly recovered. He looked over his shoulder at Peter, maintaining his menacing position over Caroline. "This is none of your business, *Doctor* Hunter," he growled. "Get out!"

The pungent odor of liquor hung heavy in the air. Unlike the comic pictures of drunks stumbling and saying stupidly hilarious things, a belligerent drunk could be very dangerous to everyone in his proximity. In spite of the viper in his belly urging him to strike, Peter knew he had to be much calmer, much more controlled, and much more reasonable than the raging beast standing between him and Caroline. "You're right that it's none of my business," he said evenly. "But you are scaring Caroline. Why don't you back off a bit so you and she can have a reasonable conversation?"

Josh didn't budge. "Do you think I didn't try that? She won't listen. She owes me the money she got from working all those hours taking care of you and your brats instead of seeing to me and my needs. I have the right to the same life you have," he spat with absolute conviction.

Peter tried to reassure Caroline with a look, but she was pushing against the back of the chair like a wounded animal in a trap. Before he could do anything for her, he had to get Josh out of the way. He held his hands up to show he didn't want a fight. "She has worked a lot for me, you're right. But Caroline wouldn't let me pay her for any of the babysitting, so there may not be as much money as you think…"

Josh stood up and turned on Peter, fists clenched. "Worked for you for free, did she? Of course, she did. You guilted her into it because your wife was sick, and you got her to do anything you wanted," he sneered. "After your wife was dead, you should have let her go. She'd done enough for you. But you kept on using her 'cause you knew she'd do whatever you said. She'd even have played wife for you, if you asked. Maybe she already did."

Her jailer removed, Caroline sprang out of the chair and knocked him back onto the sofa. "Stop it!" she screamed. "Shut up! Shut up! Shut up! You don't know what you're talking about! Peter and Maisie were there for me when my life fell completely apart! They loved me and supported me and kept me from being alone! Don't you ever, ever say anything against Dr. Hunter! I don't owe you one single cent! Not one cent!"

Peter took advantage of Josh's surprise to grab him by the shirt and yank him off the sofa. He dragged him to the door scrambling for balance, pulled him down two flights of stairs, and threw him out into the darkness. "Disappear, man, or I'll call the cops."

He left Josh lying stunned in the wet grass and rushed back up the stairs to find Caroline in a puddle on the floor, sobbing. He pulled her up into his arms and she clung to him, grabbing the lapels of his tux and burying her face in his chest. He held her tight and let her cry until her body stopped shaking. He tipped her chin up so he could see her face. "Are you all right?" he asked gently, stroking away the stray hairs.

She sniffed and nodded. "Yeah."

She burrowed deeper into his embrace and he

tightened his arms around her.

"Are you going to tell me again that I don't know the real Josh?" he said to the top of her head.

With a little laugh, she looked up at him again. "No, I think you have a pretty good idea."

"You're coming home with me. I don't trust him not to come back."

"Are you sure?" She sniffed.

Looking down at her, with her red nose and teary eyes, Peter loved her even more. He didn't know how long he had been denying it, but there was no denying it now. She was the one.

This was not the time to tell her, and bringing her home was not the opportunity to make his move. This was all about giving her a safe place to rest and get her sea-legs back. "Yes," he answered. "My house is quiet right now because Logan and Lacie are at my mom's. You can sleep in Lacie's room."

"Thanks."

Peter grabbed her purse from a nearby table and fished out her keys so she could lock the door. He kept his arm around her and practically carried her to the car, relieved to see Josh had disappeared. They didn't speak all the way home. Caroline leaned her head against the window and closed her eyes.

Peter resisted the urge to reach over and stroke her face. She let him lead her into the house and up the stairs to Lacie's room. He pushed her back gently until her legs hit the bed, and she collapsed. He covered her with an extra blanket from Lacie's closet, smiled down at her, and left before he lost his resolve and laid down beside her. Buddy, with his remarkable dog instincts for human need, jumped on the bed and curled up against her back.

In his own room, Peter peeled off his tuxedo, let the pieces fall to the floor, and dropped on the bed. He was asleep before his head hit the pillow.

****

As consciousness crept in, his first thought was *coffee*. The aroma gave him the incentive he needed to sit up in bed. He pulled on sweatpants and a sweatshirt and padded down to the kitchen to find Caroline sitting at the table, hands wrapped around a steaming mug. He poured himself a cup and sat with her.

"I'm sorry about last night," she offered.

He dismissed her apology with a shake of his head. "It wasn't your fault, Caroline. Keep your eye on the ball. Josh had no right to treat you like that. God knows what might have happened if I hadn't been there. Don't apologize for him."

She nodded slowly. "Why *were* you there? Why weren't you with Hillary?"

There was a long pause while Peter thought about his answer. He couldn't talk to her about his revelation while she was still so vulnerable. She had to be strong when he told her so he could be sure that, whatever her response was, her reaction was honest and real. "Things didn't work out with Hillary. She wanted more than I was ready to give."

She swirled her mug, looking at the ripples in the liquid. "Really?"

"Yeah," he smiled sheepishly. "Imagine that, huh? Guess I must be a little crazy."

"I don't know about that." She sighed. "You have to go with your gut."

He thought about what his gut wanted to say to her,

and he knew that impulse had to be resisted. For now. "I was driving home and saw your light on, so I stopped to see if everything was okay. Obviously, it was not."

"No," she agreed, her head hanging. "What do I do now?"

Peter considered the situation. Josh could easily return to take out his anger on her. She wouldn't be safe there until they could get the locks changed. "You'll stay here with us," he said firmly. "It's not safe for you to be there by yourself when he could come back at any time." He eased his tone and smiled. "You can stay with Lacie in her room. It will be the slumber party she is always asking for."

Caroline smiled sadly. "I am so sorry to bring this down on you."

"I already told you. You did not do this. He did."

They sat in silence, nursing their coffees, until a car pulled up in the driveway and the children came crashing in.

"Caroline! You'll never believe what we did," Lacie squealed as though seeing her was no surprise. "Grandma took us to Jump-o-rama. Logan bounced so high he touched the ceiling, and I did my first flip!"

Logan was right behind her, but stopped cold the minute he stepped in the door. "Hey, Caroline," he said suspiciously, looking back and forth between her and his father. "What are you doing here?"

Caroline pulled Lacie into her lap. "Josh got out-of-control mad, and your dad rescued me," she said honestly. "I slept in Lacie's room."

His unasked question answered, Logan visibly relaxed and nodded his approval to Peter. "Josh sucks." He moved to the refrigerator and stood in front of the open door. "What's to eat?"

Ruth walked in smiling, but when she saw Caroline at the table, her expression became decidedly unpleasant. "What happened to Hillary?"

"She stayed in Washington." Peter's curt answer offered no invitation for comment. He was in no mood to have his mother in his business.

"And how did Caroline get here?" she asked, as though Caroline couldn't hear her. Ruth was in his business, whether he wanted it or not.

"She's here because Josh stinks," Logan chimed in, relieving Peter of the need for explanation.

"Who is Josh?" she asked, undeterred by Logan's explanation.

"He's my boyfriend, Mrs. Hunter," Caroline explained. "Or rather, he was my boyfriend. Dr. Hunter saved me before he did something terrible."

"And did you call him away from Hillary to come and save you?" she asked, looking down her nose at Caroline as though she was going to squash her like a bug.

Peter stood up and slammed his hands on the table. "No, Mother. I had already come back when I drove by her apartment and saw the light on. I checked to be sure she was okay, and found her boyfriend about to take a fist to her face."

Ruth was stunned to silence. Her expression softened and she said to Caroline, "These men. Honestly. Good ones are so hard to find."

"I'm lucky you raised Dr. Hunter to be one of the good ones," Caroline replied.

"It was important he know how to treat a woman. God knows, his father was no role model." Ruth turned her attention to Peter with a disapproving glare. "And what happened to Hillary?"

"She and I want different things out of life," Peter said. "She's a lot of fun, but she has no interest in being tied down with a family."

"What about my nurse? When are you going to call her?" she pressed relentlessly. If she was aware of his exhaustion, she was ignoring it.

Caroline looked puzzled. "Nurse?"

Peter waved it off. "I'll get to it, Mom. Give me a break. I've had a long night."

She turned to go, reaching for the doorknob. "Fine. I'll remind you on Monday."

Peter looked for a way to stall her. He grabbed the first thought that came to mind. "This is Thanksgiving week. Let it rest until after the holiday, okay?"

She turned back to him, crossing her arms and tapping her foot. "And will you be bringing my grandchildren for Thanksgiving? It's easy enough for you to drop them off when you have something else you want to do."

Peter rubbed his temples. The guilt trip was unnecessary, and she knew it. They had never missed a Thanksgiving at her house. One of these years, he was going to stay home just to teach her a lesson. "Of course, we'll be there, Mom. We always are."

"You can come, too," she said to Caroline in a sweet voice that had Peter scratching his head. Her change in tone was making him dizzy. "If you don't have any place else to go."

"I don't. Thank you very much," Caroline answered in an appropriately humble tone.

Handling his mother was another of Caroline's

essential qualities. "Good. It's all settled. Thanks so much for keeping the kids, Mom. We'll see you on Thursday." Not subtle, but they had plans to make that didn't need her interference.

"Fine." Ruth turned to leave. "I'll call you later with what to bring."

"Great. Thanks." Peter got up and kissed her cheek. "Logan, Lacie, tell Grandma thank you and goodbye."

"Thanks, Grandma. It was great." Logan sounded sincere, but seemed careful to avoid the expected kisses and hugs.

Lacie, however, was happy to oblige with an enthusiastic hug and kiss. "Grandma, it was so fun. Thank you for taking us to Jump-o-rama."

"You're welcome, sweetheart," she said, smoothing Lacie's hair. "Let's go shopping soon."

When her car was out of the driveway, Peter called a family meeting around the table. "Guys, we can't take Caroline home. I'm afraid Josh will hurt her." The kids had seen Josh in action, and there was no need to sugarcoat the situation.

"Josh sucks," Logan chanted again.

Peter nodded his agreement. "Caroline needs to stay with us until we can be sure she is safe."

Lacie had moved from Caroline's lap to her own chair, and leaned forward like she was going to jump on the table. "She can stay in my room. She can help me pick out my clothes so you won't get so mad."

Peter looked sideways at Caroline.

She grinned at him. "She has your number, Doc."

"I guess that's settled, then. We'll go over after breakfast and get her things."

"I think I'd better go with you, Dad. If Josh shows

up you may need my help to take him down," Logan offered between bites of cookie.

After his defeat in their encounter the night before, Peter didn't expect to run into Josh, or else he would never consider putting Logan in danger. He was pleased and proud that Logan thought of it, however, even though he didn't want to teach him to solve problems with a fight. "Actually, Logan, I think that is a good idea. Thanks."

"I'll go too, and help you pick out what clothes to bring," Lacie offered.

Caroline was touched to tears. "Thanks, guys. Let me repay you by cooking breakfast before we go."

"That'd be great," Logan said through a mouthful of cookie. "I'm starved."

Peter went upstairs to shower and dress. This was the way life was supposed to be.

Chapter 24

Over the next four days, there was no sign of Josh. Peter went to Jilly Joe's and was told Josh had called in to quit and disappeared. Not knowing where he was made Peter uneasy, but having Caroline stay with them made his concern more of a nagging watchfulness than an on-the-edge fear.

Caroline's inclusion in their routine was seamless. The only difference from normal was that she was living with them and went into the office with them every day. Her interventions with Lacie were a welcome relief and got them all out the door a lot more smoothly in the mornings. Peter expected they hadn't seen the last of Josh, but he hadn't made any effort to contact Caroline. It was time to move on.

Thanksgiving morning dawned bright and cold, with the first frost of the year creating lacy patterns on the windows. Peter came downstairs to find Caroline wearing a path in the floor between the kitchen, where she was baking brownies, and the family room, where Lacie was watching the Macy's parade. Logan sat at the table eating, as always.

Peter poured himself a cup of coffee and leaned against the counter to face her as she washed dishes. "It has been great having you here," he said, trying to imply his feelings with his tone. Was his subtext getting through?

"Absolutely," Logan agreed. "You are a much better cook than Dad."

"Thanks," she chuckled. "You're easy to please, and I've loved every minute of it. Thank you for taking me in." She looked up at Peter. When she saw his face, she leaned back, and her hands dropped into the soapy water, the bowl she was washing forgotten. "It's probably safe for me to go home now," she said, slowly.

It sounded more like a question than a statement, and he knew he was getting his point through. "Why don't you wait until after the weekend?" Peter asked, holding her gaze. "We always put up our Christmas decorations right after Thanksgiving, and we could really use an extra pair of hands."

"Okay," she murmured. "I can do that."

****

Whether by accident or design, Ruth Hunter did not have Peter and Caroline sitting together at the table for Thanksgiving dinner. Instead, Peter found himself wedged between his mother and the nurse she had been badgering him about for weeks, a striking, model-like blond named Samantha.

"I told you that you would have so much in common," Ruth purred. "And you make such a handsome couple."

Peter glanced down the table at Caroline, who carried on an animated conversation with his sister. Both seemed entertained by something Lacie had said. Caroline looked at him and smiled, but her expression darkened slightly when she took in the stunning appearance of his companion.

"Your mother tells me you are a veterinarian."

Peter reluctantly shifted his attention from Caroline to Samantha. "That's right. And you are a nurse. She thinks we have a lot in common because we are both involved in medicine." He wanted to add, *But Caroline is the one who really knows what I do.*

"Actually, we do," Samantha said. "I work with a horse rescue group on the weekends."

Peter sat up straighter. "Really? Who?"

"Thompson's Farm. There are three of us who locate the horses and bring them in where they can either live out their days in peace, or be rehabilitated and placed."

"How do you find them?"

"People call in, of course, and sometimes we'll hear from a concerned veterinarian who's seen something he or she doesn't like." She smiled sheepishly. "Sometimes I see something I don't like from the road, and I stop to investigate."

He raised an eyebrow. "Does that ever get you into trouble?"

"Sometimes," she shrugged. "But it's worth it."

"Can I help? Do you have a vet already?"

"Actually, our vet just moved to Cleveland."

"Georgia or Ohio?"

"Ohio." She smiled. "We could use some help on the veterinary front. Has to be a volunteer, though. They eat like...well...horses, and most of our money goes for food."

"I can do that." He nodded at Lacie and Logan sitting at the end of the table. "I'll bring my kids with me to help care for the horses. They know all about dogs and cats, but it would be good for them to have some experience with large animals, too."

"That would be great." She leaned in to whisper so Ruth couldn't hear. "I've been resisting your mom's matchmaking, but I would have called you myself if I realized it would be good for my horses."

"Me, too," he whispered back with a sideways glance Ruth.

"Don't worry about dating." She winked. "I'm already seeing someone, but she wouldn't listen."

He chuckled. "Yep. That sounds like her."

"Besides, I believe you are already spoken for."

She had caught him looking down the table at Caroline, whose gaze was fixed on him despite her conversation with his sister.

"I hope so," he replied.

Because Ruth seemed satisfied that he and Samantha were planning a romantic tryst, Thanksgiving turned into a joyous occasion. Peter even found a few minutes to pull his sister, Ginny, aside to thank her sincerely for her attention to their mother.

"I can't say it was a pleasure, but I didn't mind," she responded, putting a hand on his arm. "In spite of what she thinks, you have a full plate and no one to share the load." She nodded at her husband, who talked football with Logan. "Allen is pretty good about helping with the kids on the weekends so I can grab a few minutes for myself, so it's okay that my weeks are full."

The car was quiet on the ride home. Lacie fell asleep the minute they pulled out of his mother's driveway, and Logan watched something on his phone with his ear buds in. Caroline, staring straight ahead without speaking, seemed lost in thought in the passenger seat.

Peter found himself preoccupied. What was Caroline thinking?

She didn't raise her eyes to face him, but instead looked at her hands clasped tightly in her lap. "You were having a pretty intense conversation with Ruth's nurse. She must have been really interesting, and she is certainly beautiful. If I didn't know, I would think she was a model."

Peter nodded. "You know, I commented on the same thing. She said she modeled some to earn money during nursing school, but she is actually really down-to-earth. She volunteers at a horse rescue. I told her I wanted to help, so she was filling me in on their operation."

"Did you make the love connection Ruth wanted?" she asked.

Was it a casual interest, or something more? "No, she's already seeing someone. We connected over the horses."

Across the car, he felt the stress go out of her body. Now was a good time to set "Operation Woo Caroline" in motion. "Caroline," he asked, "I don't want to do anything inappropriate, and I will understand if you say no. But would you be interested in having dinner with me, just you and I?"

"No children?"

"No children." Peter held his breath for her reply.

"Sure." She nodded.

"Okay. How about next Friday after work?" He wanted to give her a week in her own place so she wouldn't feel like she owed anything because she was still living in his house.

"I can do that," she agreed. "I have no plans."

"Great." He focused on the road ahead, congratulating himself over her acceptance.

A sliver of shadow appeared on the edge of his happy thoughts. He tried to fight it, but it pushed its way in until it was a black hole in the middle of his bright light. He gripped the steering wheel hard enough for his knuckles to turn white and glanced at her in his peripheral vision. He would have her where he could confess his feelings. But how would he say it? And what if he had misread her signals? What if things didn't work out when they tried?

Chapter 25

Peter called to hire Audra Lechleiter to babysit for his dinner date with Caroline. It gave Donna a little more information than he wanted to share about his business, but he didn't know many teenagers he would trust with his kids. Audra might not be pleasant, but he knew his children would be alive and unharmed when he got home.

"I trust you, Audra, but I have to say, I don't expect Logan and Lacie to be too happy to have you babysit. They said you weren't very friendly the last time you watched them."

"Don't worry, Dr. Hunter." Audra's tone was so congenial he wondered if he had dialed the right number. "I only treated the kids like that because two of them were my little brothers. Outside the house, I am awesome. I will be their favorite babysitter of all time."

Peter had his doubts, but on Friday, a smiling young woman arrived who bore only a slight resemblance to the Audra he had met. She actually had a bag of games to play, and, though Logan made himself scarce, she won over Lacie before Peter made it out the door.

As soon as the house was out of sight, he turned his full attention to the evening at hand. With the women on Maisie's list, he had experienced every emotion from irritation to anxiety to amusement, but none of them had been like this. He felt like his entire future rode on the events of this one night.

His enthusiastic strides toward the stairwell of her apartment slowed to a trudge when he passed the patch where he had left a drunken Josh laying in the dewy grass. As he climbed the stairs, uncertainty weighed him down like rocks piled on his back. Would things be different between them now that she was home? Would seeing him standing at the spot where he had charged in to save her raise the wall of a terrifying memory between them? What should he say to her? Should he acknowledge what happened that night, or should he allow her to forget it as a thing of the past?

When she opened the door, the vision before him drove every planned greeting from his brain. He thought she had been beautiful when they went to dinner before Halloween, but that had only been a hint of the possibilities. Her crimson dress hugged every smooth curve, and her hair was gathered softly at the nape of her neck, baring her shoulders and allowing sweet, seductive strands to frame her face. Her eyes shone like cut sapphires.

This was not going to go the way he expected. He had considered himself a modern-day knight courting a damsel in distress. That was not the person standing in front of him. This woman was equal to him in every way.

"Do you want to come in?" she asked, leaning against the open door.

He swallowed. What did a man say to such a vision? Finally, he managed to stammer, "We really should go. We have reservations for eight, and it's seven-thirty."

"Okay," she responded, and the smile was his Caroline. She turned in to get her coat.

Peter put the pieces together in his head. "His" Caroline was more than the woman he knew and loved. He knew her well, but he did not know her *all*.

He chose a restaurant called *Riverrun* based on a recommendation by his sister for someplace cozy and romantic. Nestled in a curve of the Chattahoochee River, its winter garden sparkled with white lights. The maître d' showed them to a table with a semi-circular booth in a private alcove which gave them a perfect view of the lights shining in the river and made it seem as though they were the only people in the restaurant.

Peter wasn't ready to launch into his confession of love. He needed to ease into the conversation by establishing a sense of normalcy. The feelings may be newly acknowledged, but the relationship was not, and to pursue Caroline as a romantic interest, he had to touch base with Caroline the old friend. It was easy to hide behind the menu, look up when the waiter came for their drink order, then look back as though he hadn't decided what he was going to order.

Finally, the waiter took their orders and the menus, and he had no choice but to look Caroline fully in the face. He felt her eyes piercing through him, trying to peek at the thoughts on his mind.

Now that it had come to it, what was he going to say? Everything he had practiced was addressed to the woman who wore scrubs in the office and blue jeans to babysit. He had no frame of reference for discussing his feelings with the version of Caroline that made him feel like a tongue-tied teenager.

Caroline reached across the table and squeezed his

arm. She might not know exactly what he planned to say, but as always, she seemed to know he needed her support to say it.

He took a swallow of his drink. "Caroline, I brought you here because I need to talk to you."

She let go of his arm and sat back, dropping her hands into her lap. "Sure. What's up?"

He took another swallow. Could she tell how nervous he was? He swirled his drink. "You and Maisie wanted me to get back in the saddle, and I've tried. Suzanne is very nice, but she and I have nothing in common. Donna can help with all the complications of parenting the kids, but she's way too controlling for my taste. Hillary is great, but I could never be with a person who wouldn't put my kids first in our lives."

She sighed "There *is* one more envelope."

He leaned forward and captured her eyes so she couldn't look away. "I don't need another envelope. Maisie wanted me to have someone to share my life with, who would love the children but also be a woman for me. What she didn't realize was that I would fall in love on my own. She planned for the husband she knew, but after two years without her, I am a different man than she could have anticipated." He reached across the table for her hand. "We were all so close, and you were part of that closeness. We were all family, and you were a member of that family. She couldn't have known—you are the 'someone' this man needs."

Caroline choked on the words. "I am?"

"Yes." This was the leap of faith that left no hope of turning back if she didn't share his feelings. "I love you, Caroline. It snuck up on me when I wasn't looking, but now I see it so clearly. None of those other

women worked for me because none of them was you."
He paused. He knew the entire rest of his life depended
on her next words. If he had read all her signals right,
she felt the same way he did. But if he had been
wrong—and signal reading wasn't one of his
strengths—it would tear a hole in their relationship he
may not be able to repair. Not only would he be
devastated and embarrassed, but the atmosphere at the
clinic would become charged with the awkward tension
between them, and the children would lose their
primary mother-figure.

A tear overflowed and ran down her cheek. "I love
you, too." She turned her hand so their fingers
intertwined. "I've known for a while, but I was afraid I
was too close to Maisie for you to ever see me this
way."

He nodded slowly. "Maisie was so important to us,
that I didn't recognize the way we were changing
without her. No one can ever replace her for me, for
Logan and Lacie, or for you. But you have always had
your own unique place in our family. And now,
especially for me."

Another tear escaped and left a shining trail on her
face. "I'm only truly happy when I'm with you."

He scooted around the booth so he could put his
arm around her. He raised their entwined hands and
looked at them. "Such beautiful hands," he said.
"Hands that do so much for so many. Without these
hands, my world would still be spinning out of control,
off into space with no tether to pull me home." He
leaned down and kissed her.

When they parted, she dropped her head against his
shoulder. "I didn't know what I was going to do when

you selected someone else. How could I leave you and the children, but how would a new woman force me out of your lives?"

"Like I would let anyone push you away."

She smiled. "I had actually already done a couple of job searches online, just in case."

He gave half a chuckle. "I would've taken care of that with one lousy reference. I'd make sure no one else would hire you."

"Good to know." She sat up and leaned on the table. "Now what?"

Peter sighed deeply. "I don't know. Obviously, I hope whatever we decide, we decide together."

She nodded. "That's a good start."

Their food arrived, and Caroline slid a few inches away on the booth so they had room to eat, but stayed close enough that their legs still touched.

Peter looked at his plate and wondered how something so mundane could fit into one of the most important conversations of his life.

"Have you talked to the children about this?" She lifted a delicate morsel to her mouth.

"Not yet. I wanted to see how you felt first." He took a bite of his meal. He didn't really taste the food, but the action gave him just enough pause to gain perspective. She was with him, and they were moving forward together. It was all going to be okay.

"I feel pretty good," she replied with a grin. "I think you can tell them now." She took another bite, but showed no awareness of what she was eating. "We're back to 'Where do we go from here? Dating seems anticlimactic when we already know everything about each other."

"But do we, really? I was still learning things about Maisie all the way to the end. I think we can have a few more unpredictable conversations."

Her brow furrowed. "Like what?"

He looked down at the trout on his plate. "I don't like fish."

She giggled. "I knew that. I couldn't imagine why you ordered it."

He shook his head and chuckled. "Okay, so that's not much of a revelation. But we will find other things." He took the fork from her hand and raised her palm to his lips. "What we've been doing unintentionally brought us here," he said. "If we do it on purpose, we can go even farther."

She cupped her fingers around his face. "That works for me."

The waiter appeared and, seemingly oblivious to their full plates, asked if they wanted dessert.

Peter looked at Caroline, and she nodded. "I think we'll just take the check."

They walked across the parking lot and, leaning against his car, Peter pulled her against him. He wrapped his coat around them in a cocoon of warmth and kissed her, tentatively at first, testing the taste of her. She responded as she had the night after the concert, opening for him and melting into him. This time, he gave over to his impulses with absolute abandon, all his reservations and inhibitions blown away. Finally, they parted with their breath smoky in the cold air. Without loosening his embrace, he leaned away from the car to open the door. He reached into the backseat, pulled out Maisie's package, and handed it to her.

315

She hugged the envelope tight. "Maisie's list? Why?"

"I have so much of her all around me every day that she will always be with me. But she knew the time would come to let her go, and this is that time."

"You never looked at number four." She moved close again and dropped her head to his chest.

"*You* are my number four," he replied, kissing the top of her head.

****

Caroline agreed that Peter should talk alone with Lacie and Logan about the change in their relationship. Although she had been part of their lives for as long as either of the children could remember, having her in their mother's place would be very different from the way they had always known her. It was important they were on board with it before anything else happened.

He called a family meeting at the kitchen table, getting mugs of hot chocolate for Logan and Lacie to match his cup of coffee. They sat forward in their chairs, cradling their cups in imitation of their dad. They were so attentive, he wondered why it had taken so long for him to use this method of delivery.

"I have something important to tell you," he began. "Caroline and I have decided to be more than just friends."

Logan let go of his cup and sat back. "You're dating her?" His voice was serious and mature.

Peter recognized from Logan's tone that he understood the implications of his father's answer. "Yes, I am."

"Yay!" Lacie squealed, clapping her hands. "I love Caroline!"

Peter smiled at Lacie's joy. "I do, too, Little Bit."

Logan crossed his arms, and cocked his head to one side. "No more Ms. Martin, or Ms. Lechleiter, or Hillary? Only Caroline from now on?"

"Yes," Peter replied somberly. He braced himself for the next question.

Logan's eyebrows went up reminding Peter disconcertingly of his grandmother. "Are you going to marry her?"

"I would like to, but what you guys think is important, too."

His son sighed deeply. "I won't call her Mom." His voice was tinged with sadness.

Peter rested his crossed arms on the table and leaned toward his son. "I don't expect you to, and neither does she. Caroline loved Mom as much as we did, and she has no intention of taking her place. She is our Caroline, and that is someone completely different. We love her, but that doesn't mean we will ever forget Mom."

Lacie tried to be as serious and grown-up as Logan, but it just wasn't in her. "Are we going to have a wedding? Can I be a flower girl?"

The corners of Logan's mouth twitched up before he broke into a full smile. "It's okay with me, Dad. Caroline is a great cook."

It was a cover for the depth of his emotion, but Peter understood. "Okay, then. All I have to do is ask Caroline."

****

Christmas was coming fast, and Peter knew what he wanted to do. There was no need to wait for years, or even months. As soon as he had seen the love glistening

317

in her eyes, he knew he had to buy her perfect blue stone to match their deep sapphire color. He selected one surrounded by weaving vines of diamonds, fresh and alive like Caroline herself, and hid it away with a prayer that it wasn't too soon.

Caroline came to stay over Christmas Eve, and she helped him arrange Santa's gifts under the tree. Logan was getting his camera, and Hillary had already pledged to follow through with her offer to teach him. Lacie was getting her doll-sized castle, handmade by Suzanne Martin's carpenter to fit perfectly in her room.

Christmas morning, with gift wrapping debris scattered all across the floor, Peter and Caroline sat on the sofa nursing their cups of coffee while Lacie and Logan were absorbed with their gifts. The moment was right. Peter pulled a small, unwrapped box from its hiding place in the side table.

The kids dropped their gifts and froze like statues, waiting for the scene to play out.

Peter got down on one knee in front of Caroline. "Caroline," he said, "I love you." He nodded at Logan and Lacie. "We all love you. Will you become a real member of our family? Will you marry me and stay with us for the rest of our lives?"

Caroline couldn't speak. Tears streaming down her face, she nodded, and finally choked out, "I love you, too. All of you."

He put the ring on her finger.

She leaned down to kiss him, and then held out her arms to the children. Lacie climbed up in her lap with a big hug and a kiss. Logan sat on the right, put his arm around her shoulders, and squeezed in the twelve-year-old-boy equivalent of a hug.

Peter took his place the left and put his arm over Logan's.

His family was whole.

Chapter 26

Two years later, as Peter walked through the house turning out the lights, his eyes were drawn to the picture of Maisie Caroline had picked out for the family room. He moved in for a closer look. He had taken it at the annual Labor Day picnic before she got sick. She was glowing and healthy, a loving wife and mother.

He hadn't heard her voice since he'd realized he didn't need the last person on her list, and he wondered if their conversations had been his imagination after all. He hoped, wherever she was, she was glad about the way things had turned out. After all, it was what she said she wanted for him. He was married. He was happy. He was in love.

He checked on his sleeping children. Lacie still slept with her bear, but, at eight-years-old, there was no more hint of the baby she had been. In the dim light of Logan's room, Buddy raised his head, but did not move from his place at Logan's back. It was unusual for Logan to be asleep so early, but the high school football coaches pushed hard, and they ran him until he was exhausted every day.

He finished his trek down the hall, turning off lights along the way, to their bedroom. Suzanne Martin had redecorated to Caroline's taste, which tended toward simpler lines and more muted colors. It was a new room, it was their room, and it was exactly what it needed to be.

He was surprised to see Caroline sitting up in bed, waiting for him. She had been through the early exhaustion and middle energy rush of pregnancy, and was back to exhaustion as they eagerly awaited the arrival of the newest member of their family. Peter stretched out next to her and patted the baby in her belly. "Little Hot Shot keeping you awake?"

"I have something for you." Caroline's shoulders were hunched as though she expected to be scolded but hoped to be praised.

"What is it?" he asked suspiciously.

She held out an envelope marked with a "4."

He closed his eyes and drew a deep breath. "I thought you threw that out."

She shrugged. "I planned to. But my curiosity got the better of me. I didn't want to open it because, after all, it wasn't addressed to me. But I thought that someday you would want to see who Maisie suggested."

He wasn't mad, but he also wasn't happy. He looked away as though he didn't want to see it. "I don't want to know," he said. "I have you, and you are all I want."

She shook the envelope and bit her lip "Can I open it? I've been dying to know for the longest time."

"Go ahead." He picked up a book from the nightstand and pretended to read, but his real focus was on her in his peripheral vision.

Caroline's eyes opened wide, and then she smiled and shook her head. "You have to read this." She handed him the letter and watched his face.

The handwriting was still familiar, though he

hadn't seen it since surrendering the package to Caroline. It had been important for her to know he'd realized his love for her on his own, and didn't need any more of Maisie's suggestions to help him get on with his life. He had never intended to read this fourth letter. And yet…

My precious Peter,

Now you know it was Caroline all along.

You needed a little shove to consider dating again, and then realize what you wanted. When it came down to it, though, it was important for you (and for her) that you figure it out for yourself. There's no room for a third person in a marriage, particularly a previous wife, and I love you both too much to wish that for you.

Is she pregnant already? I hope so. Caroline will be a wonderful stepmother, but she deserves a baby of her own, and it will be good for you all to be connected by blood as well as affection. Logan and Lacie will be great older siblings. Logan will carry the baby around at the mall and the park and the beach because babies are "chick magnets." Lacie will dress him or her up like a doll in all the latest fashions. Their little brother or sister will adore them from the word "go," trying to be tough like Logan or stylish like Lacie. It will be a house full of love, and what could be better than that?

I hope the picture of me you've kept in the family room is the one you took at the Labor Day picnic before I got sick. That was a good hair day, and I still had a little color from the beach. It is how I want you to remember me.

I love you with all my heart, my darling, in this life and beyond. Kiss our babies for me.

Maisie

A word about the author...

Beth Warstadt is a Tennessee girl married to a Connecticut Yankee living in suburban Atlanta. She got her Bachelor's and Master's degrees in English from Emory University, after which she sold college textbooks, the source of the broad base of knowledge she uses in her writing. Her stories are set in the real world with little touches of fantasy to make them fun. She and her husband live in Suwanee, Georgia, and have two grown sons.

Thank you for purchasing
this publication of The Wild Rose Press, Inc.

For questions or more information
contact us at
info@thewildrosepress.com.

The Wild Rose Press, Inc.
www.thewildrosepress.com